SECOND NATURE

AMBER BOUDREAU

GenZ
The Future of Publishing

ISBN:
978-1-952919-79-4 (ebook)

978-1-952919-80-0 (paperback)

GenZPublishing.org
Aberdeen, NJ

For my Aunt Bev.
I think she would have liked this one.

CHAPTER 1

Mavis Corvid's day began with attempted murder and only got stranger from there.

The murder attempt caught her attention soon after she arrived at work. In the front of the garage, where she'd spent the past four months shuffling papers and helping customers, the rush of wings reached her ears. On the other side of the large plate-glass windows, a crow landed in the empty parking lot. Its inky, iridescent wings ruffled as it inspected a shiny bit of tinfoil on the cement. A second later another crow landed with a raucous call, and the two hopped around each other.

Mavis knew 'murder' was a poetic term for a group of crows. What she didn't know, and constantly failed to recall, was where she'd picked up that interesting tidbit of useless information. She'd tried to remember things from her past, lots of times, but her amnesia remained frustratingly intact. Since leaving the hospital, she'd come to accept that she might never remember who she was or what had happened to her, but now and then she stopped and wondered. This was one of those times.

The first crow peered at her through the glass, head cocked to the side.

How could she know a group of crows was called a murder, but not remember she was deathly allergic to strawberries? Six months ago, questions like that used to keep her up at night. Not so much anymore. The more time and space she put between herself and the moment she woke up in the hospital, memory-less, and physically unable to walk, the easier it was to pull herself away.

No other crows landed, keeping the murder charges at 'attempted.' A truck sped by, kicking up a swirl of dust, and both birds flew away. Mavis watched to see if they would come back, but they didn't. She drew a deep, calming breath, pulled her focus from the past, and turned to her morning duties.

The counter with her computer, where she spent the majority of her time, took up a little less than half of the front of the garage. Behind the counter, shelves mounted to the walls held an array of colorful binders above the filing cabinet. In front of the counter sat a low oval coffee table, magazines fanned out on top, with four gray chairs arranged around it. Eustace Park Automotive wasn't the only body shop in town, but it was the best. Yes, she was biased. The computer might not have been hers, it belonged to the shop, but she was the one who used it the most. Aitch, the owner and her boss, had his own computer networked to hers in his back office.

Mavis got to work, wiping down surfaces and, sweeping and mopping the white linoleum until it gleamed. Then she cleaned the front windows until they shone streak-free. The cleaning was part of her daily routine, so there wasn't much in the way of dirt. Not since she'd started working there.

It had taken a couple of weeks' worth of guesswork to determine if she was doing anything right, but when she didn't get fired for cleaning up or organizing the paperwork and computer files, she figured she was okay. The front of the garage had gradually become her space to keep as she liked. For instance, the faded and torn muscle-car posters that used to line the walls had come down and never gone back up. She'd only meant to wipe down the plastered surfaces, but she'd had to scrub hard to remove the posters' dirty outlines. Afterward, she'd preferred the clean, blank walls. Aitch had scanned the space through narrowed eyes and grunted—his preferred method of communication. They'd since moved on to real words and he still hadn't said anything about putting the posters back. Now there were two gallons of sea-foam green paint waiting for her.

Mavis' regime of clean did not extend beyond the front of the garage. The one time she'd dared straighten a workbench in the back had not ended well. First, there had been muttering, followed by cursing, and finally shouting. Mavis didn't remember the exact words Aitch had used, but she remembered the volume and the inflection well enough. She had been so sure she was about to be fired tears blurred her vision. Aitch had stopped, mid-tirade, pointed his wrench at her, and told her not to touch anything in the back of the shop ever again. And so, she hadn't. She needed the work. She didn't have anywhere else to go.

Finished cleaning, Mavis turned the computer on as the back door banged open and slammed shut.

"Good morning," she called out, listening to the clink of a ceramic mug and the sound of liquid being poured. She'd turned the coffee maker on as soon as she arrived, arguably her most important job of the morning.

Aitch passed the open doorway and mumbled, "Morning," into his cup of dark roast. That was it. No good. Just morning.

Not the first time, she thought Aitch was far too young to

3

be such a sourpuss. If she had to guess, she would say he was around thirty, making him a few years older than her. Forgetting for the moment that he was her boss, he wasn't bad-looking. His dark, wavy hair was a little long on top, but it was all there. And when he wasn't scowling or glaring, his features were pleasant enough to notice that his eyes were a striking shade of light brown. Working on cars in the shop kept him fit, and if it didn't, the bench press and free weights in the back corner of the garage helped.

Mavis perched on the stool behind the counter and started on the paperwork. At eight on the dot, she flipped over the sign in the window from 'CLOSED' to 'OPEN' and unlocked the front door. Wheels whined in their tracks as Aitch rolled up the big metal doors on either side of the garage, those on the street, and the ones facing the fenced-in lot out back. There were a few afternoon appointments on the calendar, but unless they had a walk-in or got called out for a tow, she had plenty of time to go over the books and balance sheets.

Twenty minutes had gone by when the front door opened and Louis Raymon slipped inside with a sideways shuffle, watching his back. His dark blue button-down hung open over a white tank top and low-hanging jeans. His black hair had been combed into submission with enough product to make it shiny and immobile. His shoulders relaxed as he turned to face Mavis. The worried look on his face faded into a grin. "Good morning, beautiful."

Mavis raised a single brow.

Louis' slim shoulders came up in a "can't blame me for trying" shrug as he sidled over to lean on the counter across from her. Louis was a fifteen-year-old, pint-sized lothario—when he remembered to be. The rest of the time, he was a neighborhood kid who dropped by before or after school whenever he had the time or whenever his 'friends' were hanging around outside. He called them his friends. Mavis silently referred to them as future defendants.

One afternoon, when she'd been outside watering the plants, Louis was there with five other boys crowded around him. They were all taller and older than he was. One moment they were joking and laughing; the next, their youthful bodies were stony and rigid. They spoke words she couldn't make out in a harsh cadence. Before the static tension boiled over into action, Mavis stuck her thumb over the end of the hose. She admired the light as it refracted through the spray into a rainbow—right over their heads.

Mavis apologized immediately and profusely. Her finger slipped—new hose. She laughed at herself, eyes welling with a touch of hysteria. She might have overdone it. However, the older boys, having realized they had an audience—or witness —gave up on giving Louis a hard time and left without causing a scene.

Louis had turned up the next day and introduced himself. He told her his friends were just messing around. They hadn't been about to pound him into the dirt, despite how it looked. Then he asked for her life story. That was how he said it: "So, what's your life story?"

Mavis told him the truth as she knew it. She tried to keep it simple, but still ended up using words like "permanent retrograde amnesia" and admitted she didn't remember anything from before she woke up in Shady Creek Hospital. Then she told him he needed new friends and mentioned the front door to the garage was always open—during normal business hours, anyway. He hadn't been in for a couple of days, so she wasn't surprised to see him this morning.

"No cookies today?" Louis asked, peeking behind the counter.

"Nope. Maybe tomorrow."

Louis pursed his lips and nodded, his gaze roving the walls.

"What's on your mind?" Mavis asked.

His carefree persona fell away as he leaned across the counter. "I think"—his eyes darted over her shoulder to the garage, and he lowered his voice— "I think my math teacher might be a werewolf."

Mavis didn't laugh. Instead, she sat a little straighter.

Werewolves were real.

"Why do you think that?" she asked.

The tension drained away from Louis' face and shoulders, as if he was relieved to be taken seriously.

"We had a substitute last month, right after school started —the day after the full moon."

Mavis squinted. "Is that all you've got? It's kind of thin. Could be a coincidence."

"No way. He's all worn out from having to change and he has to take the next day off."

She thought about it. "Okay, say you're right and he is a werewolf. What are you going to do about it?"

"What do you mean?"

Mavis placed her hands on the counter. "Well, are you gonna stop going to class?"

Louis' face went blank, and she could tell he hadn't thought that far. She was pretty sure just being right was the important thing for Louis, but she was curious about how he would act on his suspicions. She didn't want to have to point out that even if his teacher was a werewolf, it shouldn't stop him from learning algebra.

"I guess if you don't like the grade he gives you, you could report him to one of those icky websites," she said.

The tips of Louis' ears turned red and he stammered, "I— I wouldn't do that. I just don't want to see what happens if he gets mad in class one day, wolfs out, and bites someone's head off."

Mavis winced at the delightful imagery. "I don't think it works that way. Does your teacher—what's his name?"

"Mr. Dubois."

"Does Mr. Dubois have a temper? Does he have a history of getting mad in class?"

Louis' gaze flicked to the corners of the room. "Not really."

According to what Mavis had seen and read, the agonizing change from man to werewolf took time. A video of the transformation had gone viral and was best viewed with the volume turned off. During the full moon, werewolves didn't have a choice. They had to change. She'd read that a strong surge of emotion such as anger or fear could trigger the change, but it didn't happen instantaneously.

Mavis knew Louis was serious about school, but still, she asked, "Are you going to skip class?"

Louis' eyes widened. "I wouldn't do that, either."

"Glad to hear it, because you're gonna be late."

He checked the clock on the wall over her shoulder and backed toward the door.

"Later, mama. By the way, you look hot in that shirt." He shot her a wink and was gone out the door so fast he was a blur.

Mavis tsked and shook her head. Despite Louis' attempt at flattery, Mavis was not dressed to impress. For the sake of variety, today's t-shirt had a V-neck, but it didn't plunge any lower than the hollow of her throat. The deep teal color complemented her gray eyes, but she hadn't planned on it.

As she went back to invoicing, her thoughts turned to werewolves. As soon as she'd learned of their existence, she'd started reading everything she could on the subject. Werewolves had revealed themselves about a year ago. No one knew why they'd chosen to tell the world, but they had. And once the wolves were out of the bag, there was no putting them back, probably because they shredded it into teeny tiny pieces. Individual werewolves came out in several professions, including first responders, private security personnel, and accountancy. They were often pillars of their communities, average men and women facing the same everyday struggles as non-werewolves. Recently, packs had started to emerge in different regions of the states and across the globe.

Stateside, the legislation remained pending on whether werewolves would have to register as lycanthropes or not. Some people didn't think the werewolves should have a choice. A couple of gossip websites made names for themselves by outing suspected werewolves. However, the only true way of knowing if someone was a werewolf was to watch them change on the night of a full moon. Not too long ago, one website had claimed a popular politician went fuzzy on the regular. The politician refused to comment. However, he did relax on the front porch of his palatial home in plain view of any curious passersby the night of the next full moon. The politician remained human, and the resulting traffic jam lasted well into the night.

Mavis jumped when Aitch's boots thudded onto the tiles behind her.

He pulled down a red binder from the top shelf and flipped through it until he stopped, running an oil-smudged digit down the paper. His fingers drummed against the page for a moment. "Add the cost of an air filter to Mrs. Wolverton's bill and call to let her know she can pick her car up this afternoon." He closed the binder and put it back.

"Do you think Mrs. Wolverton is a werewolf?" Mavis asked as she navigated to the correct invoice in the computer files.

"No." He paused. "Why do you ask?"

She could feel his eyes on her and turned to see him standing framed in the doorway, a line between his brows.

She shrugged. "Just something Louis said."

"And what did Louis say?"

"Nothing. Never mind. Mrs. Wolverton couldn't be a werewolf anyway. Besides, the name's a little on the nose. Like a werewolf called Wolfgang. No one would think a werewolf would be so obvious."

Aitch stared at her, his eyes narrowed, but he kept quiet like he was trying to figure something out. His watching unnerved her. He folded his arms. "And why is that?"

"Why is what?"

"Why couldn't Mrs. Wolverton be a werewolf?"

"Well, she's gotta be pushing what, like, seventy? Older werewolves don't exist. Well, they probably do—they just don't look old. You know what I mean?" Mavis added, "Also, a female werewolf would be kind of rare. At least, I think so. There don't seem to be too many of them. In the figures I've seen, females appear to make up far fewer than half the number of males." She needed to stop talking.

Aitch blinked, unfolding his arms. "Don't forget to call."

"I won't—" she said to his back. He had already turned away.

Mavis left a message on Mrs. Wolverton's voicemail, finished going over the paperwork, and refilled the shelf of snacks for waiting customers. As she finished, the computer screen dimmed. Unless Aitch wanted her to look something up, she didn't need to use it. The idea of disappearing down the electronic rabbit hole of the internet didn't appeal to her. Instead, she slipped the paperback mystery novel she was reading out of her backpack and let herself get sucked into the story.

Several pages later, an instinct born of working in customer service made Mavis glance up, where she saw a car pull into the lot. The vehicle was newer, with dark tinted windows, but she could make out a driver and a passenger. The driver's door opened, and a familiar figure stepped out. His blue button-down Oxford shirt was tucked into khaki trousers. Mavis knew the dark aviators he wore hid his blue eyes. The only thing missing was his white doctor's coat.

Dr. Chase Stombaugh was one of the first people she'd met when she'd woken up in the hospital. He'd seen to her treatment, helping her get back on her feet both literally and figuratively. He'd gotten her the job with Aitch and released her back into the wild. She'd seen him once or twice around town from afar, but not for a while and never at the garage.

The corners of Mavis' mouth lifted. They froze into place when the passenger door opened and a woman wearing a dark blue tank dress and spiky heels stepped out, her long dark hair unbound. Mavis had never seen Katrina wear anything besides scrubs, but the clothes didn't fool her. It didn't matter what she wore—Katrina was hard to forget. Mavis watched as she dipped back inside the sedan and came out with a purse, the strap going over her shoulder. Her head tilted one way and then the other, as if she were taking in the building as a whole. Although her eyes were hidden behind a pair of round sunglasses, the line of her mouth made it clear she found the place wanting.

Mavis stood and smoothed her t-shirt over her hips, brushing at the wrinkles. She didn't even own a pair of shoes that weren't flat. Today she wore runners, not because she ran, but because she walked everywhere. She didn't know how to drive, so why would she own a car?

The doc came around to Katrina's side and touched her arm. Though his back was to Mavis, she could see his jaw move. Whatever he said made Katrina smile in a way Mavis had rarely seen and never for a sustained period. Katrina had never smiled at her, not once in the entire time she'd spent trying to teach Mavis how to walk again. It hadn't bothered Mavis at first. Her focus on getting the use of her legs back caused her to barely notice the lack of positive feedback. But as she improved, Katrina's open hostility became an issue. She'd eventually asked to be removed from Katrina's care, in essence firing her. Since then, Mavis had only seen her in passing. Katrina's coworkers were more encouraging. They were the physical therapists she credited with getting her back on her feet, not Katrina.

The doc turned and strode toward the entrance with Katrina right behind him. He opened the door and held it. Her lips parted in a blinding white smile. As soon as she stepped inside and came face to face with Mavis, however, her mouth straightened.

Mavis ignored her. "Hi, Doc! Nice to see you again." And then, she acknowledged the other woman with a nod. "Katrina." The greeting was not returned.

"Hello, Mavis." The doc removed his aviators and hung them from his shirt pocket, stepping around Katrina and coming to the counter. His eyes met Mavis'. "How are you?"

Mavis knew he wasn't just asking to be polite. However, with Katrina standing there listening to their every word, she didn't feel like going into detail. "I'm good. Things are good."

"I'm glad to hear it."

When he didn't say anything more, she asked, "Is there something I can help you with? Does your car need some work?"

"Is Heinrich in?"

The doc pronounced Aitch's full name the way a native German speaker would. He was the only person she knew of who called Aitch by his first name and got away with it.

"He's in the back. I can go get him—"

"No, that's all right. If you don't mind, I'll just pop in and say hello."

"Sure. Go right ahead."

He didn't rush away. Instead, he murmured something to Katrina first, who still hadn't removed her sunglasses. Then Katrina turned, sat in one of the waiting chairs, picked up a magazine, and leafed through it.

The doc skirted around the end of the counter, through the door and into the back of the garage.

Mavis didn't know what to do. She didn't feel like reading with Katrina sitting there, pretending to be interested in a magazine. Nor did she feel compelled to engage her in conversation. Katrina had never had much to say to her; Mavis couldn't imagine she would have anything to say now. Mavis nudged the mouse of the computer to wake it up, but there was no work to be done except pretend.

From her peripheral vision, she watched as Katrina finished one magazine and traded it for another. At this rate, Mavis figured she would be through their limited selection in about four minutes.

Staring at the blank screen, Mavis came to a decision. "Would you like something to drink? Water? Or coffee?"

Katrina paused in her flipping of pages, raised one hand, and rubbed her fingers together. "How about a magazine not coated in grease?" Her words dripped with disdain. She sniffed and went back to flipping pages.

Eight whole words. Seven if you discounted the article 'a,' which wasn't much of a word, but Mavis decided to count it in this case. So, eight whole words. Practically a record.

"It *is* a garage," Mavis said with a shrug.

Katrina flipped past another page with a loud rustle.

Maybe the doc wanted something to drink.

Mavis backed away from the counter toward the door to the garage.

Once Mavis was through the doorway, she pursed her lips and blew out a breath. In front of her, the vehicle lift suspended a car into the air with its undercarriage on display. The smell of machine oil grew stronger the farther she stepped into the shop. A breeze pulled at the tarp covering an old car body and a pile of spare parts in the back corner.

Aitch and the doc stood facing each other on the far side of Mrs. Wolverton's car. They were about the same height and age, but the doc was pale and fair-haired, while Aitch was dark-headed with a deeper skin tone that had nothing to do with having a tan.

Mavis watched the doc lay a hand on one of Aitch's shoulders.

Aitch's gaze went from the doc to his hand and back, his expression rueful. "Your wiles don't work on me, remember?"

The doc chuckled softly and lifted his hand free before he let it fall back to his side.

Aitch stepped back, wiping his hands on a rag, and caught sight of Mavis. "What's up?" he asked.

"Just wondered if the doc wanted a cup of coffee."

The doc smiled. "That would be great, thank you."

Aitch waited until she turned away before speaking to the doc in hushed tones. She couldn't quite make out what they said.

Mavis filled a mug and carried it two-handed around Mrs. Wolverton's car. Aitch and the doc stopped talking. She handed over the coffee.

The doc took it with a grin. "Sugar?"

Aitch scoffed. "You can get it yourself. She's not waiting on you, hand and foot."

The doc frowned. "Well, of course not. I didn't mean—"

"I don't mind," Mavis said.

"I do. You work for me, not him. Was there anything else?" Aitch asked.

Mavis wasn't sure if he was talking to her or the doc.

"I was hoping you would take a look at my car actually," the doc said. He sipped his coffee and winced.

"Right. Sugar." Mavis turned.

"Mavis?"

Her shoulders tensed at Aitch's tone. She faced him again.

"Why don't you go pick up lunch?" he asked and added before she could check her watch, "I know it's early. Take your time."

She hesitated, gaze darting between the doc and Aitch. Whatever it was they wanted to talk about, they didn't want her to overhear, that much was obvious. However, if the doc was going to be around for a while, should she offer to pick up something for his lunch as well?

Aitch watched her struggle a moment before he put her out of her misery. "Don't worry about the good doctor. Or his associate. They won't be staying long," he said.

His statement reminded Mavis that Katrina was waiting out front and that she didn't want to have to talk to her any more than necessary. Discretion being the better part of valor, she decided to play it safe. "Be back soon," she said, heading out the big bay door in search of lunch and a sympathetic ear. She knew where to find both.

CHAPTER 2

O ut of sight of the garage, Mavis crossed the road at the corner. She knew when she wasn't wanted. The way the doc and Aitch clammed up in her presence made her wonder what they were talking about. They were friends, but she didn't understand why the doc didn't save himself a trip and call Aitch on the phone.

She hadn't seen the doc once in the four months since she'd been discharged from Shady Creek Hospital. When her memories didn't immediately return, she got on with getting her strength back. Either the memories would come back, or they wouldn't. No one could tell her when, or even if, that would happen, so she pressed on—moving forward, carving out a life for herself in the foothills of the Sangre de Christos in Eustace Park, New Mexico. The only reason she had gotten the job at the garage was because the doc recommended her for it. Either Aitch couldn't find anyone, or his sterling personality drove them away.

Mavis was grateful for the work, and she knew the garage benefited from her being behind the counter. Customers told her so, to her face, with Aitch standing right behind her.

Being acknowledged for her good work made her feel like her presence mattered. She couldn't afford for Aitch to think he didn't need her. There was nowhere else for her to go. Nowhere she could remember, anyway. No missing person matching her description had been reported in Eustace Park, the surrounding areas, or the state for that matter. No one knew who she was. Before she had seen her reflection for the first time, she could have passed herself walking down the street and not have looked twice. The face in the mirror triggered no memories, but at least it was an okay face. Her nose was maybe a hair too large, but it worked, so she couldn't complain.

Part of her new work-life included picking up lunch from the Main Street Bakery, a couple of blocks over and one block north of the garage. Aitch had a standing order of a BLT on sourdough with extra B, fries, and Mavis could get whatever she wanted, as part of his arrangement with Maurice, the owner. The double-wide storefront was tucked between a vacuum repair shop and a tattoo parlor. The bell over the door rang when she opened it.

A counter ran the width of the room, about six feet from the back wall, which had a pass-through to the kitchen behind it but was otherwise covered in mirrored glass. Inside, she slid onto a round blue vinyl stool at the counter. Despite the name, the Main Street Bakery wasn't a bakery at all, but a diner. All of their pies came frozen out of a box. She'd tried a slice one time and never again.

A few late-morning stragglers hung around at tables in the corners, but the lunch crowd hadn't shown up yet. One diner stared at the newspaper spread open in front of him, suit jacket thrown over the adjacent chair. Opposite his table, an older couple in matching flannel shirts played checkers.

Wes stepped out of the kitchen, dressed in a spotless white apron wrapped around his narrow waist and tied in front over a black t-shirt and jeans. He saw Mavis at the counter and checked the clock on the diner's wall as he came over, his wiry limbs allowing him to move with quiet efficiency.

"You're early," Wes said as he flipped over a mug and reached for the carafe of coffee behind him.

"Aitch told me to take my time, too."

Wes poured the coffee into the mug. "Well, then, what can I get you?" He set the carafe back on the warmer, lifted the cup, and took a sip. His eyes met hers over the rim. "Pie? Fresh out of the box."

She kept a straight face and said, "No thanks. Maybe a Coke?"

Wes, a twinkle in his eye, filled a glass with ice from behind the counter. "Why so early?"

"Visitors."

He filled the cup with soda from a gun and handed it across to her. "Visitors? Not customers?"

Mavis reached over the counter, grabbed a straw, and unwrapped it. "Do you remember the doc I told you about? The one from Shady Creek?"

"The cute one?"

Mavis rolled her eyes. There was nothing wrong with her ability to make new memories, so she knew she had never used the word 'cute' to describe the doc. She didn't think he was Wes' type, but she could be wrong. "He's not any cuter than any other doctor." Even as she said it, Mavis felt her cheeks warm.

Wes smirked.

She ignored him. "He came into the shop this morning with Katrina, my old physical therapist."

Wes frowned as he came around the end of the counter and slid onto the stool next to hers. "The one that was always such a jerk?"

Wes had a good memory. He listened when they shared meals, which they often did because they lived in the same apartment complex. And, Wes was an amazing cook. If it was left to her, she'd be eating out of a box every night, or skipping dinner altogether and making a meal of bologna and cheese. Scratch that—probably just cheese.

She nodded. "Yeah, that one."

"Huh. You think they're together?"

"I don't know. It's weird. He—they've never stopped by before."

"Did he drive? Maybe he needs his car looked at."

"Maybe," she said, but she didn't think so. They wanted her out of the way. That thought fed the idea that she was a topic of conversation, but she slapped it away and looked on the brighter side. She didn't have to put up with Katrina if she wasn't there, so maybe she should just enjoy it.

"So, the doc and the physical therapist are together? Isn't that against the rules somewhere?"

Despite Wes calling out the doc as cute, Mavis had never thought of him in any other sense beyond the strictly professional. Same for Katrina. It did strike her as odd, though. Their temperaments were so different, at least around her. The doc cared about his patients, but as helpful and kind as he was, Katrina was the opposite. She did her job and that was it; nothing more, nothing less. No pleasantries—no nothing. It hadn't bothered Mavis at first, but as time went on, it became clear something was amiss. Mavis had never received anything from Katrina beyond strict professional courtesy and since leaving the hospital, it appeared she would not even be given that.

What did someone as warm as the doc see in the cold Katrina?

"I don't know. They don't work for me. They're adults—they should know what they're doing."

"Hmm." Wes watched her a minute before asking, "You still coming over tonight?"

"Yep. I'm making cookies."

"Deal. What are you having today?"

Mavis knew the menu by heart. "Soup of the day and half a Reuben, please."

Wes got up to put her order in, and Mavis grabbed a newspaper someone had left behind.

The front-page headline of the national news was an article about werewolves, though it wasn't so much about werewolves as about those who opposed them. Anti-werewolf demonstrations were popping up in cities and towns across the country, including some capitals. So far, the protests were peaceful. They were typically planned around the full moon. Still, it had been a year since the werewolves reveal, and as the anniversary approached, tensions were rising. It was only a matter of time before the protests escalated into violence, according to statements from officials.

Wes topped off both checker player's coffees and refilled Mavis' soda before he sat down again.

"Did you see this?" Mavis asked him.

Wes sighed. "I did, but I was hoping you wouldn't. I know you've got a thing for werewolves."

"I do not have a thing for werewolves. I don't even know any."

"How do you know?"

Mavis narrowed her eyes. "Good point. Do you know something I don't? Are you trying to tell me something?"

Wes laughed with his head thrown back, a full, throaty roar.

Mavis' lips compressed into a line. She waited. Wes used the bottom corner of his apron to pat the corners of his eyes.

"Werewolves are just like us, right?" Mavis asked. "Except they have a medical condition."

Wes snorted. "A dangerous medical condition."

"One that makes them go fuzzy every 28 days."

"Don't forget potentially violent. You call it a medical condition, but if someone with cancer scratches you, they're not going to give you cancer."

Mavis' eyes narrowed as she tilted her head to the side. "I think it would take more than a scratch." Everything she'd read indicated it took a savage and thoroughly brutal mauling to be turned into a werewolf, if the victim survived. If they didn't succumb to their injuries, there was a high probability they would turn at the next full moon.

Wes drank his coffee. "You know what I mean."

She chewed the inside of her lip, considering. She'd done some reading late at night on her own and plowed through a lot of information. All of it she took with a grain of salt. But every now and then she came across a personal account that read differently. Certain elements and themes cropped up again and again. Those were the kernels of truth Mavis kept an eye out for.

"But you're right," Wes interrupted her thought. "They only have to change around the full moon, so I guess if they can get themselves somewhere where they can't hurt anyone" —he shrugged—"I don't have a problem with them."

Mavis pushed the ice around her drink with her straw. "It depends on the wolf."

"What do you mean?"

She shook her head. "It's just a theory."

"Go on."

She squinted at him. "Are you sure you want to hear this?"

"I'm hoping you'll get it out of your system, but keep your voice down." He glanced around the diner at the other customers.

"Okay. After a human gets turned into a werewolf, they have to learn how to work with their wolf. It takes time, but, let's say, three months after the initial bite they learn to hunt animals and not humans. There must be exceptions, of course. Like, what if the human that's turned isn't stable to start with? Also, no one knows how long werewolves live, but as humans, they don't age. What if something changes as they get much, much older and they get a taste for humans again? Both scenarios could increase the number of attacks, and therefore, create more werewolves."

Wes looked like he wanted to say something, but before he could reply, the counter bell rang. Her order was ready.

"That was educational, even if it was just a theory. See you tonight," Wes said.

She grabbed the bag of food and waved, heading out the door. One block south. Two blocks east. She retraced her steps, hoping the whole way that the doc and Katrina were gone. The parking lot came into view with the doc's car still there. Disappointment made her pace slow. Through the front windows, Mavis could see Katrina seated in the same chair as before, except now her head was bent low over a smartphone, probably crushing candy to pass the time.

Mavis kept walking and didn't cross the road until she was past the windows. She approached the garage from the north-east, where both big bay doors remained open. She wasn't trying to sneak up on anyone, but when she heard raised voices, she stopped and pressed herself to the outside of the building.

"—not my fight," Aitch was in the middle of saying.

The hair on Mavis' arms stood up. He sounded angry.

"It's everyone's fight," the doc said, his voice cold and flat. "Broderick wants to meet. Your garage is neutral territory." He paused. "I need all the help I can get, Heinrich. I'll do whatever I have to do to get it. Don't make me beg." The doc's voice tripped over the last word.

Silence. Aitch sighed. Then he growled, a rolling sound

she'd never heard him make before. "Fine. Midnight, tonight. Seconds only."

Seconds only? What did that mean? They could use the garage to meet, but only for a couple of seconds? That didn't make sense. Mavis stood so still and so quiet, she heard the wind before it blew past her rustling the bag she held.

"Your BLT is here," the doc said.

CHAPTER 3

The doc and Aitch stared in her direction as Mavis came around the corner. Their immediate scrutiny made her eyes widen and her stomach clench. Did they suspect she'd overheard the last of their conversation? Neither one moved. She made a big show out of checking the time on her wrist. "What? I'm right on time."

Aitch blinked first. "Maurice give you any trouble?"

She lifted the bag. "No. Wes was there. We chatted for a bit. Where do you want this?"

The doc, silent and watchful, finally blinked and shifted his gaze to the bag she carried.

Aitch pointed to the corner with his chin.

Mavis dug out Aitch's lunch and placed it on his work-bench. The two did not continue their conversation now that she was there. The thought of taking her meal out front and eating with Katrina gave her heartburn. "What kind of work does your car need, Dr. Stombaugh?" She could get started on an invoice instead of indigestion.

"It's fine," Aitch said. "The doc was just leaving."

The doc grunted—too much time around Aitch. "I was.

Thank you for the coffee. And the conversation." He handed Aitch his mug.

Aitch set the mug aside and stuck his head back under the car he was working on, dismissing them both.

The doc came around the car and held up an arm for Mavis to go ahead of him. Out front, Katrina spotted the doc and jumped to her feet. However, he paused and turned to face Mavis.

"I wanted to ask you something," he said.

Mavis set her lunch down and rested her hands on the counter. "Sure."

"There's a new patient at the hospital. Her case reminds me an awful lot of yours. Would you be willing to talk to her? Tell her a little bit about yourself?" He smiled.

"There's not much to tell, really," Mavis said. She believed it, too. She'd never recalled a single thing about who she had been before she woke up in the hospital.

"I know you think that, but you could tell her where you started. How far you've come." He was still smiling, but the folds of skin around his eyes betrayed him. They were deeper on one side than the other, giving her the impression that while he was smiling, he was also wincing.

"Your patient has amnesia?" She almost added the words *like me* but stopped herself.

"Yes, she lost her memory, but she doesn't have the distractions you had, so I'm afraid she's a bit down. I was hoping you could talk to her. Let her know things get better."

Distractions? Did he mean not being able to walk? Waking up to find her legs didn't work had bothered her more than realizing she had lost her memory. Getting her legs working again had been all she thought about in the beginning. The work had kept her mind from wandering down a dark path by keeping her physically and mentally engaged in a task. Setbacks were to be expected, progress celebrated.

"Um, okay. When were you thinking?"

The doc's smile seemed genuine this time. "Could you come to my office tomorrow morning? Say, nine o'clock."

"Tomorrow? I have to work."

"I took the liberty of clearing it with Heinrich already. He said you could have the morning off." The doc reached out and laid a pale hand on top of hers. "I hope you don't mind, but I thought you would say yes."

Over the doc's shoulder, Katrina's head jerked to the side, nose wrinkling. She still wore her sunglasses, but Mavis was sure her eyes were on their hands. Mavis' gaze dropped to the counter. The doc's hand was bigger than hers. His warm palm curled over the back of her cold one, his long, tapered fingertips going to the space between her thumb and forefinger, squeezing gently.

The gesture brought her to a stop as her stomach turned over. Her feelings for the doc had never grown beyond the platonic, yet she didn't mind him touching her hand. So why did her stomach react the way it did? Mavis frowned. The doc couldn't have known she would agree to talk to his patient. He should have asked her first. Then she would have talked to Aitch. The two of them *had* talked about her.

The only thing that kept her from being put off by the doc's presumptuousness was the fact she didn't mind talking to another patient in her same circumstances. His high-handedness must have been what caused her stomach to flip. Mavis raised her gaze to his. "I'll be there."

"I'm glad to hear it. Thank you." The doc let go of her hand and grinned. "See you tomorrow."

When he backed away and shuffled around Katrina to hold the door for her, Katrina stormed through without a backward glance at either of them. She didn't wait for the doc to open her car door either. After she'd slammed it behind her, she sat with her arms crossed.

The doc sent Mavis one last wave, still smiling as he got in the car and drove away.

Metal rang against metal behind her. Mavis jumped and froze. She'd heard a lot of loud noises working at the garage, but this one sounded different. Her heart pounded, waiting, but no shout of distress met her ears. Mavis poked her head around the doorframe into the back.

Aitch stood, hands on his hips, glaring at his workbench.

"Everything okay?" she asked.

"Fine," he said, without looking at her.

Mavis didn't question him further. She ducked away from the doorframe and returned to her post, where the aroma from the food she'd ordered wafted near, making her stomach rumble. It was close enough to lunch time. She ate behind the counter as she usually did.

The rest of the day passed without further incident, but toward the end of business hours, Mavis was busier than usual getting things ready for her absence in the morning. One of the last things she did was make sure the coffee maker was filled and ready to go. After she locked the front door, she flipped the sign and tracked down Aitch.

The steel doors were shut tight. He wasn't tinkering away under any hoods or lying under any cars, so she went to his office. The desk sat covered in papers, spare parts, and grime she was forbidden to touch. It wasn't an issue. She hadn't stepped more than a foot inside his office since her brief interview four months before. The only chair was rolled under the catastrophe of a desktop.

Aitch stood next to the locker where all the security footage for the garage was stored. When he pressed a button on the computer tower, a tray slid out. The shiny silver disc went straight into a flimsy plastic case. The insurance company required Aitch to keep CCTV footage of the premises, inside and out. Mavis knew because she'd seen the bill and read the contract. The footage was first stored on a DVD, and then backed up to a hard drive, but the disc needed to get switched out every so often.

"The coffee maker is all set for the morning. All you have to do is press the button. And I'll take care of any tidying up when I get in." Mavis set her bag down and pulled on her hooded sweatshirt. She pulled her hair free, zipped the sweater closed, and reclaimed her bag, ready to go. "Thanks, by the way."

Aitch glared at the plastic case in his hand as he wrote the date on it. "What for?"

"Giving me the morning off tomorrow."

"You want to go back to the hospital?"

That was a weird way of putting it. It wasn't like she was going there to stay. "The doc asked for my help. Says he's got a patient that reminds him of me. I think I should talk to her."

Aitch tossed the DVD aside, shut his eyes, and squeezed the bridge of his nose. "His patient is female?"

"The doc didn't drop any names, but he did refer to the patient as 'her.'"

"Of course." He lowered his hand, raising his gaze to hers. "How are you getting there?"

Mavis had been hoping to walk, but if she told Aitch that, she was afraid he would offer to drive her. She would decline. He would want to know why. She didn't want to hurt his feelings by telling him that she could think of about a hundred other things she would rather do than share an enclosed space with him. She would end up saying yes to the ride and then be stuck in his truck with him. Aitch wasn't bad in small doses and large spaces, but being around him put her on edge. If she had to spend large quantities of time with him so close, her nerves would be shot. She didn't want to have those kinds of feelings around her boss, and being with him outside of work wouldn't help. "I'll catch the bus. Don't worry. I'll be in as soon as I can."

"I wasn't worried. Good night."

"Good night."

As she turned to go, Mavis couldn't help but notice that Aitch pressed the same button on the tower as before without loading a new disc into it. The empty tray slid shut. Her breath hitched as her pulsed kicked up a notch. Aitch knew better than to not replace the DVD. Maybe he didn't want certain activities or meetings to be recorded on the CCTV that night.

Only one way to find out. She was kind of glad she didn't have to work first thing in the morning, because she planned on staying up late and being in the garage at midnight.

CHAPTER 4

Mavis altered the route to her apartment to include a stop at the grocery store. There were a few items she needed to make the cookies she promised Wes. The regular checkouts were full, which didn't bother Mavis. Self-checkout was a wonderful thing. She wanted to get in and out without having to make small talk. The one time a cashier had told her she looked familiar had sent her into interrogation mode, asking them if they'd ever seen her, or someone who looked like her before. The cashier had said no and brushed her questions aside, telling her she must just have one of those faces. At the time, Mavis didn't know what that meant. Now she knew it meant she was plain-looking, her features ubiquitous enough to belong to anyone. The encounter had left her so discombobulated she'd avoided the regular checkout whenever she could ever since.

The diversion to the grocery meant she approached the Fairwood Arms apartment complex from the rear. Her tiny efficiency was on the bottom floor of the back corner of the two-story building. Shaped like a U, the two arms of the stucco brown structure pointed away from the busy road, opening toward an undeveloped wooded area. Mavis passed the tall wrought-iron fence that cut off the U. Nothing else like their courtyard existed in town. A hidden oasis of green filled the space. Every apartment had access to it and a twelve-by-fifteen-foot water feature set in the middle of the quadrangle through their sliding glass doors. The pool was only two feet deep, but it was lined and plumbed. Water circulated through a fountain in the center.

Her landlady, Mrs. Lin, tended the courtyard with a dedication that bordered on the fanatic. That afternoon, a garden hose uncoiled over a large flat paving stone as Mrs. Lin sprayed the potted plants and ferns filling the tree-less spaces. A plastic visor shaded her eyes. She lifted her free hand in an airy wave as Mavis walked by but didn't let go of the sprayer.

Mavis turned the outside corner and stopped at her front door. Juggling her keys, she let herself in, popping the groceries on the counter. Her backpack landed on the floor. She stepped out of her shoes and crossed the single room to pull the sliding glass door open. Fresh air and natural light flowed in and bounced off the bare white walls. Wes always tried to convince her to put up pictures or shelves, but she couldn't do it. She'd tried tacking up a poster one day and felt claustrophobic afterward. As long as the walls were bare she could deal with the tiny apartment. Her bathroom didn't even have a tub. Instead, it held a shower stall, pedestal sink, and toilet. If she stood at an angle, there was just enough elbow room to wash her hair. Otherwise, she could soap up the walls, get in, turn around, and be done.

Mavis loaded the cookie ingredients from her kitchen into the grocery bag. She let herself out the sliding glass door, not bothering to put on shoes. Winding around the pool in the middle, she passed the flower bed where Mrs. Lin weeded, done with the watering.

Mavis climbed the steps at the front and walked down the

opposite arm of the building. She rapped her knuckles against the door frame. "Knock, knock!"

"You know it's not locked," Wes said.

She scooted inside and went straight to the kitchen.

Wes had a real apartment—one with more than one room. More than two, if you counted the bathroom, which she did because he had a bathtub. His couch was set flush against a shared wall in front of a flat-screen television hooked up to more than one type of gaming system. Mavis edged her way around the table. There were already some serious aromas coming from the kitchen, where she slid her bag of groceries onto the counter.

Mavis sniffed appreciatively. "What is that?"

Wes stirred a pot on the stove. "Just a little something. Don't get excited. It's not done yet."

"Then I'll start on cookies."

Mavis pulled items out of the bag. Wes handed her a large mixing bowl. Two sticks of butter went into it, followed by a cup of granulated white sugar. When Wes asked her about the rest of her day, she told him about the doctor's request.

"When do you meet this mysterious patient?" Wes knew her well enough. He didn't have to ask if she'd agreed to do it or not.

"Tomorrow."

"Mr. Aitch is giving you the day off?"

"He already gave me the morning off. Dr. Stombaugh asked him about it before I got back and he said yes." Mavis packed the one-cup measure with brown sugar and added it to the bowl. She grabbed a large wooden spoon from the utensil drawer and started mixing the contents. When Wes didn't say anything, she asked. "What?"

He frowned. "It just seems kind of, I don't know, forward? He didn't know you would say yes."

She stared at him. "You knew I would say yes."

"True. It's just—I don't know. You've been out of the hospital for a while now. You haven't seen the doc that whole time, and he just pops up out of nowhere and asks you for a favor on short notice? You might have had plans or something."

Her lips pressed together as she peered at him, brows raised in question.

"It's possible. You could have gone and gotten yourself a boyfriend between then and now."

She couldn't suppress her laughter.

"I'm serious. It could happen. But whatever—I know you want to help. You're like that, but you don't owe that doctor anything. He was doing his job. You're not his patient anymore."

"All true statements," she said. Contents creamed, she pulled out the vegetable oil and measured a cup full.

Wes watched her. "What are you doing with that?'

She poured the oil into the bowl.

He searched the counter. "You are following a recipe, right?"

"Recipe? What recipe?" Mavis grinned. In truth, the recipe was in her head, one of those things she knew without remembering how she knew. She'd made them more than once and they'd turned out perfect, but she didn't want to eat them all. Not again.

Wes turned his back to stir the pot on top of the stove.

Without Wes' attention on her, Mavis thought about what he said. She knew she didn't owe the doc anything for what he'd done for her medically, but she felt like she owed him personally. Maybe helping the doc out this one time would make her feel like she'd repaid him for helping her find the job with Aitch. After all, if she hadn't gotten the job, she couldn't have found her apartment, and then she wouldn't have met Wes, et cetera. The doc hadn't 'just done his job.' He'd gone above and beyond. That small act of kindness had led to so much more, including her being in the apartment she was standing in now, avoiding a meal eaten in solitude.

Mavis finished mixing the contents of the bowl. She wasn't much of a cook, but she could bake. Cookies were her favorite, but she had been known to bake cakes and bread. Whenever they had pizza, she made the dough.

Wes got her attention. "We're having scallops. Now would be a good time to pay attention to how they're prepared."

Mavis watched with interest and followed along until it was time to put the cookies in the oven. The stuff Wes was stirring in the pot on top of the stove turned out to be grits. He put together a green salad and tossed it with a vinaigrette dressing he whisked together right there on the spot. Honestly, eating with Wes was better than going to a restaurant. He plated the food while Mavis pulled out the cooling racks. She shuffled cookie trays in and out of the oven. Then it was time to eat.

Wes filled her in on all the behind-the-scenes gossip at the restaurant. She knew most of the people he worked with well enough to say hello to, but Wes was the only one she'd struck up a real friendship with. Their living in the same apartment complex helped. Wes liked meeting new folks and waiting tables, but Mavis knew he wanted to own his own business someday.

"And that lawyer, Jacque, from down the street came in today."

"How very French."

He sipped his beer. "I slipped him my number."

"How did you do that?"

Wes' eyes gleamed as his lips curled. "I noticed he wasn't done with his coffee and offered to get him a to-go cup. He said yes, and I wrote my number on the side."

"So stealthy." The timer went off, and Mavis went to switch the cookies. "Then what happened?"

"Nothing yet." He glanced behind her. "How many cookies are you making?" His brows drew together as he stared at his counter.

Mavis brought cookies into the shop whenever she baked. Louis would eat some if he came by. Aitch would too. He never said thank you, but she knew he ate some of everything she brought in. At least, she didn't think the plate was emptying itself.

"A batch is supposed to make forty-eight." She didn't question how she knew this, but did some quick math. "This batch made sixty-five. I guess I could have made them a little bigger. I'll leave you some."

Once dinner was finished, she tossed everything into the sink and ran the water until it got hot. She hoped her searing of scallops in the future would turn out as well as Wes' had.

"You don't have to do dishes," Wes said.

"They aren't going to do themselves. We've been through this."

"Save me the pots and pans," he said.

She never did. Wes never put up too much of a fight about it, but she suspected he was tired of washing dishes at the restaurant.

As the sink filled, Mavis spotted a full bag of garbage in the can. The dumpster was on Wes' side of the apartment complex, so she let herself out his front door. As soon as she opened it, she saw something twitch on top of the lidded dumpster. It was getting dark, but the yellow sodium lights fought the shadows in the parking lot.

"Hey, that cat's back," she called. The first time she'd seen it, she had jumped about a foot and recoiled in disgust. The four-legged creature didn't so much resemble a cat as a bag of knuckles with fur on. What fur it did have was orange, patched, and matted into clumps like it had been chewed up and spit out. Whatever got a hold of it must have had time to reconsider and decided there were, in fact, some things it would not eat.

Wes peered out the front door. "Well, go on. I don't expect he's gonna bite you, but be careful. That cat must be a badass."

"Why do you say that?"

"You ever see any other strays around here?"

Mavis tilted her head to the side. "I guess not."

The cat watched her walk down the stairs. Up close, she knew its eyes were golden brown. The thing didn't hiss or swipe at her, but it did warble and growl now and then as if it were trying to speak. It didn't have a collar or tags.

Mavis lifted the side of the dumpster lid the cat wasn't sitting on and tossed the trash bag inside. The cat didn't try to get at anything inside. Maybe it hung around and made a meal of the rodents that did.

The cat squeezed its eyes shut. Not a blink. A squeeze. "What's up, cat?"

A low rumble came from its throat.

She hesitated, then reached out a hand.

The cat sniffed and ducked its head like it was granting her permission to pet it.

Mavis wasn't fooled by its nonchalance. She pushed one finger against the cat's forehead, which was enough to send the cat sprawling onto its side in rapture. Its tail waved and stirred the air as it looked up at her in encouragement.

"Do not make friends with that stray," Wes called from his front door.

Mavis huffed out a laugh. Was that what she was doing? "Gotta go." She turned and went back upstairs. Before she shut the door, she watched the cat climb to its feet and resume its post, watching the apartments.

Soon it came time to leave and Wes bid her goodnight and wished her luck at the hospital. It wasn't like she was the one who needed the help, but she thanked him anyway. She slipped outside. The courtyard would remain lit until ten on the dot.

Mavis passed Mrs. Lin. This time she was seated by the pool in a lawn chair, her feet up on the ledge. The bright red glow of a cigarette burned brighter as she drew on the other end. Mavis stopped to silently offer her landlady a cookie. Mrs. Lin took one with a nod of thanks, and Mavis continued to her apartment. Behind her, Mavis thought she heard a small exclamation of surprise and the word, "crispy," but she couldn't be sure.

Back in her apartment Mavis yawned and stretched, almost touching the opposing walls of her single room. If she was going to sneak back to the garage by midnight and hide, she couldn't nap now. She didn't trust herself to wake up in time. Reading was out of the question. Her book might have been a page-turner, but it didn't matter. She'd fallen asleep with similar books open on her lap plenty of times.

The green light on her tablet winked at her from the counter where it was charging. She would trade a book on her lap for the chance to glance through the sites she'd book-marked—ones she trusted to report werewolf news objectively. There were discussions on every topic related to werewolves, including theories about why they had disclosed their existence in the first place. No one knew. Sites devoted to ruining lives by either disclosing private information or fetishizing werewolves were blocked.

A story about a stage actor in L.A. caught her eye. He'd moved to the west coast after several years in the Midwest, looking for a break. In the interest of full disclosure, he'd told producers he was a werewolf, and instead of showing him the door, he would be appearing on stage soon in an ensemble family melodrama set in the 1960's.

On another site, a thread on pack hierarchy dominated the discussion. Everyone knew werewolves ran in packs and the top dog, so to speak, was the alpha. Supposedly the rest would consist of a mix of other dominant and submissive wolves, but nobody knew for sure. The few packs that had chosen to register identified only their alpha in writing, presumably as a point of contact for anyone who wanted to get in touch with them. The rest of the pack members listed weren't assigned a rank. The question of how a wolf became alpha in the first place remained a mystery, but consensus held that it involved a fight between the alpha and whoever wanted to be alpha. Whatever happened to the loser wasn't widely disclosed.

One user suggested rank followed the Greek alphabet, but they were joking. Someone by the name of SirHowlsALot suggested a simple yet elegant solution. The leader was the alpha. The second-in-command would, therefore, be known as the second, and so on down the line.

This comment had Mavis thinking of the conversation she'd overheard earlier between the doc and Aitch. The doc said the garage was neutral territory. That was why he wanted to meet with—what was the name? Broderick. That was why he wanted to meet this Broderick guy there. And Aitch had said yes, but for seconds only.

No, that didn't sound right.

Mavis lowered her tablet, her gaze unfocused. Maybe Aitch meant they could only bring their seconds-in-command. If that were the case, Aitch knew way more about werewolves than she had ever expected. Although, if she was right, that would also mean that the doc was a werewolf, and not just any werewolf, but an alpha.

Mavis' jaw slid open and stayed that way for some time.

CHAPTER 5

Mavis, dressed in the darkest clothes she owned, pulled up her hood and tucked her hair away inside as she exited her apartment. She had an hour to spare until midnight. Nerves caused her to break into a jog down alleyways and back roads she knew weren't as well-lit as the main streets.

As she ran through the night, she thought about the doc. Not once in any of the times he'd visited her in the hospital and seen to her care had he ever done anything that would make her think he was a werewolf. Of course, she hadn't been paying attention to the calendar. He could have timed his visits and not done rounds the day after the full moon. Thinking back, Mavis had only ever seen the doc get agitated on two occasions, and one of those had been an honest-to-God medical emergency. Neither time had he done anything to indicate he could turn into a werewolf, which she might have expected when his emotions were running high.

The first time had come after she'd woken up to find a small box of chocolates on her bedside table. On top of the box was a card, where someone had written *Feel Better Soon* in big block letters. She thought one of the nurses or physical therapists (not Katrina) had left it to cheer her on. She'd eaten the chocolate and not given it another thought until later, when the doc came by to check up on her.

He'd spotted the box right away and frowned. "What's this?"

"Just some chocolates," Mavis said.

The doc picked up the box from the bedside table and lifted the lid.

Mavis was a little embarrassed that the box was empty, but there hadn't been that many chocolates in it, to begin with, and she'd been hungry.

The doc spotted the card and brought it close to his face, like he was all of the sudden nearsighted. His frown morphed into an all-out scowl. "Did you eat whatever was in here?"

"They were just some chocolates—"

By then, the doc was already headed toward the door. He stuck his head out and bellowed for the nurse. Mavis lay there and listened to the doc berate the poor nurse who answered his shout. In the end, no one knew where the box of chocolates had come from. When she asked what was going on, the doc said they were monitoring all of her meals and no outside food or drink was allowed. She hadn't known that. Mavis promised not to eat anything else that mysteriously appeared on her bedside table, and the doc calmed down.

The second time Mavis had seen the doc get upset, she'd been having lunch when he'd stopped in to check up on her. Intense physical therapy that morning had left her starving. Eating in front of the doc seemed rude, but he must have noticed how her eyes kept going back to the tray. He told her to go ahead and eat, and so she did while he paged through her chart.

A bite of fresh strawberry got caught in her throat. She coughed, but that didn't take care of it. She swallowed again, thinking that would help, but once the fruit was down. She just couldn't seem to catch her breath. Her neck grew hot, and suddenly her breath was whistling in and out of her throat. She raked her nails across her neck, clawing at her throat and trying to get some air.

The doc glanced up from her chart and noticed her frantic motions. "Mavis?"

She wheezed and grabbed her throat, staring at the doc, terrified. Words were beyond her.

He rushed to the door and threw it open, yelling down the hall. "I need a shot of Epi! Now!"

Mavis remembered thinking: *Is that what this is? An allergic reaction?* She knew what epinephrine was, but she didn't remember ever having to have it before.

Spots crowded her vision. The air hissed in and out of her like someone trying to pump up a bike tire with a hole in it. Through blurred eyesight, she made out the doc as he raised his fist and hit her in the thigh. It hurt. Just because she hadn't been able to walk didn't mean she'd lost the feeling in her legs. As soon as he injected her with a dose of epinephrine, the doc rubbed the spot, almost like he was sorry.

Her wheezing faded, replaced by full breaths as her throat opened and her vision cleared.

The doc stopped rubbing the injection site, whipped the stethoscope from around his neck, and pressed the business end to her chest. His fingertips pinched her wrist as he checked her pulse.

"Thank you." Her voice sounded like wet fabric dragged over gravel, harsher than she'd ever heard it. "What happened?"

"Must have been the strawberry," the doc said, frowning down at the offensive fruit. "I'm going to check you over and then order an allergy test."

The test revealed she was indeed allergic to strawberries, but not to any of the other most common food or environmental allergens they tested her for. If she had known she was so violently allergic to something, she would have avoided that something at all costs.

Her amnesia remained whole and complete.

Those were the few times Mavis had ever seen the doc stressed or heard him raise his voice. The rest of the time, he was calm, relaxed, and maybe a little sad. She wasn't sure about that last one. It was just a feeling she got sometimes.

But could he be a werewolf?

If anyone was a werewolf, the cantankerous Aitch fit the bill better than anyone. The thought had crossed her mind more than once. He was certainly grumpy enough, but Mavis knew he wasn't a werewolf. When she'd first started work at the garage, she'd stayed late a couple of evenings to familiarize herself with the business and make sense of the paperwork. Aitch had put in some extra hours under the hood of a customer's car at the same time. She hadn't noticed until she walked home that the full moon had risen. Aitch couldn't be a werewolf.

Mavis stuck to the shadows as she approached the garage. It was completely dark. She let herself in through the same door she had that morning, but when she turned toward the keypad to punch in the code for the alarm, there was no need. The alarm had already been disarmed.

She listened hard. No one there. Aitch must not have turned the alarm on when he left because he knew he would be back. That worked for her. She could focus on finding a place to hide.

Mavis took out the flashlight she kept in her kitchen and flicked it on. She kept the beam lowered and crossed the garage to the tarp in the corner. Underneath were the remains of an old car and a pile of spare parts she couldn't identify. Whatever the car was, it used to be electric blue, but now it was on blocks with no rear doors, roof, or hood. The tarp hung straight down from the frame where the rear passenger doors should have been and covered the opening to the back seat. She lifted the tarp and aimed her flashlight at the interior. Not only were the doors gone, but the rear seat was missing. Still, there was plenty of room to sit inside on the floorboard. She tried it out. Inside, she was completely covered, but she couldn't see anything either. In the toolbox, there was a flathead screwdriver. She used it to slit a hole in the tarp. After the incision had been made, Mavis put the screwdriver away, slipped under the tarp into the car, and checked her watch. Twenty minutes to midnight. She turned off her flashlight.

Fifteen minutes had passed when she heard tires on the concrete outside, different from the noise of regular traffic passing by. The same door she had come in through opened and shut. The lights came on, and the sound of booted feet came straight toward the covered car.

Mavis clutched the flashlight to her chest and held her breath.

The boots stomped past her hiding place, and the rear garage door rolled open.

Her pulse pounded as she peeked through the hole.

Aitch stood in the open doorway facing outward, arms crossed. Between the nearby streetlights and the waxing gibbous moon, there was enough light for Aitch to cast a shadow over her hiding spot. A minute later, a pair of head-lights washed over Aitch as a car turned in behind the garage. As the sedan came to a stop in front of the open door, the deep-throated rumble of a pair of motorcycles came around the end of the garage. The car's engine turned off as its head-lights winked out. The pair of motorbikes came to a stop about ten feet away from the passenger side of the sedan.

The two men who rode the bikes cut their engines and killed their headlights. Silence struck swift and complete.

The two men eased their kickstands down. They weren't wearing helmets. Their gazes locked on the sedan, but only one of the riders bothered to get off his bike. He wore black leather over skintight black clothing. His square jaw was covered in dark stubble and his short dark hair stuck up at all angles, windblown and tangled. Dark eyes watched the sedan over a boxer's nose and a full-lipped mouth. The other biker wore a leather vest over bare skin and blue jeans. He leaned back and crossed tattooed arms over a wide chest.

The driver's side door of the car opened and the doc stepped out. He wore a neutral expression as if he had mysterious meetings at the garage in the middle of the night all the time. He walked around the rear of the car and opened the passenger door in no rush at all.

Katrina stepped out with a smile for the doc and a neutral stare for everyone else. The dress and heels from earlier were gone, replaced by a leather jacket over jeans and a t-shirt with a pair of heeled boots. Katrina looked like she could have slid off the back of one of the motorcycles. Wait. Did that make Katrina a werewolf? For some reason, Mavis had an easier time believing that than the doc being a werewolf. Did that make Katrina the doc's second?

Katrina stepped away from the car. The doc closed the door.

Aitch stepped between the two parties. He wasn't a werewolf, but he certainly commanded authority. "This is neutral territory. Will you abide by the laws outlined in the accords?"

The biker who'd climbed off his bike nodded.

"Say it," said Aitch.

"I and mine agree." The biker's voice was a gravelly bass. "Doc?"

"We agree," the doc said.

Aitch grunted. "Good."

The doc addressed the standing biker. "Broderick. Joe." He nodded at the seated biker, who dipped his head in return.

Broderick raised his arms and smiled, but something was off about it. The smile didn't reach his eyes. It was more a baring of teeth. "Brother!"

Mavis sat back. This was the doc's brother? She leaned forward again.

The doc crossed his arms. "You called this meeting. What do you want?"

"Is that all the greeting I get after, what, a whole year?" Broderick lowered his arms.

"Don't make me repeat myself."

Broderick sighed. "Where is our father?"

"I don't know."

Broderick raised his chin in the air. "Then he is dead."

The doc dropped his arms. "Father is not dead. You would know it. As would I." The doc's voice changed, taking on a hint of an Irish accent.

"If he isn't dead, then he might as well be. A pack needs a leader."

The doc squinted at his brother. Thinking of this Broderick dude as the doc's brother left Mavis reeling, and finding no similarities between the two made it even harder still. In her head, if she straightened Broderick's nose, a hint of a family resemblance between the two could be seen, but that was all.

"You're not just talking about one pack. You're talking about all the packs. You want to take over for Father as alpha to the alphas. You want to be the Aldwulf," the doc said. Then he leaned his blond head back and laughed.

Broderick did not seem to find the comment funny. He

crossed his arms and widened his stance. "I suppose you think you should be Aldwulf?"

The doc's mirth abruptly fled. "No, I don't."

"The werewolves need a leader," Broderick said.

"We have one."

Broderick uncrossed his arms and growled. "Then where is he? He exposes us to humankind and then abandons us. And you do nothing."

The doc lifted his hands. "No one knows where he is. There's nothing to be done."

Broderick bared his teeth again. "Someone might."

Now it was the doc's turn to growl. "No. No one knows."

"That's not what I heard."

"I don't care what you heard. No one knows what happened to Dad or where he is."

Broderick chuckled low and steady. "You're so transparent, little brother." His gaze slid to Katrina, and his laughter died.

Aitch chose that moment to speak. "Are we done here?"

Broderick's gaze shifted between the three of them. "If Dad isn't back in the flesh by the next full moon, I'm taking over."

The doc jerked, blinking several times. Broderick stared at his brother, waiting.

The doc's frown turned into an all-out glower, but just as he was about to respond, a metal scraping noise came from inside the garage, right behind the tarp Mavis was hiding under.

CHAPTER 6

Mavis froze.

Everyone outside turned to peer into the darkness straight at where she sat under the tarp covering the old car.

Mavis sat back, not making a sound. She covered her mouth with her hand to muffle her breathing, which was suddenly very loud to her ears.

"I'll check it out," Aitch said.

Mavis' head turned to follow the sound of footsteps around the tarp-covered car to the far side. What were four werewolves and Aitch going to do when they found her? They would want to question her at the very least. Her mind stuttered and skipped over what she might say. Some of it went like *I heard there was a clandestine meeting and I wanted to know what was going on.* Or, *I felt left out.* It all sounded terrible.

The tarp began to lift.

Mavis pressed the flashlight to her beating heart. She saw the tops of Aitch's boots, his denim-covered shins—

A cat meowed.

The tarp dropped back into place like a curtain. Then,

purring. The sound of Aitch's booted feet walked away from the car.

"It's just a cat," Aitch said.

Mavis' eyes closed in relief, but her muscles twitched as she came to terms with the fact that she wouldn't have to run for her life. Not that she would have gotten far. She eased forward and saw Aitch holding a long, furry body, the tail hanging over his arm

"Friend of yours?" Broderick asked.

"You want to be Aldwulf," the doc said.

Broderick raised his hands. "I don't want to be, but the packs need a leader. I'm prepared to do what I have to do to avoid senseless werewolf bloodshed."

"By killing me and taking the title for yourself."

"The other alphas will accept one of Gloin's sons as Aldwulf. If you don't want to lead us, then I will. You've got three days."

Broderick turned on his heel and stalked back to his motorcycle. He threw his leg over the large black machine. The two bikes rumbled to life, and the riders took off into the night.

No one said anything until the motorcycles' engine noise faded.

"Son of a whore!" the doc swore.

Mavis' eyebrows shot up.

"How the fuck did he find out about Mel?"

Mavis had never heard the name before. Who was this Mel person? They seemed to be the someone Broderick thought knew where his father was.

Katrina's lip curled at the name, as if the mere mention of it disgusted her.

"More than a few people know what happened," Aitch said.

"I ordered my people not to speak of it."

Aitch shrugged. "People talk."

"Not werewolves who've been ordered to keep quiet by their alpha," the doc said.

Katrina glared into the night, her hands curled into fists. "You should have let me kill him."

The doc smiled. "You may still get the chance, dear one, especially if he doesn't give up the absurd notion of becoming Aldwulf. Not while Dad is still out there somewhere."

"And you have no idea where?" Aitch asked.

The doc shook his head. "No, but I know he's alive. For now. I've tried to reach him through the pack bonds, but the connection went cold the night he disappeared. If we could find him, this could all get resolved."

Aitch bent from the waist to set the cat down on the ground. The purring stopped. Mavis took a look at the feline that had almost spoiled her first attempt at spying. Her eyes widened. It was the same cat she'd seen on the dumpster outside her apartment building hours before. Could it have followed her there? The ugly orange stray took off into the darkness.

Aitch brushed off his hands. "Sounds like Broderick plans to settle it one way or another, come the next full moon."

"He can try," the doc said, but Mavis saw him swallow.

The meeting broke up after that. The doc opened Katrina's door and walked around to get behind the steering wheel. Aitch watched as the sedan reversed and then rolled forward out of the lot. A second later, he pulled the garage door shut and locked it.

Mavis relaxed. All she had to do was sit tight and wait for Aitch to turn off the lights. She expected he would turn on the security alarm as he left. When she was sure he was gone, she would leave her hiding spot, use the code to let herself out, and turn the alarm on behind her.

Any second now.

Had Aitch made it to the door yet?

With a loud whoosh, the tarp disappeared from the car. Mavis screamed.

Aitch stood next to the car with the tarp in both hands. "What do you think you're doing here?"

Mavis winced and hunched her shoulders, caught.

Aitch tossed the tarp aside and stalked around the car. "Do you have any idea what would have happened if they caught you here? Huh? Do you?" He smacked the car's frame hard enough for it to make a dull ringing sound.

Mavis didn't answer.

Aitch made a sound of disgust. "You're too stupid to know how lucky you are."

Mavis shot to her feet. "I am not stupid." Standing in the car made her taller than Aitch by about four inches. It wasn't much of an advantage, but she would take it.

"How did you know about tonight?" he asked.

She had no reason to lie. "I heard you guys talking about it earlier when I came back with lunch."

"And you just decided to invite yourself along and eavesdrop?"

"Are the doc and Katrina werewolves?"

Aitch braced both hands against the frame and scowled up at her.

"Is the doc an alpha? Is Katrina his second?"

Aitch stood up straight away from the car and lowered his hands. "You are too damn nosy for your own good."

All Mavis heard was what he didn't say. He didn't deny any of her questions which, in her mind, confirmed her suspicions.

"You're coming with me," he said, walking away.

"What? Now?"

"I know your ears work fine."

"No."

Aitch stopped and turned. "Excuse me?"

"I'm not going anywhere with you."

He took a step back toward her. "If it makes you feel any better, I don't want to go anywhere with you, either, but how else am I going to tell you everything you need to know about werewolves so you can survive your trip to the hospital in the morning?"

That was a strange way of putting it. Mavis had forgotten for the moment that she was due to see the doc in the morning and be introduced to his patient. What did Aitch mean by *survive*?

She crossed her arms. "Fine, tell me here."

"No, Mavis. You've proven the garage isn't exactly sound-proof, and you never know who could be listening. We're going to my place. I'll be driving you to the hospital tomorrow morning," he added. Then he stalked off.

Mavis scoffed. No way was she going anywhere with Aitch. Never mind he probably knew more about werewolves than anyone she had met or talked to online. When the were-wolves wanted to meet, they came to his garage. There had to be a reason this place was considered neutral territory. What else did Aitch know about them?

Inwardly, she groaned. She was doing this. She was going to willingly spend time with Aitch outside of work. All in the interest of learning more about one of her favorite subjects, she told herself.

Mavis hopped down from the car. "Can we stop by my apartment?"

He grunted. She hoped that was a yes. When Aitch switched off the lights, Mavis hurried to catch up.

<<<<>>>>

Aitch drove to her apartment without Mavis giving him

directions. Eustace Park wasn't that big. He'd probably heard her mention the Fairwood Arms in passing or he'd seen her address written down. She jumped out, ran inside, grabbed a few things, and crammed them in her backpack along with a change of clothes. Two minutes and she was back in the truck, ready to go.

Aitch didn't talk while he drove, but Mavis could feel him thinking. Being in such a confined space with him made her hyperaware of the smallest details, like how his knuckles went white from gripping the steering wheel too tightly, and also, how he avoided even glancing in her direction if he could help it. The farther they drove, the more she pressed herself into the corner of the passenger seat, trying to make herself as small as possible.

She'd never had a reason to go to Aitch's home before. Wherever he lived, it was well outside of town. The two-lane highway bent and twisted its way west while signs of civilization fell away. They hadn't passed another car once since they left town. After what felt like forever, Aitch turned onto a gravel drive that ran into a rutted lane. The road climbed up and leveled out, the headlights illuminating a single-story house built out of rough-hewn logs, the bark peeling and bleached by the sun. Aitch parked in front of the attached two-car garage. He cut the lights and the engine.

Mavis rushed to open her door and escape the inside of the cab. Outside she drew several deep breaths and remained silent, following Aitch to the front door. When he stepped inside, he held the door open for her. As soon as she was out of the way and the door was closed, Aitch went straight into the kitchen to pull a long-necked bottle of beer from the fridge. A second later, he seemed to remember that he had a guest who didn't know their way around. He flipped a switch, and three pendulum lights came on over a kitchen island. Two stools were pushed under the edge of the green stone countertop on the opposite side of the kitchen.

Her gaze darted around the open floor plan. To the left, a large dark brown leather sectional sat in front of a flat-screen television. Past the dining room was a hallway that probably led to the bedroom. The walls were painted a neutral color of earthy sand. Bright striped rugs in umber, turquoise, and red covered the hardwood floors. Several Southwest-inspired prints hung on the walls, along with a few black-and-white photographs. She wasn't sure what she had been expecting, but she liked it. There were no auto parts or pictures of cars to be found anywhere. Maybe he only kept that stuff at the garage.

Aitch removed the cap from the bottle and took a long swallow. "You want one?" he asked.

"No, thank you." It was kind of him to offer, but there were questions she wanted answers to. Mavis dropped her bag and joined him in the kitchen. "Tell me about the doc and Katrina."

Aitch tipped his beer. "Have a seat."

If he was standing, so was she. Mavis went to the island, leaned against it, and crossed her arms.

Aitch didn't say anything for a minute, staring into his bottle. Finally, he took another drink and finished the beer. He put his empty bottle by the sink and took another one out of the fridge. "What I'm about to tell you doesn't leave this house. The more humans know about werewolves, the more danger they'll be in."

Mavis wasn't sure if he meant the werewolves or the humans.

"I'm only telling you because you need to know," Aitch continued.

Mavis nodded.

"Tell me you understand."

She glared at him. "I understand."

"The first thing you should know is that werewolves have an incredible sense of smell and exceptional hearing."

"Okay." That made sense. Wolves were part of the canine family, and dogs had the best noses.

Aitch went on. "Even in their human form, werewolves retain both." He pointed his beer bottle at her. "You're lucky you chose to hide under that old, oily tarp and kept real quiet. It covered your scent and suppressed it. What they smelled of you, if anything, could be excused by your working there. If they knew you were there—" Aitch shook his head, uncapping his second beer. "Anyway. Fact is, a werewolf's nose is so good, they know when you're telling the truth because they can smell a lie."

Mavis' brows went up. "So, they're like human lie detectors?"

"Yes. If they're in the same room and close enough to smell you. Now, what are you going to do tomorrow morning when the doc asks you about your evening? What if he questions you further and you have to lie about knowing the doc and Katrina are werewolves? Have you thought about that?"

Mavis' mouth fell open before she snapped it shut and swallowed. What would she say?

Aitch sipped his beer. "Now you know why it would be better if you didn't know."

CHAPTER 7

Mavis held up a hand. "Hold on. No one is going to come out tomorrow and ask me if I know the doc and Katrina are werewolves. Why would they? I'm going there as a former patient to talk to a current patient. There should be no mention of werewolves."

Aitch's brows rose. "There shouldn't be, you're right, but if they get the slightest whiff that something's off, they might start poking around, asking questions you don't want to answer. This might come as a surprise, but werewolves can be a pretty paranoid bunch. More so now than ever."

What did he mean by that? Did it have anything to do with what she'd overheard tonight? Or the fact that they were coming up on the anniversary of their outing? "Do you know why the werewolves came out?"

Aitch looked away.

Mavis wouldn't be put off so easily. She pushed away from the counter. "Is Broderick the doc's brother? And what, or who, is the Aldwulf?"

Aitch put up both hands. "Knowing even a little about werewolf politics is dangerous, and you want to know more?"

Mavis couldn't say why, but she'd been interested in were-wolves ever since she'd heard a nurse mention their existence in passing. Mavis had latched onto the comment, wanting to know more. The nurse hadn't been able to tell her very much, so she'd started to do some research, reading everything she could find on the subject during her stay in the hospital. Now here she was, thirsty for knowledge, and Aitch was holding a glass of it over her head—a source, right in front of her who had first-hand experience. She nodded eagerly.

Aitch tipped his head back. "Am I going to get any sleep tonight?"

"Talk fast and we'll see."

He finished his second beer and switched to a bottle of water. When he remembered to offer her one, she took it.

"I'm only telling you this because I'm afraid of what you'll say if I don't." Aitch heaved a sigh. "The doc is alpha of his pack, which includes Katrina. She's his second. That means she's the second most dominant wolf in the pack. Broderick is alpha of another pack. The Aldwulf is alpha of the alphas, the most dominant wolf of all. His name's Gloin. And yes, he's Chase and Broderick's father."

"Werewolves can have kids?"

He narrowed his eyes. "Are you gonna keep interrupting me?"

Mavis threw up her hands but kept her mouth closed.

"Only under extreme circumstances can werewolves have children, but yes, Gloin has two sons. Soon after the news broke that werewolves existed, Gloin disappeared. All of the alphas took it hard. There's been a kind of mourning period for the old man, even though he's not dead—not as far as anyone can tell, anyway. But that time is coming to an end. Before alphas start fighting to become the next Aldwulf, Broderick wants to take the title for himself. He thinks the rest of the alphas will have an easier time accepting one of Gloin's sons instead of someone outside of his lineage."

When he didn't add anything else, Mavis took it as a sign she could ask questions. "But the doc is Gloin's son, too, so he could take the title of Aldwulf, right?"

"He doesn't want it."

"Can he, I don't know, abdicate?"

"It's not a throne, Mavis. If Broderick wants to become the new Aldwulf, he's going to have to kill his brother and remove all doubt that he alone has the right to the title. That's how it works. If he leaves Chase alive, he'll always represent a threat to Broderick and vice versa. If Chase somehow manages to take out Broderick, he'll be Aldwulf for as long as it takes another wolf to kill him. And believe me, they will. The doc's heart isn't in it to be Aldwulf."

Mavis nodded. "But none of that explains why the wolves came out in the first place."

Aitch's jaw clenched as he stared out into the night through his living room window. His hand rubbed the back of his neck "No one knows for sure."

He wasn't telling her everything. "Why do you think they did?" Mavis asked.

Aitch lowered his hand. "I've got a theory."

She leaned forward. "Let's hear it."

Aitch tipped his head back before he faced her again. "You'd have to know Gloin. He's a chess player. He gave the go-ahead for Andrew Tull, the alpha fireman out of Montana, to tell the world what he is. The picture they released of him pulling that kid out of a house fire was on the front page of every newspaper world-wide. It couldn't have looked any better."

Mavis listened, and didn't interrupt.

"After that, Gloin disappeared. I don't know what happened, but if you think about it, with all the cameras in this day and age, someone's bound to have seen something they can't explain. I think someone threatened Gloin. His priority would have been to control how werewolves came out to humans, which he did. He arranged for the picture of Tull to be released to the world with the news that he's a werewolf. Gloin's nothing if not a PR wizard."

"You talk about him like he's alive."

"Yeah, well, the alternative doesn't bear thinking about."

And yet, Gloin went missing when his pack, or rather all of the packs, needed him the most.

Mavis thought back over everything she'd heard at the garage, recalling how angry the doc had gotten after Broderick left. "What about this Mel person?"

Aitch stood up straight and frowned. "What about Mel?"

"Broderick seemed to think he might know something about where Gloin is."

"Mel went missing around the same time Gloin disappeared. Broderick thinks the two might be related."

Mavis tipped her head to the side, considering. "That does sound too good to be a coincidence. Could this Mel know something?"

"No. Mel doesn't know anything about Gloin because Mel's dead. Broderick just doesn't want to accept that."

"Why are you so sure this Mel person is dead, but Gloin isn't?"

"I have empirical evidence of the former and won't believe the latter until I'm standing over Gloin's dead body."

When he put it like that, it sounded like this Mel person was a dead end. Literally.

Mavis crossed her arms. "Let me see if I've got this right. No one knows where Gloin is, and on the night of the next full moon, Broderick is going to challenge the doc to become the new Aldwulf?"

"There's a bit more to it than that, but you've got the gist of it."

"And the next full moon is three nights from now?"

"Yeah."

"What happens if Broderick becomes the Aldwulf?"

Aitch shook his head. "I don't know. Changes in pack leadership never go well. I've seen it before. There'll be lots of scrabbling for rank and position, which almost always means bloodshed."

"What are the pack bonds?"

"They're how an alpha communicates with the rest of the pack, or how the pack communicates with one another. When one of them dies, they all feel it."

"They would all know if Gloin was dead, then?"

"Right. That's why I think he's alive, but he may be incapacitated in some way and unable to reach out to anyone for help. No one knows."

Mavis wondered how Aitch knew so much about packs and ranks and the Aldwulf. She was sure she knew the answer already, but she had to ask. "Are you a werewolf?"

Aitch threw his head back and laughed. If she didn't feel like he was making fun of her ignorance on the subject, she might have joined in the hilarity.

His laughter tapered off. "No. No, I'm not a werewolf."

"Then how do you know so much about them?"

He sobered. "I was raised with them." His jaw clenched tight. There had to be more to that story, but he turned his back on her and ran water in the sink. The subject was closed.

"It's late," Aitch said eventually. "What time do you need to be at Shady Creek in the morning?"

It seemed like such a long time ago now, but she told him the doc had asked her to show up around nine.

Aitch spoke to the sink. "We'll leave here at eight, then."

"You're still going to take me?"

"Not taking you would raise even more suspicion than my giving you a ride."

"Then there must be a way to beat a werewolf's nose," she said.

He turned off the water and faced her. "No, there isn't, but you can confuse it."

"How?"

"We'll talk about it in the morning. Get some sleep. The guest bedroom's down the hall on the right. The bathroom's right next to it." Aitch started down the hallway without a backward glance.

Mavis took her bottle of water, grabbed her bag, and found the guest room. It was bigger than her apartment, with a queen-sized bed set against the middle of one wall. A white duvet covered it, looking as soft and billowy as a cloud. A yawn hit her at the sight of it. On one side of the bed stood a nightstand with a lamp. On the other side was a heavy chair with curved arms.

Mavis toed off her shoes, fighting another yawn. Rifling through her backpack for pajamas revealed there were none inside. She'd grabbed clothes for the next day but nothing to sleep in. After crawling around in the garage, she didn't want to sleep in her clothes—the bed linens were too clean—but she didn't feel comfortable sliding between the sheets naked, either.

She hung her head and opened the door back to the hallway. The bathroom was empty, a nightlight throwing off a soft, warm glow. She knocked lightly on the other closed door and called Aitch's name.

A grunt sounded on the other side, so she knew she was in the right place. The door swung inward a second later. Aitch stood on the other side in a pair of flannel pants and a scowl. The sparse covering of curly black hair on his chest matched the hair on top of his head.

Mavis kept her eyes up, letting her peripheral vision do the soaking in. "I'm sorry, but I seem to have forgotten pajamas. Do you have a t-shirt or something I could borrow?"

Aitch turned away, but he didn't slam the door in her face. He walked his broad back across the floor to a tall dresser. His room was larger than the guest bedroom, with a four-poster king-size bed in some kind of dark wood. On either side were bookcases, each one overflowing with paperbacks and hardback books.

Aitch came back with a plain white t-shirt in his hands and gave it to her. "Anything else?"

Mavis thought about it. "Extra toothbrush?"

"Bottom drawer of the bathroom vanity."

"Great. Thank you." She hugged the t-shirt to her chest, turned, and walked back to the guest room, closing the door behind her as gently as she could. She felt if she moved too fast, she would break something loose between them.

Inside, she pressed her back to the wood and listened hard. She could have sworn she heard a footfall as if Aitch had started to follow her, but then stopped. Did she want him to stop? Of course, she did. What if he hadn't stopped? As she stood there, she heard his door softly click shut.

Why was her heart racing? It wasn't like she'd never seen a half-dressed man before. At least one had appeared in every magazine she'd ever read. She pushed away from the door, stripping off her soiled clothing. The t-shirt Aitch loaned her smelled like laundry detergent and hit her across the top of her thighs. All things considered, it felt like wearing a comfy mini dress. For a second, she thought about going to the bathroom to brush her teeth but she decided to wait until morning. She didn't want to risk running into Aitch, not when she was wearing nothing but his t-shirt.

The bed was as soft as it looked. What would happen the next day? Her worries didn't keep her up long. As soon as Mavis rolled into a ball on her side, she was asleep.

CHAPTER 8

Mavis could have sworn she'd just closed her eyes when a terrible banging awoke her. This was followed by a voice saying, "Rise and shine. Time to get a move on." The voice sounded like Aitch's, but that couldn't be the case. It was probably just a lucid dream. Why would she be dreaming about Aitch's voice?

Mavis stretched to her full extent without banging into anything. When she remembered where she was and what they were going to do that morning, she jerked awake. Her legs dangled over the edge of the bed after she sat up. Everything Aitch had told her about the doc, Katrina, and werewolves came back to her. She rubbed the sleep from her eyes and tried to think.

Another knock on the door almost made her slip from the edge of the bed. "There's a towel and washcloth on the bar in the bathroom for you. You can use the soap and shampoo in the shower, okay?"

"All right, thanks!" Mavis called.

She picked up her change of clothes and cracked open the door to the hallway. No sign of Aitch, but she did smell bacon. She darted to the bathroom, closing and locking the door. She hadn't brought any toiletries with her, so she was happy to use whatever Aitch had in the shower. The size of his bath seemed indulgent, causing her to linger longer than she might have normally. Teeth brushed and properly dressed, Mavis gathered her clothes from last night, stuffed them in her bag, and headed to the kitchen. Aitch stood at the counter, drinking from a mug.

"You *do* know how to make coffee," Mavis said.

"I never said I didn't. Eggs and bacon are on the stove. Help yourself." Aitch motioned with his cup.

"You didn't have to cook."

"I was cooking anyway. Be ready in ten." He stalked out of the room down the hallway.

"I can be ready in five," Mavis muttered to herself. She found a plate on the counter and helped herself. She was done with the eggs and onto her third piece of bacon when Aitch came back.

"This is for you," he said.

"What is it?"

Aitch lifted his hand between them. A chain spilled over his fingers. Hanging from the end of it was a silver leaf pendant, about an inch in diameter.

"I'm not really a jewelry person," she said.

"I don't care. This is silver. I don't expect you to have to use it, but having a bit of silver on your person when you're dealing with a bunch of werewolves can come in handy. It'll also help confuse your scent." He opened the clasp and stepped in close behind her.

Her breath caught in her throat. "I can do it—"

"Let me," he said.

Mavis swept her hair to the side, hoping he would finish quicker if she helped.

Her assistance had the opposite effect. She watched the

silver leaf draw near in slow motion, felt it settle against her collarbone. Aitch's fingertips brushed the nape of her neck and lingered. Her hair stirred with his breath. Mavis cleared her throat.

"How would I use it, if, you know, I had to—had to use it?" she asked, releasing her hair.

His hands fell away. The necklace dropped into place. "Silver hurts them if they come into contact with it. You've heard about silver bullets, right? I've seen a wolf take one to the head. It was the only thing that stopped him." Aitch moved away, avoiding her gaze. He stepped around the end of the counter.

She picked up the silver leaf, examining the detail in the veining and stem. "This is no bullet."

"Right. Don't throw it. You would have to press it into fur or flesh for it to do any harm, and even then it might only give you a second or two. Let's hope you never have to find out. Ready to go?"

"Yeah." Mavis tucked the silver leaf inside the rounded neck of her long-sleeved t-shirt. She estimated it would take three-quarters of an hour to get to the hospital. She could do this. It was one car ride. She would concentrate on her breathing and remain calm. Whatever it was between her and Aitch that made it hard to share a confined space, they couldn't let it get the better of them. Still, her feet dragged all the way to the passenger door of Aitch's truck.

Soon enough they were headed down the drive through a thick forest. Mavis wouldn't have seen any neighbors last night because there weren't any. On the main road, they headed back the way they had come the night before. The hospital was on the other side of town to the north.

"Are there ways to tell if a person is a werewolf just by looking at them?" she asked.

Aitch didn't grunt or answer. Maybe he hadn't heard her.

Half a minute later, he responded. "No. You can't tell just by looking at someone. Like what you said the other day, about there not being any older werewolves? You were right. A lot of them are older than they appear, but they don't look so in human form. No one knows exactly how old Gloin is, but he looks about the same age as his sons."

"So, what do I do if the doc or Katrina ask me a question I don't want to answer?"

"Don't answer. Deflect. Rephrase. Get as close to the truth as you can. Their noses are good, but they're not infallible." He glanced in her direction and caught her eye. "How are you going to answer if the doc wants to know if you spent the night with me?"

Mavis felt her cheeks grow warm. She didn't spend the night with him. Not like that. "Why would the doc want to know if I spent the night in your guest bedroom?" She emphasized the last two words.

Aitch chuckled. "Because you used my soap and shampoo this morning."

Mavis looked down at herself. She sniffed. "You have got to be kidding me."

He laughed, enjoying her discomfort. "Even that silver you're wearing won't cover an out-and-out lie."

Mavis felt tricked. He had known what he was doing when he'd offered her the use of his toiletries that morning. Well, she could play along. She wondered how far Aitch was willing to take their pretend relationship. "So, did I come over after your rendezvous at the garage, or did we spend the evening together?" She fluttered her eyelashes at him. "Did you leave me all alone in that big bed of yours?"

Aitch's hands tightened on the wheel. He wasn't laughing anymore. A muscle jumped in his jaw.

She'd never teased Aitch before. It was kind of fun, but not her style. She couldn't be interested in her boss. Not like that. Besides, as far as she knew, the only reason he was helping her was because he felt responsible for her. She was his only employee, after all. He didn't want her to get into trouble with the werewolves. Besides, teasing him cut both ways, and her stomach rolled into a knot at the thought of spending the night in his bed. She pressed her knees together and went back to staring out the front window.

"You could say you came over to watch a movie," Aitch said after a minute of stilted silence. "You fell asleep on the couch, stayed the night. I drove you in so you wouldn't be late."

Mavis didn't look at him. "What movie did we watch?"

"What movie?" Aitch asked, his tone incredulous.

"Yes. This is why I hate lying. Everyone has to keep their stories straight."

"What about *Halloween*?"

It was October. "I hate scary movies."

"Seriously?"

"Yes."

They argued about what movie they were supposed to have watched for the rest of the drive. Aitch turned on to a long gravel road that meandered around the natural bends in the landscape until the last half-mile when it straightened into a lane lined with tall evergreens on either side. Within ten minutes of the turnoff, their surroundings went from wild to manicured. The lawns and walking paths surrounding the grand old pile of stones known as Shady Creek Hospital were meticulously kept for the residents. She had been a patient, not a resident, treated and released because she could hold down a job and function on her own in society. There were some people inside who could not function on their own. They had nowhere to go and wouldn't be leaving anytime soon because, for the most part, Shady Creek was a mental hospital.

As Aitch parked, they decided on *The Princess Bride*. She'd watched it recently and Aitch owned a copy. He turned the ignition off. She took off her seatbelt and went to open the door, but his voice stopped her.

"How would you have gotten here if I didn't give you a ride?"

"Like I said, I would've taken the bus."

"I thought you hated lying."

She let go of the door handle. "I would've walked. I like walking. I like being outside." She turned back to face him.

Aitch stared back at her, an inscrutable expression on his face. He was across the cab from her, but the space between them seemed to shrink in an instant. Their argument had distracted her from their close quarters, but meeting his eyes across the bench seat reminded her Aitch could easily reach her from where he sat. Likewise, if she leaned forward, she could touch him, but why would she do that? Her heart thumped in her chest.

His eyes searched hers. "I like being outside, too."

Was he trying to put her at ease? Did he sense her sudden nerves? Did he honestly want her to think they might have something in common?

Mavis fumbled for the door latch, opened it, and jumped out of the truck. "All right. Well, thanks for the ride." She closed the door.

She didn't expect Aitch to open his door and climb out after her.

CHAPTER 9

"What are you doing?" Mavis asked.

Aitch shut his door. "I thought I'd wait. Grab a cup of coffee."

Mavis slung her backpack over her shoulder. "There's coffee at the shop. All you have to do is press a button."

"But I'm here now, and it's a long drive back to town. Don't worry, I'm not going to interrupt your meeting. Unless you want me to." He arched his brows.

Mavis turned on her heel and strode past the few other parked cars to the main entrance, not waiting for Aitch. She pushed through the tall oak doors. Inside, she blinked, her eyes adjusting to the interior. Natural light spilled in through the tall windows across the parquet flooring and surrounding woodwork. A fresh, clean scent with an underlying note of disinfectant invited her to relax, but she'd been away from the place too long for it to have much of an effect. The smell made some people uncomfortable, but it had never bothered her.

An older woman with a chin-length silver bob sat behind a solid-looking reception desk made of heavy, blonde wood.

Mavis didn't recognize her, but she had never really seen much of the hospital beyond the doc's office and top floor where her room had been. The woman asked Mavis for her name, consulting the computer, fingertips flying. Mavis admired her skills and wished she could type half as fast and well. It would make doing invoices a breeze.

"You can go ahead. Do you remember how to get there?" the receptionist asked.

Mavis winced even as she nodded. The woman was just doing her job. She had no way of knowing Mavis didn't have a problem forming new memories and could find her way around the hospital in the dark. She just couldn't remember who she had been before she woke up there.

The main door opened and Aitch came inside. Mavis ignored him as well as the elevator, taking the main staircase to the second floor. As she approached the doc's outer office, she heard voices. She stepped inside. No one there. The voices carried through from the doc's inner office, but from their pitch and tone, it sounded like they were wrapping up.

She sat down to wait.

Not even a minute later, the door opened and a tall young man emerged. She couldn't tell exactly how tall—his shoulders were rounded and stooped, his chest concave, and he had his arms crossed like he was trying to fold in on himself. A shock of dark hair fell across his forehead making his fair skin translucent. He wore a long-sleeved white t-shirt and dark blue jeans—not the clothes she associated with a resident, but Mavis wasn't so sure that he wasn't. The way he carried himself made her think of a fragile porcelain plate set close to the edge on a high shelf. She guessed he was about her age, perhaps a little younger. His early twenties, maybe.

Mavis stood.

The dark head lifted to reveal bright blue eyes. He started to say something, saw her, and stopped. He went still. She wasn't quite sure how he managed it, but he paled further. On top of his sudden stillness, his features went rigid. "Hello," he said and swallowed. His eyes focused over her right shoulder, and he repeated himself. "Hello." He focused on her again. "I —I'm sorry for your loss."

Mavis frowned. Did he mean her memory? Or had she suffered some loss she didn't know about? Did he know who she was? She pursed her lips, ready to ask him what he meant, but he turned away.

"I'm sorry," he repeated. His face crumpled. He buried his face in his hands as sobs tore through him, his thin frame shaking. The intensity of his cries unsettled her.

Behind him, the doc witnessed the entire exchange. He stepped up, settled an arm around the younger man's shoulders, and spoke in a low, soothing voice. "It's all right, Forrest. Why don't I take you back to your room? Would you like that?"

Forrest's sobs tapered off. He lowered his hands, his arms hugging himself. He kept his face turned away from her, but what she could see of his cheek was splotchy from crying. As the doc led Forrest away, he held up a hand, his index finger extended, letting her know he would return soon.

Mavis sat back down. She'd spent two months at Shady Creek and never run into anyone like Forrest. While her interactions with other people had been limited to doctors and staff, his reaction to her being there reminded her of the kind of hospital she was in. What loss was he sorry for? She didn't know of any losses besides her memory. Her thoughts threatened to drag her into an anthill of unanswerable questions, so she forced herself to dismiss his comment as the ravings of a delusional young man.

Two minutes later, the doc came back. "I'm sorry you had to see that. Forrest is new here and we're working on getting him settled. He's usually much calmer. I'm not sure what set him off. Please." The doc held out a hand for her to precede him into the inner office.

If Forrest was a new patient, he could not have known her. Perhaps he thought everyone who came to see the doc had suffered a loss. "Is he going to be okay?" Mavis asked, standing.

"He calmed down once he was back in his room."

Mavis stepped into the doc's office. He closed the door and went around the desk. His familiar white coat was back in place over his blue button-down shirt. Today he wore a patterned blue tie knotted high and snug against his throat.

He sat. "How are you?"

Mavis flashed him a smile and sat in one of the two visitor chairs in front of his desk. "I'm well."

"Before you meet with the patient I was telling you about, I wanted to check in with you, see if anything new has come up."

"You mean, has my memory returned?"

"In part, yes."

"No. I haven't remembered anything from before. My amnesia remains."

The doc studied her a moment.

Mavis blinked, then swallowed. Of course, he would know if she was telling the truth. Between her hurry to put some distance between her and Aitch, and then being distracted by his patient's outburst, she might have tried to forget the doc was a werewolf.

"And how's work?" the doc asked.

"It's good."

The doc nodded, his nostrils flaring. "How's Aitch?"

Mavis sucked in a breath. Why was he asking about Aitch specifically? Could he smell his scent on her skin? She couldn't deny she'd been with Aitch that morning, so she didn't. "He's good. He gave me a ride."

"Really?"

"He insisted."

The doc sat up straighter. "How so?"

Mavis could have slapped herself in the forehead. She could have just said yes and left it at that, but she'd slipped up by telling him Aitch had insisted on bringing her. Now what?

"He didn't want me to have to walk, since I don't drive and all."

The doc leaned back and ran a hand down his tie. "I'm sure he's just keeping an eye out for you. You've done a wonderful job with the garage. It's never looked better."

"Thank you," she said, her lips curving into a smile. It was nice of him to say so. Lord knew, Aitch never had.

"Have you thought about what you might want to do with yourself?"

Mavis frowned. "I don't know what you mean."

"I have to be honest with you, Mavis. When I got you the job with Aitch, I didn't expect it to turn into a long-term situation. I'm asking what you think you might want to do with yourself when you're done working at the garage."

She frowned, barely holding herself back from parroting his words back at him.

The doc stacked his hands on top of his desk. "Let me put it another way. If money were no object, where would you go? What would you do?"

Those were loaded questions—the type of questions that would keep her up at night if she allowed. She could certainly see the appeal of a fresh start somewhere else. Somewhere she didn't know anyone and no one knew her. But she couldn't leave, could she?

Her existence might be considered meager by many standards, but Eustace Park was her home. The only home she could remember, anyway. She didn't have any family. No one was looking for her. She was on her own. If money were no object, she could just pick up and leave with what little she had with her right then—travel, see the world, or at least more than New Mexico.

Not for the first time, Mavis wondered what capital-T Trauma had caused her to lose her memory in the first place. In her mind, it must have been a catastrophic event. There weren't just unanswered questions surrounding that life-altering moment, but also about the type of person she'd been before it. Had the old Mavis traveled and seen the world? Had she enjoyed it? Or could she not wait to get back to wherever it was she came from? That train of thought brought up even more questions—had she been a good person? Did she have any friends? People who cared about her? If so, where were those friends and family now, and why hadn't they tried to find her? No, she had come to accept the fact no one was looking for her.

She considered the possibility that her life, as it was right then, was her fresh start.

Mavis blinked and shook her head. "I don't know."

"You could learn how to drive."

"I'm not sure."

"Think about it. You might decide you'd like to go to school, learn a trade."

She didn't know what to say to that, but she thought some sort of response was needed, so she replied, "I'll think about it."

"Great. Please do. You have potential, and whatever you choose to do, I'm sure you'll excel." The doc pushed back from his desk and stood. "The fact that you have such a bright future is important for my patient to know. Thank you again for coming in today and speaking with her. I know she's eager to make your acquaintance. We can head up now."

"Up?"

"Yes. She's on the fourth floor. Near your old room."

CHAPTER 10

Mavis and the doc took the elevator up to the fourth floor, standing together, but separate in the way that people forced to share an enclosed space did. The doc watched the numbers. Mavis kept an eye on the doors.

Beside her, the doc stirred. "You said Aitch gave you a ride this morning?"

"Yes."

His nostrils flared and he turned toward her. Too late, Mavis realized she should have insisted they take the stairs. Inside the elevator, there was no way the doc wouldn't notice just how much she smelled like Aitch. Damn him.

The doc's gaze focused on her neckline of her shirt. "I didn't think you wore jewelry."

Her hand flew to the silver maple leaf still tucked inside her shirt. The pendant remained hidden, but the chain circled her neck in plain view. "Aitch gave it to me."

The doc's eyes narrowed. "Did he? You weren't wearing it yesterday. Are you—no, it's none of my business." He shook his head, but his brows drew together down low.

"I went over to Aitch's place last night and fell asleep. He let me stay instead of taking me home so he could give me a ride this morning." That was the truth if one didn't pay too much attention to the timeline of events. "We're not—"

The elevator doors dinged open cutting her off.

"As I said, it's none of my business." The doc stepped out of the elevator.

Mavis tucked her chin and followed the doc. She didn't want to dig herself into a verbal hole she couldn't climb out of. Aitch had said the silver around her neck would help confuse a werewolf's nose, but it would only do so much.

Nothing had changed. The hallway they walked down was entirely the same as it had been the day she left. Washed-out geometric prints filled metal frames on the pale blue walls. Institutional white tile stretched in every direction, spotless. The place had an outdated feel, but it wasn't worn-down.

Mavis knew her way around this part of the hospital well enough, but she let the doc take the lead, since she was technically a visitor now. If she were still a patient and they were returning to her room after an appointment, she wouldn't have thought twice about leading the way.

They passed a deserted nurse's station, the computer terminals humming away, and kept walking.

Mavis' steps did not slow as they passed what had been her room for the duration of her stay, but her head turned, and she peered at the closed door as if she could see through it into the room beyond. The sunlight would be pouring through the windows, lighting up the bright white wall across from the foot of the bed and illuminating the picture there: a tall ship, its sails full of wind, its bow pointed away from the windows and toward the exit. They continued down past Mavis' favorite balcony and around the corner. The doc slowed, stopping in front of a door she'd passed by but had never passed through before.

"Before we go in," the doc said in a hushed tone, his hand on the doorknob, "I want you to feel free to discuss any aspects of your treatment. As much as you feel comfortable sharing. She's curious about you." He pushed the door open.

Inside was a lounge with two loveseats facing each other over a wooden coffee table. An older woman stood across the room at the window. The woman turned as the door finished traveling through its arc. Her arms hugged her torso, one hand to the opposite shoulder, the other to the opposite hip. She wore a pair of blue pajamas with a long, gray cardigan, the pockets sagging open. Her dark brown hair hung straight down to her shoulders, parted in the middle around an oval face and brown eyes. Though her brows lifted at the intrusion, she didn't smile.

"Mavis, this is Sandra, the patient I was telling you about," the doc introduced them. "Sandra, this is Mavis."

Mavis stepped into the room.

Sandra watched her, brows lowering.

"I'll leave you two to get acquainted. Just call when you're finished." The doc lifted his hand toward the phone on the wall. He turned to Mavis. "Thank you again for coming." He left the room, closing the door behind him.

Mavis swallowed and faced Sandra, this mysterious woman who reminded the doc so much of her. She raised a hand in greeting. It seemed awkward to cross the room and offer to shake her hand when Sandra's arms were still wrapped around herself. "Nice to meet you."

Sandra released herself from her self-imposed hug and motioned to the loveseats. "And you. Please, have a seat."

After Mavis sat, Sandra took the seat across from her. She leaned over the end of the loveseat and reached into a bag Mavis hadn't noticed. It was made of a faded, sturdy-looking canvas with a large flap over a single deep compartment. From inside the bag, she withdrew a long wooden incense holder, curved on one end, along with a thin stick of incense itself. She stuck the end of the stick into the holder and lit the other with a cheap plastic lighter. As soon as the stick produced a thin trail of smoke, she pulled out a small tin, opened it, extracted a round pill, and popped it in her mouth. She saw Mavis watching her.

"Allergies," she said. "Do you mind if I burn some incense?"

Mavis glanced around the room. Every window was shut tight.

Sandra waved a hand through the smoke. "It won't set off the smoke detectors, and I already asked the doctor if it would be okay. I like this particular scent. It helps me relax."

"Okay. Sure. I hope I'm not making you nervous."

Sandra's brown eyes narrowed a fraction in an assessing sort of way. Then she relaxed. "No, of course not."

Mavis cleared her throat. "The doc said you can't remember who you are?"

Sandra replaced the tin and drew out a notebook and pen. "Yes. that's right. I've lost my memory. I take notes to help me cope with my condition. Do you take notes?"

Mavis shook her head. "I've never had a problem making new memories. I just can't remember who I was." She sniffed. The incense smelled of something sweet she couldn't identify. The scent stuck in the back of her throat and coated her tongue.

"You don't remember anything from before your..." She paused, perhaps hoping Mavis would fill in the blank, but Mavis didn't have anything to fill it with. "Your accident?"

"No. I've tried, but there's nothing there for me."

Sandra scribbled something in the margin of her notes. "When you say you've tried, what do you mean?"

Mavis shrugged. "Relaxation. Hypnosis. That kind of thing. What about you? Do you not remember anything?"

Sandra wrote something down before she looked up. "Do I remember anything? I get flashes of things from time to time. Like an image. All of a sudden, it's there and then it's gone. What about you? Anything like that for you?"

"Not at all." What Sandra described sounded strange to Mavis. She'd never caught a flash of anything from her former life. At first, she would have given up a lot for a glimpse of the life she led before, almost anything. But now, as time went by, she found she'd give less and less. When had she grown so comfortable with herself and not knowing? She should want to know, right? Like Sandra.

Mavis rolled her shoulders. She and Sandra were two different people. Their experiences were going to be different.

The way Sandra spoke about these flashes made it sound like her memory might return someday, which made Mavis wonder what the doc thought they had in common, other than their affected memories. "What are your flashes like?"

"Just flashes. Like someone holds up a photograph and then puts it away."

Mavis glanced down. "Do you write down what you see?"

Sandra fingered the edge of her notebook. "Yes. Yes, I do."

"Maybe you should draw them instead."

"Draw? Yes, maybe I should, but I'm not much of an artist." She looked down at her notes. "So, you've never had anything like that happen to you?"

"No." Mavis frowned. "You already asked me that."

Sandra inhaled sharply as she raised her gaze to meet Mavis'. "Right. Sorry."

Here they were, two women with memory problems, and she made the other feel bad for asking the same question twice. Mavis felt like a jerk. "No problem. That's great that you get flashes, though. Maybe you'll get your memory back in time. But don't worry if you don't."

"Don't worry?"

"I think that's why the doc wanted me to talk to you. I haven't remembered anything since before I woke up here in the hospital, but I'm doing okay. I've moved on. I have a job, an apartment—friends." She smiled as she thought of Wes and frowned when she thought of Aitch. "I guess my boss is my friend." Mavis stopped and shook her head. Why had she said that out loud?

"Your boss?" Sandra asked, making a note.

Mavis fidgeted. The cloying scent of the incense was getting to her. "I think he's trying to be my friend, even though he's not very friendly sometimes. At least not to me. Not until—" She stopped herself before she said anything about last night, or that morning. Her knee started bouncing. "So, I guess what I'm trying to say is that even if your memory doesn't return, you can still move on from here and have a life outside these walls. Do you know what happened to make you lose your memory?"

Sandra blinked and wrote in her notebook. She raised her head and looked around the room. "Car accident. What about you?"

Mavis' brows merged as her knee continued to bounce up and down. She rubbed her hands together and twisted her watch around her wrist. Her eyes watered, and she blinked. Hadn't she told Sandra she didn't remember anything before she woke up in the hospital? They hadn't even told her how she came to be there. Mavis had always wondered, but too much time had passed to worry about that now. She was pretty sure she'd said as much already. "I don't know. Were you driving?"

"Yes, but I don't remember why."

"That's awful. I don't drive." Mavis had no idea why she said that.

"You have a job, an apartment, a life. What do you like to do in your free time?" Sandra asked.

Sweat broke out across Mavis' forehead and upper lip. If she could stop fidgeting, maybe it would stop. She made her knee stop bouncing. Then her toe started tapping. "I like to read and go for hikes. I'm also curious about werewolves." Her mouth snapped shut. She should not have said that. Why did she say that? What was wrong with her? Mavis sprang to her feet and began to pace between the windows and the door behind the couch where she had been sitting.

Sandra remained seated, watching her. "I'm sorry? What about werewolves?"

Mavis fanned herself with her open hand. "Is it hot in here? It feels hot in here." She stopped and checked the windows, but they didn't open. She fanned herself harder.

"What do you find curious about werewolves?" Sandra asked again.

"Nothing. Everything. I just find them fascinating."

"What do you know about them?"

"Only what I've read." She needed to change the subject. She wasn't supposed to reveal anything Aitch had told her last night and she'd already blurted out enough random information. Her head wasn't working right. She couldn't concentrate.

Sandra wouldn't let it go. "Do you know any werewolves?"

"I—" Mavis stopped. Sweat ran down her sides. Her heart hammered away at her breastbone.

Sandra watched her from the couch, her complete focus on Mavis. The intensity of her gaze took Mavis by surprise. Why was she so interested in whether Mavis knew any werewolves? Was she a werewolf? Could she smell a lie? Mavis couldn't say she didn't know any werewolves, because that would be a lie. Then she would have to reveal how she knew about them, and she knew she would. She could feel the words building on her tongue, behind her teeth, waiting to spill past her lips like bile. She covered her mouth to hold back the trickle of words. If they started, she wouldn't be able to stop them. She had to get out of there.

"I need some air."

Mavis crossed the room in a rush and threw open the door. She caught a glimpse of Sandra's face, her eyes wide, her mouth a circle of surprise, but she didn't get up from the couch.

Outside, Mavis turned the way she and the doc had come earlier. The balcony—that was a good place to go. Plenty of air there. She hadn't stepped foot in her favorite place since she'd left the hospital, but her feet knew the way.

She pushed through the door and went straight to the solid stone railing. The balcony was only partially covered. Many times, she'd enjoyed watching the rain come down from the shelter of the overhang closer to the door. The sun shone down now, making the mortared rocks beneath her palms warm. Mavis had the place to herself, as she often had when she had been a patient.

The fresh air helped clear her head despite her spasming limbs. She pressed her hands to her chest and focused on the treetops in the distance. With each breath, her focus sharpened until she could peer through the branches about fifty yards away across the manicured lawns. A magpie hopped from branch to branch, the white on its wing catching her attention. Her heartbeat slowed.

A rough scrabbling noise sounded behind Mavis. She hadn't heard the door open, so she didn't turn around.

A sharp push between her shoulder blades sent her tumbling forward over the railing, head first. A scream caught in her throat.

CHAPTER 11

Mavis came back to herself slowly, and then all at once. She blinked her eyes open. Above her, the trees waved in the wind. Her whole body ached like she'd been pushed through an old washing machine's wringer rollers, the kind she'd seen in a cartoon somewhere, but she was alive to feel it somehow. She lay face up in a pile of leaf litter and debris on the forest floor, naked. She closed her eyes and rested her head back against the earth.

"Mavis!" a voice bellowed.

She gathered her strength and raised a hand in the air, stretching toward the treetops. Light filtered through her fingers.

"Mavis!"

The voice yelling her name sounded an awful lot like Aitch. Maybe she should just stay where she was. The dirt wasn't so bad. Energy depleted, Mavis closed her eyes. Her hand fell back to the ground.

"Mavis!" This time his shout held the note of discovery.

She kept her eyes closed, too weary to open them again.

The rush of footsteps was followed by the snap of

fabric. A blanket settled on top of her as something landed in the dirt beside her. "Mavis," Aitch breathed her name. "I've got you." Solid arms—one under her shoulders, the other under her knees—lifted her into the air. Her left side pressed against a warm, solid wall. It occurred to her to protest, but she didn't have the energy, and she let the indignity slide.

Aitch carried her for a while. She wasn't sure how long she bounced against his chest to the rhythm of his steps. Somewhere along the way she lost the fight to stay conscious.

<<<<>>>>

The lights in the dream came up slowly from pitch black to not quite so dark and hovered there. She faced a mirror or, at least, she thought she did, because the person in it shared her looks. The face she recognized, but not the individual behind it. She had the right features in all the right places, but it wasn't her. As Mavis stared, the mouth pinched in disapproval, the eyes hardening. Mavis flinched away from the visage. The person in the mirror did not. She sniffed with contempt; her lip curled in disgust.

A machine beeped. The smell of disinfectant hit her nose. She was back at Shady Creek. The first time she'd woken up there, she hadn't remembered who she was. Now she felt a similar sensation but different. It wasn't her name, because she knew that. She remembered who she was. No, this was something else. Something important.

Mavis blinked her eyes open. No picture of a tall ship graced the wall across from the foot of her bed. She was glad they hadn't taken her to her old room. This one was larger than the one in which she'd spent the majority of her recovery. From the light streaming in the window, it was still daytime, but was it the same day? Before, when she first woke up, she would blink, and hours—sometimes days—would pass at a time.

Whispers slid past Mavis' ears, none of the words catching.

"Hello?" she croaked, her throat sore.

"Mavis." Aitch turned up at the side of the bed. He wore the same clothes from that morning.

She hadn't lost much time, then. She started to push herself up, and then stopped. The blanket Aitch had thrown over her outside covered her, but underneath she was naked.

Aitch put up a hand. "Take it easy. I found your things. You can get dressed when you feel up to it."

"But why am I naked?"

Someone snorted.

Mavis peered around Aitch to see Katrina standing across the room next to the doc. She was dressed in pale blue scrubs, like she'd been pulled away from her work.

"Why is she here? She doesn't even like me," Mavis said, surprising herself. Their relationship had always been one of quiet, mutual disdain, but it didn't seem as if Mavis could stop her mouth.

Katrina snorted again. "You got that right."

Anger made Mavis push herself up, holding the blanket close to keep it from slipping. "Are you kidding me? I don't need any physical therapy right now, so why don't you go away?"

Katrina took a step forward. "Oh, I don't think so."

"Katrina, please." The doc put his hand on her forearm.

It was like a switch flipped. Katrina relaxed. She didn't smile—not that Mavis cared—but she unbent enough to step back, lean against the wall behind her, and cross her arms in a decent imitation of someone at ease.

"Will someone please tell me what is going on?" Mavis'

head turned from the doc to Aitch and back again. Katrina, she ignored.

The doc took a step forward, but it was Aitch who sat on the side of the bed, facing her. "Mavis, you have to think. Try and remember what happened."

She thought back and remembered her conversation with Sandra. "I needed some air. I went to the balcony." Her favorite place.

"Good. If you can remember that, you can tell us what happened next," Aitch said.

Mavis peered into her lap as if it had all the answers. Her fingers plucked at the blanket. She remembered the tree with the magpie in it and then the pressure between her shoulder blades. The ground rushing up to meet her. Why was she not splattered all over it? Gravity had a way of winning in these situations. Why not this time?

Mavis plucked at the blanket again and, for a second, instead of her fingers, she saw feathers, white and inky black. The magpie? She blinked, and the sight was gone. The sensation of falling hit her low in the stomach, but what came next was something else. The sensation of lift.

Mavis sucked in an audible breath, staring at her fingertips.

Aitch covered the hand she was staring at with one of his own. "It's okay. Breathe. Think back. Did you hear anything?"

Had she? She shut her eyes tight. The weight of Aitch's hand grounded her. The air roared past her ears as she fell. Mavis cocked her head to the side, listening hard. There was something else. She turned her hand over and clenched Aitch's fingers. The roaring sound filled her head, a wall of white noise, but then another sound emerged from the void. A beat, but more. A rhythmic flapping. Could it be—

Her eyes opened and she shook her head. Could a bird have saved her from falling to her death? Did the magpie she saw earlier spare her life somehow? Impossible. It didn't make sense.

Aitch let go of her hand and took her by her bare shoulders. "Mavis, think about it."

She was, frantically. No way one tiny bird, or even an entire flock, could have swooped in from out of nowhere, stopped her from falling, and carried her away into the woods to drop her in a pile of pine needles. The sensation of falling, followed by a sensation of rising. The ground rushing up to meet her and just as suddenly receding as if pushed away.

Unless—

Unless she was the bird.

The idea was so preposterous, she laughed in Aitch's face.

His lips compressed into a thin line. "Tell me what you think happened," Aitch said, his voice low and firm.

Mavis shook her head.

Aitch let go of her shoulders and took her hand again. His features relaxed. The sudden change in his demeanor convinced her more than anything that what she suspected was the truth.

"I think I turned into a bird and flew."

There. She'd said it out loud. Now they could all have a good laugh and tell her what had really happened, but no one laughed. No one even smiled.

"What am I?" she asked.

Aitch squeezed her fingers. "You're a shifter, or what we call two-natured. You're human, but you can shift to a second nature. In your case, a bird."

She stared at Aitch, waiting for him to say something that made sense. Then she turned to the doc. His hands were shoved into the pockets of his white coat, but he wore a similar expression, open and accepting.

Mavis turned back to Aitch. "You're not kidding."

"No."

"But—" A flash of treetops from above popped into her mind. "How? I don't know how I could have turned into a bird just now."

"You won't remember either," the doc said. "The first couple of shifts can be hard on the mind as well as the body. I suspect that, along with your other memories, you've forgotten your ability to do even that."

The flash of black feathers—was it a memory of the bird she saw, or the sight of her hand, transformed into a wing? How was this possible? How could she not know? How could she forget something like that? She swallowed, her stomach churning. "I saw a magpie."

Aitch nodded. "Having a visual of the thing you want to shift into can help. It was a good thing you saw it, or you might not have been able to shift. That's how you survived the fall from the balcony. But why"—he gripped her fingers tight—"did you jump?"

Mavis jerked. "I—I didn't."

From his frown, she could see Aitch didn't know whether to believe her or not. He said, "Okay," but she thought he was trying to placate her.

"I did not jump." Her gaze went from him to the doc. "Someone pushed me and I went over the balcony. The next thing I knew, I was lying in the dirt out in the woods."

Aitch gave her fingers one last squeeze and let go.

"I do not have a death wish," she said. "You have to believe me."

Aitch glanced over his shoulder at the doc. She couldn't read his expression, but she wondered if he was looking for the doc to confirm her story with his werewolf nose.

"I do," the doc said. "I find it easier to believe that you were pushed than you would try to take your own life. Your other nature acted out of self-preservation."

Mavis rested her head back against the pillow, vindicated.

A good feeling.

It didn't last.

"How did you know I could turn into a bird?" Mavis asked.

The doc glanced away and wouldn't look at her.

Aitch cleared his throat. "We didn't know for sure until today. You've been back for six months and haven't shifted once. We didn't know if you still could."

Mavis' eyes narrowed. "What do you mean 'still'?"

CHAPTER 12

"Y ou disappeared," Aitch told her.

Across the room, Katrina sighed and rolled her eyes.

Mavis glared at her, tired of the interruptions. Katrina stood up straight from against the wall, meeting her hard stare with one of her own. As Mavis watched, Katrina's eyes lightened, going from dark brown to a yellow-brown. Her lip lifted in a sneer, and Mavis thought she saw a canine start to lengthen. Katrina took a step forward.

Mavis' anger faded, replaced by fascination.

The doc stepped up close to Katrina and touched her arm. Again, the change was instantaneous. Her eyes darkened back to human brown as she looked away from Mavis.

"Maybe you should wait outside," the doc suggested.

Katrina glanced quickly up at the doc and then away. Without a word, she turned, leaving the room.

As soon as the door swung shut behind her, the doc turned to Mavis. "You shouldn't challenge her like that."

"I—I didn't."

"Perhaps you didn't mean to, but you did. Just staring her

in the eye like that is enough to set her off. Her wolf doesn't like it."

"Her wolf?" Mavis glanced between the doc and Aitch.

"He knows. I told him everything," Aitch said. "Once you ran out on Sandra, all bets were off."

Sandra had asked her if she knew any werewolves. Mavis didn't regret running out on her. If she had stayed, she was afraid she would have spilled everything she knew about them. She didn't know why she would have done that when she knew she wasn't supposed to.

"No one knew where you were or what happened to you," Aitch continued, drawing her thoughts away from the worrisome Sandra. "He knows about your visit to the garage last night, too."

"You always did poke your nose into matters that didn't concern you," said the doc.

Mavis shook her head. "Always?" she breathed the word. "What are you telling me?"

"You disappeared," Aitch repeated. "When you turned up six months ago with no memory, no one knew if you would remember being two-natured."

She licked her lips, mouth dry. "How long was I gone?"

"You disappeared about a year ago," Aitch said.

"What happened to me?"

Aitch shook his head. "No one knows."

And the big one. "Who was I?"

Aitch sat back, his mouth opening and closing, his powers of speech abandoning him for the first time since she'd woken up.

The blood pounded in her ears. They knew. They knew who she was—they knew *what* she was—this whole time. And they had never told her. The doc had asked her what her plans were, like they weren't going to tell her, as if they were prepared to let her go on without ever telling her what she was. If she hadn't been pushed from the balcony, she might never have known. Not that she understood what it meant to be two-natured, not yet. What would have happened if she had left and never found the chance to change? Would she have gone through life blissfully unaware? What if something happened further down the line that brought her ability to the surface at an inopportune moment?

"Your name was Melisandrea," the doc said, interrupting her thoughts.

Mavis sucked in a breath, turning the name over in her head, rolling it around, trying to get a sense of it. She didn't feel like a Melisandrea. "And I—she was two-natured?" Mavis asked.

The doc nodded, "Yes."

"How long did you know her?"

"Two years."

Mavis' hands fisted in the blanket. "Two years?" The words came out low and harsh. "You knew me for two years? I disappeared a year ago, show up six months later with amnesia, and you didn't bother to tell me you knew who I was?" Her voice rose. "Do you have any idea what I thought? I thought no one was looking for me. I thought no one wanted me. And now you tell me you've known who I was this whole time?" She gripped the blanket so tightly her hands shook. "You never thought to tell me, so that maybe I didn't think I was a complete waste of a human being?"

The doc stared at her. When he spoke, his tone was calm, as if he suspected she was about to lose more than her temper. "Telling you before you remembered what you were could have done more harm than good. Would you have believed us?"

"No," she responded sharply. "No, I understand why you didn't tell me I could shapeshift into a bird, but why didn't you tell me you knew who I was?" She glared at the doc.

"It was important not to influence your memory. Doing so could have been injurious to your psyche. Letting your memory return on its own was best." He glanced away and cleared his throat.

Mavis narrowed her eyes. The doc wanted something.

"Since you've shifted—twice now—have you remembered anything?" he asked.

"Like what?"

"Anything from before you came to be here six months ago?"

Mavis relaxed her white-knuckled grip on the bedding. "No."

The doc cleared his throat again. "I understand you're upset, but could you try?"

Mavis closed her eyes and concentrated. She went back to the beginning, to the darkness she'd known lying in that hospital bed, surrounded by machines; before she blinked and lost hours at a time; before she realized she couldn't move her legs; before she realized she didn't know who she was. The very first thing she recalled upon blinking her eyes open was the light burning bright and white, so intensely she had to close her eyes again right away. But was there anything before that?

Mavis opened her eyes.

"Did you remember something?" the doc asked.

She shook her head. "Not yet."

"But you think you might?" His voice sounded hopeful and wary at the same time.

"I don't know." Her head dropped back against the pillow. "I'd like my clothes now, please."

"Of course. Excuse me," the doc said and left the room.

Aitch stood up from the side of the bed. He crossed the room to a tall cabinet, pulled out her clothes, and set them on the foot of the bed.

"Where did you find them?" she asked.

"Below the balcony where you fell."

"Was pushed," she corrected him.

Her clothes were folded into a neat stack. Resting on top was the silver leaf necklace. The stack of clothes confused her. How could she have shifted into her other nature while she was dressed and not gotten tangled in her clothing?

Aitch left the room. Mavis rested her head against the pillow. She must have closed her eyes for longer than she thought because a knock on the door woke her.

"You all right in there?" Aitch called through the door.

"Just a minute," she said, and then got dressed. She remembered to tuck the necklace into her shirt. Outside, the hallway of her old wing was deserted except for Aitch.

"I know you want to leave, but you should see something first," he said.

"Shouldn't we get back to the garage?" There was already so much to wrap her head around, she wasn't sure she could take much more. She yearned for the familiar. After all, if the doc hadn't asked her to come in and talk to Sandra, she would be at work, probably on the computer or finishing her book so she could return it to the library.

"Don't worry about the garage, Mavis. You need to see this."

Mavis sighed and followed him down the hall, around the corner, past her old room, the balcony where she had fallen, the lounge where she had met with Sandra, all the way to the end of the hall. Aitch stopped in front of a door that looked like all the others. Another room she had seen but had never had a reason to enter. He stepped to the side, waiting for her to open it.

Mavis hesitated, unsure.

Aitch must have thought she wouldn't do it. He reached out to open the door, but she beat him to the doorknob. The door swung inward. She expected another hospital room, which it was, but someone had gone through a lot of trouble to try and get rid of the institutional feel of it. Colored fabrics covered the walls. Patterned rugs sprawled across the floor. Tall casement windows opened outward on a landscape similar to what she'd seen from the balcony, which made sense because both faced the same direction. Another door across the room must have led to a bathroom.

A full-sized bed made up with several pillows in colors to match the rugs was pushed into the corner across from the windows. Besides that, there wasn't much in the way of furniture; a desk with a lamp, a chair rolled under it, and a tall heavy-looking wardrobe with doors on top and drawers underneath.

Mavis stood on the threshold hesitant to enter what was clearly someone else's personal space.

"Go on. It's okay," Aitch said.

She stepped into the room. A stale, musty smell rose around her. The room belonged to someone who hadn't used it in a long time. Maybe a year? The thought tugged the corners of her mouth down, and her stomach roiled. She swallowed and crossed the floor to the desk. She switched on the lamp. A blotter sat on top with a genuine ink well, capped so its contents didn't dry out. A jar filled with a dozen different types of feathers in various sizes, shapes, colors, and patterns sat beside it. At the back of the desk was a framed photo. A fine tremor passed through her hands as she reached out to pick it up.

The snapshot held two people. One of them had her face, the same brown hair and gray eyes, but she knew it wasn't her. This was Melisandrea. The woman in the photo was smiling, her gaze not on the picture taker, but on something unseen past the end of the camera pointed at her. The hitch of her lips made it appear as if she didn't smile a lot. Regardless, the smile reached her eyes and appeared genuine, if a little reserved.

Next to her stood an attractive man she didn't recognize. He was shorter than Melisandrea and had sandy brown hair. He smiled with his head thrown back, mouth open in laughter, his gaze focused on Melisandrea.

The two people in the photo had a relationship of some kind but to Mavis, the body language captured on the print did not suggest it was romantic. A respectful distance existed between them.

"Who is this?" Mavis asked.

Aitch came into the room. Taking the picture from her, he frowned down at it.

"That's Melisandrea."

"Yes, I see that. We kind of look alike. Who is that?" She tapped the photo.

Aitch hesitated, struggling with some internal conflict she wasn't privy to. Finally, he answered, "That's Gloin."

Mavis snatched the picture back from him. "*That's* Gloin?" She stepped toward the window to peer at the photo in the natural light. The man in the picture did not look like a werewolf, let alone the alpha to all alphas, never mind the doc's father. This man was the picture of health and full of life, younger than the doc and his brother. Maybe because he was smiling, relaxed, and enjoying himself? Her fingertip ran across the glass, tracing the distance from one person to the next. Was Gloin laughing at something Melisandrea had said?

Mavis lowered the picture, her gaze seeking Aitch. He avoided meeting her eyes. Now she recalled why the name Melisandrea sounded so familiar. She sucked in a breath and then another until her chest heaved and her hands shook. "Gloin disappeared the same time as I—as Melisandrea? Mel? Me?"

CHAPTER 13

Mavis could accept the fact that she was two-natured, and that she used to be someone named Melisandrea, but the idea that she was this mysterious Mel figure, the friend of the Aldwulf who had disappeared around the same time he did, was, for some reason, a step too far. But there she was, all buddied up next to the Aldwulf. At least now her fascination with werewolves made sense.

The glass in the picture frame cracked with a tinkling sound that made Mavis jump. She loosened her grip, but it was too late. The fracture ran diagonally from corner to corner across the image, through Mel's shoulder and Gloin's midsection. Mavis set the photo down. A sudden chill had her crossing her arms. She stared at the picture without blinking, trying to see all of it at once.

"How is this even possible?" she asked.

She didn't expect an answer, but Aitch tried. "I don't know, but if there's one thing I'm sure of, you're not Mel."

"Clearly, you're mistaken." She waved at the photographic evidence on display.

"You look like Mel. Hell, you might even be the same physical person, right down to your DNA, but you're not her. Not where it counts." He turned his head to the side as if he'd said more than he intended.

Mavis' gaze darted from his face to the picture and away. "How would you know?"

"I just do. I've known for a while."

"Since when? Today?"

"No." Aitch avoided her gaze, staring out the window. "I wasn't completely sure until you came into the shop that first time. But as soon as you walked in, I knew. You're not the same person. Not really."

Mavis' pulse slowed as she focused on Aitch. "But you did know her? You knew Mel?"

"Only in passing. We never spoke more than a dozen words to each other. She didn't drive a car, so she never came to the shop."

Mavis frowned, more confused than ever. Aitch knew Mel, but not really, but enough to be confident Mavis was nothing like her? "If you didn't know Mel that well, how can you know I'm not her?"

Aitch sighed. "Mel's reputation preceded her. You're... very different from her."

Mavis couldn't tell if that was a good thing or not. The whole situation was troubling, but she attempted to work through what he was telling her. "Okay. You weren't positive I wasn't Mel until I came into the shop." Her eyes narrowed. "What about before that?"

Aitch shifted his weight from one foot to the other. "You were in the hospital," he said.

Mavis nodded. "And I never met you before the day you hired me. Why weren't you sure before then, if you only knew Mel in passing before she—I disappeared? What did you mean?"

Aitch hesitated.

"Please just tell me what you know," Mavis said.

Aitch blew out a breath. "I found you."

"You found me?" She pinched the bridge of her nose, trying to make sense of what he was saying. "You found me. Six months ago. You found me and brought me to the hospital."

"No one knew what had happened to you, but you wouldn't just take off without telling... someone." The way he said it, Mavis wondered if he expected Mel would have told him she was leaving, but he had said they hadn't known each other well. Mavis let the thought go. Aitch continued "The wolves started a search, but they weren't getting anywhere. I kept my ears open. Heard a lady in the canyon asking about some strange bird she'd seen. I decided to take a look around."

Mavis walked towards him, cocking her head to the side. "What kind of strange bird?"

"I never saw it. But I did find you more or less in the same state I found you in today." He didn't blink as he said it. Well, if he could forget seeing her sprawled naked on the ground, she could forget that was how he had found her.

"Then I guess I owe you a thank you, twice over."

Before Aitch could tell what she was up to, Mavis stepped in close, went up on tiptoe, and kissed his whiskered cheek. With the same speed, she stepped out of his space. She didn't know what had made her do it, but she was cognizant of the fact that Aitch was still her employer. However, life was short. Nothing like being pushed from a balcony to point out how suddenly it could end. She didn't want to forget to show her gratitude.

Aitch didn't say anything, but he rubbed his jaw and peered at her.

Mavis raised a hand to indicate the walls around them.

"Why show me Mel's room?" she asked. "This was hers, wasn't it? Were you hoping I'd see it and remember something?"

"No," he said, frowning. "I brought you here because everything that was Mel's belongs to you now."

Mavis turned in a slow circle, her gaze skipping over the accumulated possessions of another person's life; everything in it hers, but not really. It felt more like an inheritance. Other than a passing curiosity about the person the items belonged to—a person who was her but not—Mavis didn't know where to begin. Her efficiency was barely big enough for her meager possessions as it was. "Everything?"

"No one else is using it. Is there anything you want?"

She didn't even need to look. "I wouldn't have anywhere to put it if I did."

"It's not going anywhere. You might change your mind. Ready to go?"

They left the room almost exactly as they had found it. She felt bad about the picture glass, but apparently, it was hers. She could break it if she wanted. Eventually, she let her remorse go.

Back in the hallway, they approached the balcony. They had already passed the door leading outside when Mavis stopped. Aitch noticed she was no longer next to him and turned. Mavis walked backward until she reached the balcony door, pushing it open. She went straight to the same spot she had stood earlier, turned, faced the building, and looked up as Aitch joined her. Three feet above the top of Mavis' head, the roof came down at an angle. She craned her neck. Aitch followed her gaze and did the same.

The memory of the scrabbling noise came back to her. Earlier she hadn't thought anything of it, but since she'd been pushed, it meant the noise she heard must have been made by whoever pushed her. There—scratches above the edge of the roof tiling. Not deep gouges, but scratches.

She pointed. "Told you I was pushed."

Aitch shaded his eyes. After a minute, he lowered his hand and nodded. "Okay, but why?"

Mavis turned her back on the roof and faced the view. "No idea." What could have made the gouges in the tiles? They didn't look like marks left behind by a pair of shoes. Could they have been made by talons? Or claws?

Aitch leaned on the balcony next to her. "Being out here doesn't make you nervous?"

The view calmed her overworked nerves, but the moment when she tumbled over the edge came back to her, and the breath caught in her throat. Mavis coughed to cleared it and stared out at the scenery, unseeing. "Why would someone want to kill me?" It was the only reason she could think of for someone to push her. She certainly hadn't known she could shift into a bird and save her own life. No one else thought so either. There had been no indication of her abilities before the moment she'd been shoved from behind, which made her think someone wanted her dead. Her fingers drummed against the stone under her palm. She wondered if they were as shocked as she was that she had survived.

Aitch pulled in a deep breath and blew it out, loudly. "If it makes you feel any better, I'm not sure they want to kill *you*."

Mavis heard the slight emphasis he put on his last word. "You mean, assuming I haven't pissed anyone off just by breathing, the question is why would someone want to kill Mel? But since Mel is me, or used to be me, what are they hoping to get from my demise?" She turned the question over in her head. "My best guess is silence. Someone doesn't want me to remember."

"Remember what—how to shift?"

Mavis thought it might be something else. "You said Mel

went missing the same time as Gloin. What if Mel knew what happened to him? What if she knew where he was? If Gloin doesn't return by the night after next, Broderick's going to fight his brother to become the next Aldwulf. Seems like a pretty good reason to want Mel out of the picture. Broderick's an alpha. He could have ordered someone to push me or done it himself."

Aitch tipped his head to the side as if considering her theory. "It's possible."

Her eyes narrowed. "And we're sure Katrina didn't push me?"

A harsh huff escaped him. "I saw her talking to the doc about the time you were taking your swan dive."

Mavis sighed. "Of course, someone could just really not like Mel." If that was the case, pushing her off the balcony seemed a bit extreme. If her other theory was right, however, someone didn't want her to remember something important. But why wait until now? She'd been much more vulnerable before she left the hospital.

Mavis rocked back. "I need to talk to the doc." She turned and crossed to the door.

"Why?" Aitch asked, already right on her heels.

"I have to ask him something."

They took the stairs down to the second floor. No one sat in the waiting room, but voices came from behind the doc's closed door. She headed straight to the office door and knocked. Without invitation, she opened it.

The doc stood up from his chair behind his desk. "Mavis?"

Sandra sat in the same visitor's chair Mavis had earlier, but she'd changed her clothes. The blue pajamas were gone. Now she wore a lemony-yellow blouse and black slacks under her long gray cardigan. She didn't get up.

Mavis stared at Sandra, who sat straight and tall under her

scrutiny, one knee crossed casually over the other. "You're not a patient, are you?"

"Come in, please," the doc said. "And close the door behind you."

Aitch followed and shut the door.

"You're not, are you?" Mavis asked.

Sandra shook her head. "No, I'm not."

"What?" Aitch asked, his gaze going from Sandra to the doc and back.

"Who are you?" asked Mavis.

Sandra reached into the canvas bag at her feet, the same one as before, and pulled out a business card. She held it out to Mavis. The name Wilcox followed Sandra. After that came a whole bunch of letters. "I'm a psychiatrist."

"I asked Dr. Wilcox to come down and speak with you," the doc said.

Mavis took the card. The black embossed lettering on the creamy cardstock gave the words a snakeskin texture. "Did he tell you to lie to me?"

"No. Pretending to be a patient was my idea," Sandra said.

Mavis refused to think of her as a doctor, despite the card in her hand.

"Why?" Mavis asked.

"I thought my evaluation would go smoother if you felt we had something in common."

Mavis thought back over their conversation from earlier; Sandra's repetitiveness, her note-taking, the accident she'd lied about having. All to gain Mavis' trust. "And what did you find?"

Sandra settled back into her chair with her hands folded in her lap. "In my experience, with cases of permanent retrograde amnesia, it's unusual for the individual to have zero recall as you do. The patient usually remembers something leading up to the event that caused them to lose their memory, but not in your case, which could be a cause for concern. I'm aware some time has passed since you lost your memory. You appear to have made peace with it, which accounts for your lack of disorientation and fear. After speaking with you, I can tell your condition unsettles you, but you're not looking away from the past. You want to remember; you're just not able to, for whatever reason."

Mavis stared at Sandra while she spoke. Mavis recalled doubting Sandra's story in the middle of their interview and how she'd pushed her feelings of unease away. She should have trusted her gut. "So, why did you poison me?"

CHAPTER 14

"What the hell?" asked Aitch.

Sandra blinked rapidly, glancing at the doc, then away again. "Poison?"

The faintest odor of the sickly-sweet scent still clung to Sandra's sweater. "That wasn't just incense you were burning."

"Still, poison is a strong word." Sandra put both feet on the floor and shifted in her seat.

Mavis lifted one brow. "I was given something without my consent and it made me ill—sounds like poison to me."

The doc cleared his throat. "I allowed Dr. Wilcox to dose you."

"Son of a—" Aitch started around the desk toward the doc. Sandra gasped. Mavis laid her hand on his arm, and he stilled.

"Dose me with what?" Mavis asked.

"An opioid meant to help you relax—lower your inhibitions," Sandra explained. "I've used it in my practice to help patients recover memories, sometimes painful ones."

Mavis let go of Aitch's arm. He stayed put, for which she was grateful. If he wanted to go after the doc, it wasn't like she could stop him. "The pill you took for your 'allergies' kept you from feeling the effects," Mavis said.

"Yes."

"And it worked on me."

"To an extent. Your response was idiosyncratic. Most of my patients don't run out of the room. I couldn't tell you any more than that without running some tests," Sandra said.

Could it have anything to do with being two-natured? How much did Sandra know? Mavis caught the doc's eye. He glanced away, the shake of his head barely perceptible, but enough to indicate that Sandra didn't know anything about shifters, and, perhaps more, she didn't know the doc was a werewolf. Mavis was glad she'd gotten out of that room when she had.

"I think I'll just say no to drugs," Mavis said and held out the card Sandra had given her.

Sandra took her card back and stared at it as if she didn't know what to do with it. She must not have expected Mavis to give it back. "That's... very wise." Sandra stuffed the card in the pocket of her sweater, grabbed her case, and stood. She turned to the doc. "You have my findings. If you have any more questions, don't hesitate to call." She nodded to them all, including Aitch, and let herself out of the office. The door closed quietly behind her.

Aitch waited until the door clicked shut. A second later he lunged for the doc, his hands gripping the lapels of his white coat. "What the hell, Chase? What were you thinking?"

The doc grabbed Aitch's wrists. "I told you I was willing to do whatever it takes."

"Including drugging Mavis?"

The doc bared his teeth. "I had to know."

Aitch shook him. "Know what?"

Mavis plopped into the chair next to the one Sandra had vacated, stifling a sigh. "He had to know if I was lying."

Confronting Sandra and the doc had taken all her energy. Both the doc and Aitch turned to stare at her. "You should probably turn him loose, Aitch."

Aitch let go of the doc with a shove.

"What else did Sandra find?" Mavis asked.

The doc brushed at the wrinkles in his coat and the front of his shirt. "She's convinced your amnesia is genuine."

Mavis resisted the temptation to roll her eyes. "We already knew that. Or at least I did." Her brows drew together. "Didn't you?"

"I'm not an expert on amnesia. That's why I called Dr. Wilcox."

Mavis sighed. "But that's not all you wanted to know."

Aitch glanced at Mavis before he resumed glaring at the doc. "What else is there?"

"You don't think it's a coincidence Mel went missing at the same time as Gloin," Mavis replied, attention on the doc. "You think I know what happened to him, but I can't remember. What did the expert say?" She waved at hand at the door Dr. Wilcox had walked through. She wanted to know herself.

The doc shook his head. "Inconclusive. There's no way of knowing if your memory will ever return."

Mavis smirked. "I could have told you that. I didn't even remember being able to shift into a bird until today."

The doc stood tall. "But you did remember."

Mavis threw up her hands. "Because I got pushed off of a balcony and would have fallen to my death otherwise!"

"Exactly," the doc said. "Under dire circumstances, you remembered your ability to shift. If you experiment with shifting further, perhaps more of your memory will return."

Mavis wasn't so sure about that. She didn't know how she had shifted in the first place. If she had to be pushed off of a building every time for it to happen, she wasn't sure she ever wanted to do it again.

The doc cleared his throat. "Was there something you needed?"

Aitch stopped trying to glare a hole through the doc and turned toward her.

Just like that, Mavis remembered the reason they'd barged in. "I wanted to know if Mel had any allergies."

The doc frowned. "Yes. She had a severe nut allergy."

"But I'm not allergic to nuts." She'd consumed enough cookies to know.

"No. No, you're not. But you are allergic to strawberries."

"I remember. Vividly. I also remember the box of chocolates I received. The one with the note telling me to feel better soon."

"What box of chocolates?" Aitch asked.

Mavis threaded her fingers together and rested them against her middle. "A small, four-piece box showed up out of nowhere one morning. All of them had nuts in some form or another."

"And you ate them without questioning where they even came from," the doc spat out with a shake of his head. His reaction that day he'd found the empty box of chocolates next to her bed made a lot more sense now.

"Jesus." Aitch ran a hand down his face.

Mavis' brows lowered into a line. "Do you know why I ate them?" She didn't wait for either of them to answer. "Other than the fact that they were chocolate? It was the first time anyone seemed happy to acknowledge my existence. I thought someone was being nice." She shook her head, relaxing her brow. "Now I'm wondering if they were trying to kill me." Her head tipped to the side, considering. "Or they could have been testing me. Maybe whoever left the chocolates didn't believe I'd lost my memory. Not for real. If my amnesia was a ruse, they wanted to see how far was I willing to take it. If I didn't eat the chocolate, they would take it as proof that I remembered being deathly allergic. If I did, they would know my amnesia was for real, my potential demise aside." Her eyes widened as she chuckled. "They must have been pissed when I ate the chocolate and nothing happened."

She stopped when she noticed Aitch and the doc weren't laughing. "Anyway. Do you know who left the chocolates?"

The doc shook his head. "No. Whoever left it made sure to keep their scent off of it. Otherwise—" He didn't finish the thought and instead cleared his throat. "Did you stop by your —by Mel's room?"

Mavis thought she saw his ears perk up. She stared at the doc a long moment and then said, "I'll make you a deal, doc."

He sat down, leaning forward in his chair. "What kind of deal?"

"The minute I remember something—anything—from Mel's life, you'll be the first to know. But no more interference. I'm either going to remember or I'm not. You don't get a say in how, or even if, I do." She really shouldn't have had to say that last part, but since he'd let Sandra drug her without her consent, she thought she might as well say it out loud.

The doc didn't hesitate. "Deal, but there's someone you should meet before you go."

"Another patient?' Aitch snorted and crossed his arms.

"No. He works here." The doc picked up his office phone and punched in an extension. "Can you come to my office now? Great. Thanks." The doc replaced the receiver. "Weasel will be up in a minute."

"Weasel?" Aitch asked.

"He's quite adept at helping others get a grip on their ability to shift."

"This is a bad idea," Aitch said.

"Why?" asked the doc, glancing from Mavis to Aitch and back. His eyes widened as he came to some kind of realization. "Is that so?" He cleared his throat. "Don't you think you're letting your prejudices get the better of you?"

"Not if it saves Weasel's skin," Aitch said.

Mavis had no idea what they were talking about. She didn't have time to ask before a knock sounded on the door.

"Come in," the doc said, getting to his feet.

Mavis decided she might as well be polite and stood also.

The door opened and a young man entered of average height, which made him shorter than her. His dark brown hair was covered by a backward-facing baseball cap. The bottom half of his face sported whiskers in a short beard the same shade as the rest of his hair. He had friendly green eyes and a nice smile. She liked him instantly.

"What's up, doc? Hey, Aitch." He nodded in Mavis' direction.

"Weasel, I'd like you to meet Mavis," the doc introduced them.

Weasel stuck out his hand.

Mavis slid her palm against his and returned a firm squeeze. "Nice to meet you."

"Mavis has just discovered she's two-natured. I was hoping you could help her get a handle on shifting," the doc said.

Weasel turned to Mavis. "Really? You're a little old to be finding out you're a shifter now."

Her mouth opened, but she didn't know what to say.

The doc stepped in. "There were mitigating circumstances that kept Mavis from discovering she was two-natured until now."

Weasel nodded, assessing her in a professional way that didn't make her feel gross. "So, you can turn into a—"

"Bird." That one she knew.

"All right, cool." He spoke with a slight accent Mavis couldn't place.

"Does your name mean that you can change into a weasel?" she asked.

"A ferret actually, but they're related. What kind of bird?"

"Magpie. I shifted into a magpie earlier," Mavis answered. "I'd just seen one in the trees."

"Very smart bird. If you'd never shifted before, having that direct visual would have helped."

Aitch had said the same thing. What if she hadn't seen the magpie? Her stomach churned with the thought.

"Would you have some time tomorrow morning?" Weasel asked.

She didn't even glance in Aitch's direction. "Tomorrow's my day off, so that could work."

"Can you meet me here? We can head into the woods. It's better if there aren't too many people around."

Mavis nodded, and the room tilted. "Yes. Tomorrow. Here." She sat down quickly, but the room kept moving. She closed her eyes, waiting for the walls to stop spinning.

Aitch spoke then. "That's enough."

She felt an arm around her shoulders and one slide under her legs. Mavis' eyes snapped open and she jumped to her feet. She had to steady herself against the edge of the doc's desk to keep from falling over, but no way was she letting Aitch carry her out of there like some wilting flower. "I can walk."

CHAPTER 15

Mavis made it to the truck by sticking close to solid objects, like walls, handrails, and Aitch. As soon as she tipped her head back against the seat, she fell asleep, jerking awake only when Aitch turned off the engine. They weren't at her apartment or the shop—they were parked outside the Main Street Bakery. She squinted, taking in the traffic.

"Stay here," Aitch said.

Getting out of the truck, he went inside.

Mavis rubbed her eyes, checking the clock across the street at the bank. The hour she would have stopped by for lunch had passed, but it was a diner. They weren't going to run out of food in the middle of the afternoon. She stretched and watched cars roll by until Aitch came out carrying a bag.

He handed it to her as he got back in. "I asked Wes what you liked. He threw in a piece of pie."

"You can have it. I don't have much of an appetite."

"Shifting takes a lot out of you. You need to keep your strength up."

The scent of hot fried food called to her, making her stomach rumble. "Okay, but I still don't want the pie."

Aitch drove to the shop, which sat closed. No one clamored at the door in need of assistance, which was fine with her. She'd had what by many standards could be considered a hell of a morning, and she just wanted to sit in peace. Opening the garage in the early afternoon felt weird. She didn't bother with her regular routines, but did flip the sign in the front window. Behind the desk, she ate the turkey avocado club Aitch had gotten for her, not tasting it as she stared out the front window.

The parking lot, the shops across the street, the traffic—none of it drew her focus. What she saw instead was the view from the balcony. The trees in the distance. The ground rushing up to meet her, over and over again until the very last moment, when it receded. That was it, then—the moment her second nature decided to assert itself and remain aloft instead of crashing into the unforgiving earth. She still didn't know how she'd done it. Could she do it again? What if she couldn't? What if it had been a fluke?

The scrape of her stool against the tile echoed, along with every other little sound. Aitch hadn't opened the big bay doors in the back. The hum of the lights overhead morphed into a roar. She couldn't take it. In a burst of activity, Mavis tidied up the front of the shop. There wasn't much to tidy, so she was soon seated back at her post.

By the time the front door opened and Louis came in with his backpack square over both shoulders, she knew school was out. Where had the time gone?

"'Sup, baby girl?" He waggled his brows.

"Hey, Louis." Mavis didn't get up.

"Are you okay?"

"I'm fine."

Louis peered at her from the corner of one narrowed eye.

"When my mom says she's fine, something's always up." He glanced around the shop. "Is Mr. Aitch okay?"

"He's fine."

"You said it again." Louis stepped around the end of the counter and stuck his head through the doorway into the back of the garage. "Mr. Aitch? Is everything okay?"

"What do you want, Louis?" Aitch called.

"Nothing." He shuffled around to the front of the desk and leaned over. "He seems okay." Then he added, "So what's up with you?"

Mavis shook her head. "I wouldn't even know where to start."

Louis nodded. "Maybe you should bake something. You always feel better when you bake something. How about cookies?"

"I made some. I just didn't bring them with me." Louis didn't need to know she hadn't been to her apartment since late last night. Mavis buried her face in her hands. So much had happened since then. This was why she didn't want to be at home alone right now. Left to relive everything that had happened, she might curl up in bed and never get out again.

"Hey, it's okay. I'm sure they'll taste just as good tomorrow."

Mavis dropped her hands, huffing out a laugh. "You're right. They'll taste fine tomorrow. On my day off."

"Rats," Louis said. "So how come the garage wasn't open this morning?"

"Aitch had an appointment." Louis wasn't a werewolf. He couldn't smell a lie. "How was school?"

Louis shrugged. "It was fine."

She stared at him and raised her eyebrows.

His head tilted back, caught in a trap of his own making. "I got my math test back, and I didn't do so hot. It's hard to concentrate when you think your teacher's a werewolf."

"Can you get some extra help?"

"Are you not listening? Then I would have to be alone with the werewolf."

"Suspected werewolf," Mavis corrected him. She lowered her voice and gestured for Louis to come closer, leaning forward. "Don't lie to him. You shouldn't lie anyway. But if he is a werewolf, he'll be able to smell it." She didn't know why she was telling Louis what little she had learned about werewolves, but it felt good to share it with someone.

Louis' jaw dropped as he straightened, eyes wide. "Jules— she's a girl in my class—she told Mr. Dubois she did the homework but lost it. He didn't believe her." Louis frowned. "Then again, none of us believed her. How do you know they can smell lies?"

Mavis leaned back, glancing away. "Just something I read."

"Henry says he knows where Mr. Dubois lives. He said he and some guys he knows might keep an eye on his place."

"That sounds like a terrible idea."

Louis shrugged.

Mavis stood. "Is Henry a friend of yours? You should tell him that's harassment and to leave Mr. Dubois alone."

Louis put up his hands and stepped back. "It's not me. Geez. I'm not gonna do it. Calm down. Henry and I aren't friends. He's, like, cool and stuff. He's got a car and everything."

"Well, I've never heard of this Henry guy, which means he doesn't bring his car here for service. So, not cool."

Louis rolled his eyes.

Mavis didn't get a chance to respond. The door swung open and a woman entered carrying a leather briefcase bag over one shoulder. Mavis didn't recognize her, and she didn't see a car in the parking lot. Whoever she was, she was on foot. Her long brown hair, threaded with gray, flowed free past her shoulders. Her light-colored blouse was buttoned up to the neck and tucked into an ankle-length denim skirt belted at her waist. She approached the counter with a polite, pasted-on smile, and a stack of folded flyers.

Louis moved to the side, his gaze on the newcomer.

"Good afternoon," the woman said. "Are you the proprietor?"

Mavis' eyes narrowed. What a strange way to ask if she owned the place. Whatever this woman was selling, she was pretty sure they didn't want any. "No, I'm not. He's in the back."

"May I speak to him, please?" Her smile didn't falter.

Mavis backed away from the counter without turning her back on the woman. She spared Louis a glance. He watched the woman with open interest. In return, the woman ignored him.

"Aitch," she called. "Someone here wants to speak with you."

He didn't answer, but there was no way he hadn't heard her. He wasn't working on anything. Mavis didn't take her eyes off the woman to check his exact whereabouts. A second later, she heard footsteps and walked straight back to her spot behind the counter.

Mavis could tell when Aitch came into the room by the way the woman perked up, her gaze darting down and back up again as she checked out Aitch. Her smile became genuine.

"Can I help you?" Aitch asked.

"Good afternoon. My name is Lydia Shaw and I'm inviting local business owners, such as yourself, to a town hall meeting to discuss the growing number of werewolves in the community." She slipped the top pamphlet away from the rest and held it out to Aitch.

To Mavis' surprise, he took it. She frowned at him.

"Are you a local business owner?" Aitch asked.

"Not myself, no. I work with a group interested in preserving current lifestyles in cities across the state of New Mexico."

Which meant they were against change—or, rather, those that could change—into wolves. That's what it sounded like to Mavis. Her frown turned into an all-out scowl as her teeth ground together. Mavis wasn't a werewolf, but she was a shifter. If there were forces out to stir up distrust of werewolves, Mavis wondered what would happen if they knew about others like herself and Weasel.

Aitch glanced at the pamphlet and made an interested-sounding noise. "This meeting is the night after next."

Lydia Shaw giggled like a school girl. "Of course. Will we see you there?"

"Can anyone come?" Louis asked.

Lydia Shaw reluctantly tore her gaze away from Aitch to glance in Louis' direction. Her smile slipped a notch. "It is open to the public, but we're hoping local business leaders will make a point of attending."

Not teenagers without any influence in the community.

Louis nodded. "You said 'growing number.' But what if there are already werewolves here?" No doubt he was thinking of his math teacher.

Lydia Shaw's smile fled. "That's why the people of this town need to come together and voice their concerns."

Mavis glowered at the woman. She drew a breath, ready to tell her what she could do with her pamphlets, but Aitch's hand on her arm stopped her. She ignored the tiny arc of electricity shooting through her at his touch.

"Well, I'll be sure to stop in," Aitch said. "Can I have a few extra pamphlets for friends of mine?"

Mavis' eyes narrowed. Aitch didn't have any friends.

She couldn't have read Aitch wrong this whole time. He didn't hate werewolves. He said he'd been raised by them.

When two alphas wanted to meet, they came to his garage. So why was he being so nice to this 'Lydia' person when it was clear she had it out for werewolves?

Lydia Shaw handed over the stack of pamphlets with a smile, thanked him for his time, and left with a little wave.

As soon as the door closed behind her, Mavis snatched a pamphlet from the pile. Louis snagged one also. "What the hell, Aitch? *Concerned Citizens Unite?* The only thing missing is a picture of a werewolf with a red circle and a line through it." She opened the pamphlet. "Oh, wait, there it is."

"Calm down." He grabbed the stack of pamphlets and tossed them in the recycle bin.

"Why didn't you throw her out?" Mavis asked.

He sighed. "There was no need. Now that she thinks I'm a like-minded individual who doesn't need any convincing, she won't come back. And she can't hand out any of the pamphlets she gave me."

"She probably has more in her bag."

"I'm sure she does, but now there are a few less in circulation."

Aitch stalked away into the garage while Louis remained at the counter, lips moving as he read.

Mavis resisted the temptation to rip the flyer out of his hands.

"Learn anything new?" she asked.

He folded the paper closed. "Nah." He frowned. "But why would they have their meeting on the night of the next full moon?"

"Think about it, Louis. You know why."

Louis' face relaxed. "Because it's the one night they think werewolves won't attend. But why do you care?"

"Werewolves are people, too, Louis." She waved the pamphlet. "And this is discrimination, no matter what the 'concerned citizens uniting' call it." A sound of disgust escaped the back of her throat.

Louis didn't say anything, but he took the pamphlet with him when he left. She, too, kept one for herself. She wanted to research the group coordinating the efforts of concerned citizens, but not at work.

After Louis left, the rest of the afternoon sped by without trouble. When it was time to go, she poked her head through the doorway to the back. Aitch stood at his workbench, head bent, reading an auto repair manual.

"I'm off," she said.

"What time should I pick you up in the morning?"

She stepped the rest of the way into the maintenance bay. "You shouldn't. Tomorrow's my regular day off. You need to open the shop on time. I'll find my way to the hospital." The more she talked, the more Aitch frowned, but she kept going. "I'll see you Friday. Try not to run off any new customers." She wasn't kidding. Their regular customers knew Thursday was her day off and had been known to wait until Friday to call about work they needed to be done. New customers didn't know any better.

The paper manual crumpled in Aitch's hands. Between clenched teeth, he ground out one word: "Fine."

Mavis turned on her heel and left, thinking that Louis might be on to something. When people said they were fine, they were anything but.

CHAPTER 16

Mavis walked straight home, head down, lost in thought. Her mind replayed the day's events on a continuous loop. She paused the reel in her brain when she reached her apartment and dug her keys out of her backpack, but had to stop herself.

Her apartment door was already ajar.

No way would she have left her door open. She would never have left it unlocked, either. When Aitch had brought her by last night to get her things, she distinctly recalled closing her door and locking it behind her, turning the handle to double-check. From where she stood, the jamb appeared to be intact, the door undamaged. Whoever had opened it hadn't forced their way inside.

There was something to be said for owning few material possessions.

She would miss her tablet the most. That was about the only thing of value she owned, and even that had been bought secondhand. Everything else could be replaced. She hoped whoever had broken in hadn't messed up the place too badly.

Mavis stepped in close to the door's hinges. She reached

out, planting the tips of her splayed fingers against the door, and pushed. The door swung open in silence. Mavis leaned forward. The floor was clear, nothing tossed.

Someone stood in the middle of the room. At first glance, she thought Mrs. Lin must have let herself in—maybe someone had smelled gas—but her landlady never put her hair up. Nor did she wear heels.

"What the hell are you doing here?" Mavis asked.

Katrina had the gall to glare at Mavis over her shoulder without turning around. Then Mavis realized Katrina had probably heard her coming.

Mavis stepped inside and set her backpack on the counter. She knew that Katrina was a werewolf, dominant enough to be second in her pack, and that, for whatever reason, she didn't like Mavis. However, Katrina probably wouldn't have left the door cracked if she planned on doing Mavis any harm. Still, Mavis left the door wide open behind her. Standing on her home turf made Mavis brave, not stupid.

"Did you pick my lock?" she asked.

Katrina faced her. "I came to give you a warning."

"Go ahead."

Katrina growled, "Stay away from Chase. He's mine."

Mavis blinked. "Okay."

"Okay?" The tension in Katrina's body deflated the slightest bit. "You'll stay away from him?"

"I have no reason to get near him unless I remember something." Mavis shook her head. "And what do you mean *he's yours*? I'm pretty sure slavery was outlawed. Do you mean like you're seeing each other?" She remembered thinking the doc and Katrina looked like a couple when they came into the shop, so the news wasn't a complete surprise, but why was Katrina telling her?

"That's right. We're together. Chase loves me now. He doesn't want anything to do with you. He told me so."

Mavis held up her index finger as her stomach flipped over. "You mean, me and the doc—the doc and Mel—they used to—" Bile raced up the back of her throat. Mavis threw herself to the right into the bathroom and gripped the edge of the sink. Her mouth flooded with saliva. Mavis took shallow breaths, fighting back the urge to empty the contents of her stomach. Her knuckles whitened.

If she believed Katrina, then she and the doc—the doc and Mel, she corrected herself—the doc and Mel had been together. Like in an intimate way. Why shouldn't she believe Katrina? The woman had been nothing but antagonistic to her since day one, but she wasn't a liar. Mavis never would have imagined she and the doc—her stomach clenched again. The doc and Mel, she repeated to herself. The doc and Mel.

Mavis let go of the sink and turned on the faucet. She splashed cold water on her face, pulling a towel from the bar to dry off. Sure, she liked the doc. Or she had, anyway. More so before he'd let Sandra drug her without her knowing. Her stomach twisted. She did not like the doc in a romantic way. Nope. Never crossed her mind.

Mavis turned off the water and returned the towel to the bar. She stopped in the bathroom doorway. A breeze blew through her open front door.

Katrina hadn't moved an inch, but her posture wasn't as rigid. A frown creased her brow.

In the kitchen, Mavis opened a cabinet, and pulled out the container of cookies she'd made at Wes' the night before. She tossed the lid on the counter. "Want one?" She held out the container to her uninvited guest.

Katrina glanced down but didn't take one.

"Suit yourself." Mavis took a cookie off the top and bit into it. She set the container on the counter. "Are you the doc's second?"

Katrina drew herself up tall, or she tried to. Mavis fought

a smirk. Katrina just wasn't that tall, even in heels. "I didn't come here to answer questions."

Mavis released an irritated gust of air. "No, you broke into my apartment to tell me to stay away from your boyfriend like some jealous harpy. Does he even know you're here?"

The only thing that kept Katrina's wolf at bay earlier was the doc's presence. Would she have a raging werewolf on her hands if she made Katrina angry enough? She hoped not, but she kept checking Katrina's eye color without making direct eye contact. For now, Katrina's eyes remained their regular shade of dark brown.

"I'll take that as a 'no,'" Mavis said when Katrine didn't answer, sitting on her bed. "I'd ask you to sit, but I didn't invite you and I don't want you on my bed. I have to sleep here."

Katrina sniffed, glancing around at the sparseness of her apartment. After visiting Mel's room, Mavis knew her space was less colorful.

"Tell me something," Mavis said. She waited for Katrina to glance her way. "Did you know Mel?"

Katrina's shoulders hitched upward at the mention of the name.

"I'm not her, you know. I know I look like her, but I'm not," Mavis said. She couldn't pinpoint what made her so sure. Maybe it was Aitch's conviction rubbing off on her, but it seemed like the right thing to say.

Katrina twitched with some sort of internal struggle.

Thirty seconds passed. She didn't think Katrina would answer. She should have just kicked her out, but she was hoping to learn some things first.

"Not well," Katrina finally replied. "You—Mel—kept to herself. She was close to Gloin, but the rest of us weren't good enough for her. When she left, it damn near destroyed Chase. I was there to pick up the pieces."

"Sounds like you would do anything for him."

"I would."

Mavis widened her eyes. "Except stay away from me."

"He never said to stay away from you. If he had, I wouldn't be here."

Mavis put that together with what she'd read about were-wolves. "Because he's your alpha?"

Katrina's lips pressed into a flat line.

"You have to do what he says, don't you? Like you can't not do it, can you?" She couldn't stop her nose from wrinkling. "And you're his girlfriend. Do you have to do anything he says?"

Katrina crossed her arms. "You don't know anything, and it's not like that. Get your mind out of the gutter."

Mavis' thoughts continued to wallow. She shuddered. "Did he make you help me with physical therapy?"

"He didn't make me," Katrina said, but her gaze jumped to the side and back.

"But he did ask you," Mavis said.

"Yes. He did."

"Why was that?"

"Because I'm the best."

Mavis grunted. Too much time around Aitch. Then she added, "I wouldn't know. I never saw your best."

The lines around Katrina's mouth deepened. It was obvious Katrina took pride in her work as a physical thera-pist, but Mavis couldn't forget how Katrina had made her feel when she was trying to learn how to walk again. Katrina's bedside manner had been the number one reason Mavis asked to be removed from her care.

She tried to see Katrina's point of view. The doc had asked her to help Mavis—the woman who devastated him by leaving—learn how to walk again. She couldn't blame Katrina for wondering how long it would take before Mavis tried waltzing away on rehabilitated legs with the man Katrina loved. It explained why Katrina had always been so cold, but it didn't excuse her behavior.

"It doesn't matter. I got the hang of it." Mavis finished her cookie.

Katrina lifted her chin in acknowledgment, probably in recognition of her peers instead of Mavis' abilities. Then she unfolded her arms and stuffed her hands in the pockets of her jacket. "So, you'll stay away from Chase?"

Mavis stared at her. "God, you're like a dog with a bone." Then she guffawed. Her hand flew to her mouth to stifle her laughter. It didn't work. The stress of the day had finally caught up with her.

Katrina glowered.

Mavis' eyes watered. "It's funny because you change into a wolf." She made a rolling motion with her hand.

"I got it. I just didn't think it was funny, bird brain."

The insult made her laugh harder. "How long"—she hiccupped—"how long have you been waiting to use that one?"

Katrina sighed.

Mavis' laughter subsided. "For the last time, I don't want anything to do with your boyfriend." She wiped the corner of one eye. "I have no desire to see the doc again. Especially after he had me drugged and interrogated."

"What are you talking about?"

Mavis scoffed. "Like you don't know."

Katrina shook her head. "I don't, but I'm sure he had a good reason for doing whatever he did."

"Your unflagging loyalty is nauseating." Mavis groaned. "Keep it up and you really are gonna make me puke."

Katrina glared. "Just tell me what happened."

"The patient he told me was a patient turned out to be a psychiatrist. She drugged me and I ran away on to the balcony. You know the rest." Mavis thought about what she'd just divulged and to whom. "Am I lying? Can you tell?"

Katrina wrinkled her nose. "No. You're not. As far as you know. Chase must have had a good reason."

Mavis bounced off the bed and grabbed another cookie. "He wants to know what happened to Gloin. He thinks Mel knew, which means he thinks I know, but I don't. And I may never remember."

And if she did? Earlier, she had believed the idea that the possibility she could remember was enough for someone to try and kill her. Why else would they push her from the balcony? She still believed it. Someone wanted her dead because they were afraid of what she might remember.

"Do you think Gloin is alive?" Mavis asked.

"I don't know."

"Did you know him well?"

"Everyone knew Gloin. He was the Aldwulf."

"But did you know him, like, personally?"

Katrina lifted her chin. "No one really knew him. It was more of a feeling. You knew he was there. He cared about every single one of us—kept us grounded, kept us connected." Her head lowered, and she seemed to shrink in on herself. "But not since he disappeared. When he left—" She swallowed. "We all lost something. Just like that, we were cut off. We had to learn how to make do."

Perhaps Mavis, better than anyone, could understand what it was like to lose someone. Except the person she'd lost was herself, and she was trying everything she could think of to get her back. The way Katrina described it made it sound less like they'd lost someone and more as if they'd each lost a limb. Like they had taken their connection to the Aldwulf for granted until it vanished suddenly. They wanted their leader back, but if they couldn't have him, would they accept another?

"Now Broderick wants to be Aldwulf," Mavis said.

Katrina scowled. "That will never happen."

"But it could."

"It won't." Her words were hard as steel.

"He's Gloin's son, too. Why not?"

"Chase would never let it happen."

Mavis doubted that, but it was clear Katrina had more faith in the doc than she did. "Why not?"

"Because Broderick doesn't want to lead. He wants to rule. If Broderick fights Chase and wins, there'll be a war. Broderick said that he wants to avoid bloodshed, but a lot of innocent people could get caught in the crossfire, and not just werewolves."

Mavis swallowed. "And that won't happen if Chase wins?"

"No. Chase would be a leader. He wouldn't expect people to bow to him."

"Do you think Chase can beat Broderick in a fight?"

Katrina smirked. "He won't have to. Broderick will have to go through me first." Color bloomed in Katrina's cheeks as she spoke, and her respirations sped up. Katrina was clearly spoiling for a fight and couldn't wait to give Broderick one. Mavis pitied him.

The sound of knuckles rapping on glass made them turn toward the sliding glass door to the courtyard. Wes waved from the other side.

"Excuse me," Mavis edged her way past Katrina, unlocked the door, and slid it back.

"Hey, what happened to you today? You up for some dinner?" His gaze went to Katrina. "Your friend can join us."

"Nah. She was just leaving." Mavis turned to Katrina. "Take a cookie for the road and don't forget to lock the door on your way out." She stepped outside, pulling the sliding glass door closed behind her.

CHAPTER 17

Wes gathered cheese and bread to make *trois fromage* sandwiches. While he grilled their dinner, he attempted to do the same to Mavis.

"I just about had a heart attack when Mr. Aitch came in today. I thought maybe something had happened to you, but he said you were fine."

"The doc called Aitch to give me a ride back into town," Mavis said. No need to tell Wes she'd been so exhausted she could hardly walk.

He checked the sandwiches. "What happened with that patient the doc wanted you to see?"

"Not much."

"Were you able to help her?"

Mavis chewed the inside of her lip and stared across the kitchen at the pantry door. "She didn't need my help. Not really."

Wes frowned, perhaps picking up on her desire not to talk about it, but it didn't stop him from making conversation. "I'm sorry you wasted a trip out there for nothing."

"Me, too."

A minute of silence stretched into two, which had to be some kind of record for them. Then Wes asked, "So, who was your friend?" He pointed with his elbow in the direction of her apartment.

"She's not my friend."

Wes flipped the sandwiches. "Okay. Then who was she?"

"Katrina."

Wes' eyebrows shot upward. "That was Katrina?" He blinked, his gaze turning inward as if to replay what little interaction he had had with her. "Huh."

"What?"

Wes shrugged. "I don't know. From the way you talked about her, I was expecting someone, I don't know, taller?"

Mavis folded her arms. "Everyone looks taller than you when you're stuck in a wheelchair."

"True, true. I just thought there'd be more to her."

Mavis snorted. "There is. She's a werewolf." Her eyes widened. She should not have said that. Damn Wes and his plying her with food and making her comfortable enough to share things with him she probably shouldn't, but if she couldn't tell Wes, who could she talk to? He wouldn't say anything. Especially if she asked him not to.

Wes' mouth dropped open. "You're joking."

"Nope."

"That—she's a werewolf? How do you know?"

Mavis lifted one shoulder. She regretted saying as much already.

"How long have you known?"

"I just found out."

Wes stared at her, a deep vee forming between his brows. "I thought you'd be more excited."

"What? Why?"

He waved his spatula in the air. "Ever since I've known

you, you've wanted to know more about werewolves, and now you know one."

"I don't know her. Not really."

Wes turned off the fire under the griddle pan. "You know what I mean."

Mavis raised her shoulders. "It's not like we're friends. We're not gonna braid each other's hair and talk about what it's like for her to be a werewolf. It's probably against the werewolf code or something. And could you not mention she's a werewolf to anyone? I probably shouldn't have said anything. I don't think she wants anyone to know."

The urge to blurt out all she knew about werewolves, including who was one, weighed on Mavis. She wished she could tell Wes everything, but she didn't know how he would take it. If he had a hard time believing Katrina was a werewolf, no way could he handle knowing Mavis was two-natured and could turn into a bird.

"My lips are sealed." Wes mimed zipping his mouth shut and throwing away the key.

That put an end to the topic of werewolves just in time to eat. They stuck to gossip around the diner over dinner. After they were finished, Mavis helped clean up, and Wes asked her if she wanted to play a video game. They landed on the couch, controllers in hand, ready to race. The mindless fun somehow kept her mind occupied.

The evening slipped away. By the time Mavis left, the sun had set. Outside her sliding glass door, she fumbled the leftovers Wes forced on her, dropping the foil-wrapped package as the lights in the courtyard went out. Crouched in the darkness, Mavis checked the glow-in-the-dark hands of her watch. Time for lights out—in the shared courtyard, anyway. Her outstretched hand landed on the food.

A low growl stopped her.

At the back of the complex, the eight-foot-tall wrought-iron fence separated the courtyard from the alleyway and, beyond that, the undeveloped lot on the other side. Beyond the fence, the only things she could make out were the shadows of tall grasses and trees. She blinked, her eyes adjusting to the dark. A figure moved between the trees, low to the ground.

Mavis stood up slowly. In the darkness, the figure's shape and size were indiscernible. She could almost believe she'd imagined it.

Then, there it was again, gliding through the trees, shaggy and low to the ground, but not by any means small. Keeping her eyes on the figure, Mavis opened her sliding glass door as quietly as she could. She slipped inside, dumped the leftovers, and grabbed a flashlight before stepping back outside. She turned it on, pointing the beam across the alley into the wooded lot. Nothing stirred.

But something did brush against her ankle.

Mavis jumped, the flashlight flying from her hands. It clattered to the ground, rolling away. The cat from the garage wound its way around her legs and meowed. Mavis bent over and scratched the furball behind the ears. She sidestepped, still bent over, and picked up the flashlight.

The figure returned.

Mavis could tell now it was a wolf; the black and gray werewolf—it had to be a werewolf, it was too large to be a regular wolf—stared at her with orange-brown eyes from across the alley, completely still. Mavis blinked, glancing away as she remembered what the doc had said about too much eye contact being a challenge. She kept the wolf in her peripheral vision. It sat there, but she knew the wrought-iron fence wouldn't keep it out. Mavis could imagine it sailing over the pointed bars in a single bound and landing in the court-yard without issue.

Was she supposed to have seen the wolf? If she wasn't

meant to see it, then she didn't think she would have. If it was a warning of some kind, she would expect more teeth, but it displayed no signs of aggression. Maybe the wolf wasn't there to warn her, but to watch her. Was it someone she knew? She could think of only one person to ask. The doc's number was on the fridge.

The cat meowed again. It could easily slip through the bars back into the alley. "I'd stay on this side of the fence, cat," she said. It butted its head against her leg and then padded away, deeper into the courtyard.

Mavis stood up, avoiding any sudden movements. Turning off the flashlight, she stepped into her apartment, sliding the door closed behind her. She slid the lock home and went to the refrigerator. A business card was stuck to the front with a magnet. She took her cell phone out of her bag and tapped in the number.

The line rang twice. Three times.

"Hello?" a voice answered.

"Who's the wolf?" she asked.

Silence. Then the doc sighed. "You weren't supposed to see him."

"Well, I did." Maybe she wouldn't have if the lights hadn't gone out and she hadn't come home earlier to find Katrina in her apartment. At least Katrina had closed and locked the front door behind her as Mavis had asked. The open container of cookies sat on the counter. There might have been one less than before.

"His name is Harley. He's there to keep an eye on things."

Her eyes narrowed. "You mean he's here to keep an eye on me."

"Yes. I asked him to watch you."

She chewed the inside of her lip. "Asked or ordered?"

The doc cleared his throat. "Told him. I told him to keep an eye on your place."

That sounded like an order to her. "Does Harley the were-wolf need anything?"

"No. He'll be all right for the night. How are you getting here in the morning?"

"I'll take the bus." Supposedly he could smell a lie, not hear one.

"I thought Aitch would drive you."

"Aitch has a business to run. I can get there on my own."

The doc didn't say anything for a minute, but she could hear the rustle of fabric on the other end of the line. Smoothing his tie, perhaps? "Good luck tomorrow."

Mavis hung up

<<<<>>>>

Mavis was up with the sun the next morning. Pure exhaustion played a major role in her being able to drop off to sleep at all, despite knowing of the werewolf outside, watching her apartment. She showered and washed any lingering scents associated with Aitch down the drain. When she got out she dressed in layers, tucking the silver necklace inside her shirt. She shuffled extra gear in and out of her backpack and laced up her boots tightly, ready for a hike.

The main roads weren't busy at that time of the morning. Still, a pickup pulled over, the driver asking her if she needed a lift somewhere. The people of Eustace Park were friendly like that, but she thanked the driver and waved them on. Mavis cleared the edge of town, climbed through a fence, and set out toward the hospital taking a direct overland route through a pasture that ran up against the trees.

Her legs burned as she climbed a hill and she relished the chance to stretch her lower limbs. Her upper body had always been stronger than her legs. Now she wondered if her physical abilities, or lack thereof, had anything to do with being two-natured. Did the fact that she could shift into a bird explain why her legs hadn't wanted to work at first six months ago? Mavis couldn't be sure, but the physical activity took her thoughts back in time.

In the early days, her consciousness had teetered, waking her at random times, day and night. Events ran together in her head like watercolors, the red streaks of pain always on the edges, muddying the rest. As the pain faded, she was left with twin realizations: one, she couldn't remember who she was, and two, her legs couldn't remember how to walk.

With time and physical therapy, her legs came around, but not her memory. She could recall nothing personal before waking up in the hospital, but she knew facts. For instance, New Mexico had become a state in 1912, *dreamt* was the only word in the English language that ended with the letters "mt," and Pluto was no longer a planet—that one made her heart beat fast, for some reason. The most personal thing she recalled was a recipe for crispy chocolate chip cookies. However, the random facts never came with information about where she might have learned them or about who she was. Her fondest wish was to remember where she picked up all her useless knowledge in the first place, but nothing ever came to her. Zip. Zilch.

According to Sandra, a.k.a. Dr. Wilcox, she might never know, and telling her anything about her past might do more harm than good. The doc wanted her to remember on her own, but what if she couldn't? Would anyone ever tell her about Mel? Both Aitch and Katrina claimed to have not known Mel well enough to tell Mavis anything of substance about her. After what she'd learned from Katrina about the doc and Mel's relationship, Mavis wasn't sure she could trust anything he had to say about her, good or bad.

Whatever happened to Mel would have occurred around the same time that the werewolves revealed themselves to the rest of the world, which put it at around the same time as the disappearance the mysterious Gloin, their leader, and Chase's and Broderick's father. The framed photo on Mel's desk suggested that she and Gloin had been close. Perhaps she had seen him as some kind of father figure. That would make sense, considering that Mel had been seeing his son romantically, but then, why not keep a framed picture of her and her boyfriend on her desk instead? Mavis' skin crawled. How many people had Mel slept with? Mavis didn't get the sense from the photo that Gloin and Mel had been together, but there had been some kind of relationship between the two of them. Mavis just didn't know which kind.

At the top of the ridge, Mavis stopped to catch her breath. She pulled out her water bottle for a drink. Taking advantage of being on higher ground, she made sure she was going the right way. Her sense of direction never steered her wrong. Did it have anything to do with being able to shift into a bird? At the bottom of the ridge, a little to the north, she would hit the drive leading to Shady Creek.

She started down the hill and considered what she knew. The Aldwulf was gone, and no one knew what had happened to him. Chase, her doctor, insisted his father was alive, but his brother, Broderick, thought he was dead. Mavis may be the only person who knew what had happened to Gloin and his location, except she couldn't remember. Tomorrow night his two sons would fight to rule over all of the packs unless someone stopped them and Mavis had a niggling suspicion there were people out there who wanted that someone to be her.

CHAPTER 18

When Mavis arrived at Shady Creek, she asked for Weasel at the front desk.

The receptionist didn't bat an eye and directed her to the cafeteria, which was open around the clock. Weasel hadn't specified a time. A few chairs were occupied in the main dining room, but none of them by Weasel.

Mavis hadn't eaten much before leaving her apartment that morning. The thought of sitting down with a hot meal made her warm all over. Inside the serving area, she grabbed a tray and fixed herself a cup of tea. Two people waited at the grill. She got in line.

As the cook took orders, Weasel stepped backward through the swinging door out of the kitchen carrying a long silver tray. The backward-facing ball cap he wore gave the impression he was moving forward while doing the opposite. When he swung around, Mavis saw a beard net covered the bottom half of his face.

Weasel settled the tray onto the counter. Glancing up, he saw Mavis and grinned.

"You made it," he said.

"You didn't say what time—"

He waved a hand. "Now's good. You grab breakfast, and I'll meet you in the dining room."

She nodded and he went back through the swinging door.

Mavis purchased her breakfast and went to find a place to sit. There were plenty of seats to choose from, but she found one in the middle that placed her back to a column and gave her a good view of the grounds through the windows. A few minutes later, Weasel joined her with a tray of his own.

"Here, I got you this." He handed her a blueberry yogurt, a package of granola, and a banana. Two cartons of milk, a pile of scrambled eggs, hash browns, sausage, bacon, and another cup of yogurt remained on his tray.

She nudged her meal. "Thanks, but I already have enough to eat."

"Yeah, nah. You're gonna need more than that to get through the morning." He bent his head and lowered his voice, though no one sat nearby. "You can shift on an empty stomach, but I wouldn't recommend it."

"I'll save it for later, then. Thanks. Where are you from, anyway?"

"Christchurch, New Zealand."

"How did you end up in New Mexico?"

He tipped his head to the side. "There was an airplane involved."

Mavis smiled. "Gosh, I hope so."

"Nah, yeah. What about you?"

"I, uh, I don't know."

Weasel ate while she told him about her amnesia, waking up in the hospital unable to walk, her recovery, and that she'd only learned she was two-natured the day before. "I went by Melisandrea before, and apparently the Aldwulf and I were friends."

Weasel frowned. "I heard he disappeared."

"So did Mel. Around the same time."

Weasel nodded between bites.

Mavis sipped her tea as a familiar face appeared in the serving area—the patient she'd run into yesterday. The tall, pale, dark-haired man started when he saw her. What was his name? Forrest. That was it.

His gaze dropped to the cup of coffee he held. Weasel glanced over to see what had caught her attention. Then he waved.

"Hey, Forrest, over here." Weasel lowered his hand.

Forrest's expression fell. No way he could ignore them and say he hadn't seen them now.

In a whisper, Mavis asked Weasel, "Is Forrest two-natured?"

"Nah, he's got other problems."

Forrest approached the table, but stopped a good distance away, his gaze darting to either side. "Good morning," he said. He glanced at Mavis. "Good morning."

Mavis wondered if one of his problems was making a habit of repeating himself. He'd done it the day before as well. Perhaps it was some kind of nervous tic.

"Morning," Weasel greeted him. "Allow me to introduce my new friend, Mavis."

She hid her surprise, but upon reflection, she didn't think it was a stretch. Weasel was the type to make friends easily, which was probably why Forrest had stopped instead of ignoring them and moving along.

"We've met," Forrest replied.

"Well, not formally," Mavis said.

"Are you a patient?" Forrest asked her.

"I used to be. Now I live in Eustace Park."

Forrest blinked while staring at the lid on his coffee.

"How're the meds today?" Weasel asked.

He glanced up at Weasel and then back down. "Better. I'm going back to my room now."

"Yeah, all right. I'll bake some cookies later and bring you a stack, fresh out the oven," Weasel said with a wave.

Forrest slipped away, silent as a shadow.

Weasel turned back to his tray. "Bit of an odd duck, that one, but nice enough. I like him."

"You like to bake?"

He shrugged. "Yeah, for my sins."

"What kind of cookies are you going to make?"

"I'm not sure yet. I'll have to see what we've got the ingredients for. Do you bake?"

"A little."

"Good to know." He smiled. "You ready to get started?"

The breakfast she'd consumed turned over in her stomach. Soon she would know if shifting into a bird was a fluke or something she could do whenever she wanted. "As ready as I'll ever be."

<<<<>>>>

Mavis followed Weasel to a small clearing in the woods. He carried a backpack, like her. They were far enough away from the hospital that she couldn't see it through the trees.

"So, you've never done this before?" Weasel asked.

"Not before yesterday, no." She set her things aside and rubbed her hands together. It was early enough to still be cool in the shadows. "Is that a problem?"

"Not necessarily. It's strange, but not unheard of."

"Can I—" She stopped, unsure how to ask for what she wanted.

Weasel lifted a brow. "You want to see my other nature, don't you?"

"Is that rude? That's rude. Forget I asked."

"It's all right. That's why we're here, after all."

Weasel tossed his ball cap aside, uncovering wavy brown hair and whipped his shirt over his head.

Mavis stared. The technical term that came to mind was *physically fit*. A whole bunch of not-so-technical terms also sprang to mind, such as *cut, ripped,* and *washboard*. Weasel toed off his shoes and reached for the button of his jeans. She blinked.

"Do you have a problem with nudity?" he asked.

"My own or someone else's?"

He chuckled.

Mavis kept her eyes trained upward as Weasel stepped out of his jeans. The treetops were very green on this underwear-optional kind of day. Her face heated as she pressed her lips between her teeth until she finally focused on Weasel. That was why she was there. The air around Weasel blurred, and she drew her head back, unsure if what she was seeing was really happening. Weasel disappeared without a sound. There wasn't even a *pop*.

His clothes twitched. Something low and sleek tumbled across the ground, coming at her. A buff-colored ferret with a black mask, feet, and tail undulated closer. He stopped about a yard away to look up at her with deep brown eyes, black nose twitching. Mavis crouched down. He scampered closer, sitting up on his hind legs and pressing his forepaws against her knee. She searched for any trace of the human Weasel in the ferret in front of her but found none. His rounded ears twitched, and Mavis stroked the fur on top of his head.

A breathless "Wow," escaped her.

The ferret turned and ran a few feet away. The air around him wavered, infused with some kind of dense fog, enveloping him. When Weasel was standing right in front of her again, she got another good look at the treetops. "That was amazing."

"Well, once you get the hang of it."

Fabric rustled, making her glance over to see Weasel bent over his pile of clothes.

The backside was more impressive than the front. "How come it's not like that for werewolves?" Mavis asked. Everything she'd read and seen—thank you, internet—indicated that the change from human to werewolf and back took a lot longer and was much more painful.

Weasel stepped into his jeans and slid them up, zipping them closed, but leaving the button undone. "I'm not sure. Werewolves are cursed, for whatever reason. It takes them longer to change, and they don't have a choice when the full moon rises."

"The air went all shimmery and you were a ferret, and then it happened again and you were back."

"That's what shifting looks like from the outside."

"Did it hurt?"

Weasel raised a hand. "Slow down. You need to focus on what it means to be human before you go shifting into a bird and forgetting."

His words had her sucking in a breath, her brows drawing down into a frown. "Has that ever happened before? Someone—forgot?" she asked. Forgot what it was to be human, or how to shift back? Is that what happened to her? Had she shifted into a bird and stayed that way too long? Her heart hammered against her ribs. That couldn't be how she had lost her memory. Could it? Her vision went fuzzy around the edges, and her heart couldn't work hard enough to get the blood to her brain.

Weasel, completely dressed again, glanced her way and did a double-take. "Whoa. Are you okay? You've gone all pasty."

"Answer me."

He crossed the distance that separated them and took her by the arm. "That's never happened, as far as I know. Come over here—take a load off. This'll be easier if you're comfortable."

He led her to a fallen log. They both sat. He didn't let go.

"Why would you say that?" she asked.

"I didn't mean to upset you. No one I know of has ever forgotten how to turn back into their human form. What I meant is that before you do shift, you should focus first on what it's like to be human. It will make shifting back easier. Once you turn into a bird, communication will be limited. If I didn't teach you how to shift back to human first, it would be like teaching you how to ride a horse without showing you how to stop first." He squinted and tilted his head to the side. "Kind of. Do you see what I'm trying to say?"

Mavis nodded. "I think so." Her heart no longer wanted to pound its way out of her chest, but a fine tremor wracked her hands. "Sorry. I just thought—I don't know what I thought."

"Nothing to be sorry for. Now focus on your surroundings."

She closed her eyes and tuned in to the ground beneath her feet, the bend in her knees, the brush of her clothes against her skin. Leaves rustled and birds called overhead. The smell of earth mingled with the scent of flowers. Human. Her natural state.

"What's your favorite cookie?" Weasel asked.

"Crispy chocolate chip," she answered. No hesitation.

"Ah, a traditionalist with a twist. Good."

She opened her eyes. "What about you?"

"I am a lover of all things cookie. Talking about food might sound silly, but by recalling the little details, I don't think you can forget what it's like to be human. Our second natures aren't nearly as complicated. Besides, shifting is like a muscle. The more you use it, the stronger you'll get." He squeezed her arm and let go. "Now, I don't say this to a lot of people, but strip."

"Because if I shift while I have my clothes on—"

"You might get tangled up in them. Here." Weasel went to his backpack. He pulled out a striped blue-and-green beach towel and tossed it to her.

Mavis doubted she had anything Weasel hadn't seen before, but she turned her back anyway and took off her clothes, wrapping herself in the towel and tucking in the end.

"Ready? I'm going to help you with this part." Weasel held out both hands, palms up.

Mavis reached out and placed her palms on top of his, the tips of her fingers skimming his wrists. Nothing happened. Weasel smiled. Mavis blinked.

They stood surrounded by some kind of pinkish fog, the air shimmering in waves.

Mavis gasped. "Where are we?"

"We're still in the woods."

She peered through the haze. The trees still stood around them, only wavy and distorted.

"What is this?" she asked.

"We call it the fugue. Think of it as another plane of existence beneath our everyday one, like the fruit of the apple under its skin. It's always there. It's always waiting. The only people who can call it up are shifters. You just have to reach out and tap into it when you want to shift. Now that I've shown it to you, it should be easier for you to find your way in. Then you can change whenever you want."

Weasel released her hands and the curtain of haze parted and dissipated. They stood alone in the woods.

"How did you do that?" Mavis asked.

Weasel shrugged. "It gets easier with a bit of practice. But I will say that if you don't get at least a little bit queasy, you're not doing it right. Give it a try, but don't shift yet." He sat down on the log, at ease, and crossed his arms.

Mavis pulled at the bottom edge of her towel. "I don't even know where to start."

"Start with where you are. Remember, the fugue is always there. You're just reaching out and tapping into it."

"Wow, when you say it like that, it's no help at all."

Weasel smirked, but he didn't say anything more.

Mavis' head dropped forward, her fingertips brushing her temple as she pushed her hair behind her ears. She stared at the dirt. Below it was more earth. Eventually, rock. Whatever she was after wasn't under her feet. Supposedly, it was all around her. It was always there. Its presence was automatic, involuntary, and continuous. She did not have to consciously think about it, but now that she knew about the fugue, she couldn't stop herself from pushing her thoughts forward. The bubble separating her from the fugue quivered and broke.

A tingle shimmied down her spine as a wave of nausea washed over her. Bending at the waist, Mavis gulped and breathed through her mouth. The need to vomit passed. Mist surrounded her, obscuring everything from view. She could barely make out the blurred figure of Weasel sitting on the log. The fugue wasn't as oppressive when he was in it with her, but on her own, the pink haze threatened to suffocate her. It pressed in from all directions in a way that made her uncomfortable, almost as if she was underwater and sinking fast.

Mavis got the sense that the fugue was a dark place. Now that she knew about it and acknowledged it, she wouldn't be able to forget. However, she did want out. Between one breath and the next, the fugue receded, leaving her standing in front of Weasel.

"You good?" he asked.

Mavis nodded, unsure of how to describe her unease after

having entered into the fugue on her own. Maybe it was the same for everyone.

"Great, 'cause that was the easy part. Ready for what's next?" he asked.

"Yes." She was proud of the way her voice didn't waver at all.

"We've got to get you back in touch with your other nature."

Mavis swallowed. "How?"

"You've got to picture what you want to turn into. Do you have a bird in mind?"

A flash of black and white feathers. "Yes."

"I want you to slip into the fugue and try to shift. I'll be right here. I'm not going anywhere, so take your time."

Mavis called up the fugue. It was already easier to pluck at the veil between worlds and gain access to it. She waited for the nausea to pass.

Now what?

In her haste to shift, she may have been remiss in finding out exactly how to go about it. The last time she'd shifted into a bird had been to save her skin. If she had to recreate a die-or-take-flight situation every time she wanted to shift, it wouldn't be worth it. Her fingertips beat a rapid tattoo against her thigh before she wrapped her arms around her middle in frustration. She could do this; she'd done it before. The fact that she was two-natured had been established—now she just had to go for it. She screwed her eyes shut tight, prepared to change.

Nothing happened.

An irritated huff of air escaped her. She wasn't sure how much longer she could take the fugue pressing in on her before she had to escape it. Leaving in her human form would mean that she had failed. She unfolded her arms and raised them away from her sides, her gaze tracing their shape.

While she stared along the edges of her skin, she thought of the magpie.

It was as if her gaze turned inward.

Her skin shuddered and she was wracked by the sensation of her bones growing shorter, hollowing out, and fusing. Soft, internal crunching sounds and the occasional squelch reached her ears. Her feet grew longer front and back, her littlest toes absorbed into the rest of her three-pronged feet, each new toe complete with a curved black talon on the end.

And feathers. Oh, the feathers. Black and white plumage sprouted, covering her.

The whole process didn't take long, neither did it hurt, but it was undeniably strange. Every muscle cramped, seeking release, and an uncomfortable tingling refused to fade. Finished, she shook herself head to tail feather. The fugue surrounded her, but it no longer pressed in on her as it had before. As a bird, the fugue was no different than a swatch of sunlight filtering through a window.

With a thought, the mist fell away.

She chirped at Weasel.

He jumped. "All right?"

She flapped her wings and lifted straight into the air, settling straight back down again. Weasel watched. "Maybe you'd like to—"

In a flash, she was flapping up and away into the clear blue sky.

"—stretch your wings!"

CHAPTER 19

Flying.

It was better than any dream.

Mavis' wings beat the air, thrusting her higher and higher. Above the trees, she tangled with the wind—dipping a wing here, thrusting hard there—until she found a current to ride that allowed her to hang motionless in the air. She didn't have to think about making adjustments to her wings; her movements occurred without conscious thought, keeping her aloft. With her increased visual acuity, she focused on the hospital, easily picking out the window to the room that had belonged to Mel.

She rode the current as high as she could until it tumbled against another and she had to beat her wings to climb higher. She flew closer to the hospital and the balcony. Flying over it, she got a view of the scratches from above. They were longer than she thought, pointing straight at the edge. She soared higher over the peaked roof, noting a square panel near the center for access.

Her wings strong and stretched, she banked to return to Weasel, though the view of the mountains in the distance called to her. The struggle to keep from blowing past the clearing to sink into the landscape was a real fight. As a human, she knew the mountains were farther away than they appeared, but as a bird, her wings freed her from having to stick to roads and trails. She could fly straight toward the snow-capped peaks and be there in a fraction of the time.

A heady thought.

She reminded herself that this was just a test flight, and in a few beats of her wings, she circled over Weasel's head. He sat on the log with his arms crossed.

"Now remember, crispy chocolate chip cookies," he said and bent forward, his hands pressed to the log on either side, ready to stand.

Mavis landed on top of the crumpled terrycloth towel that lay where it had fallen after she shifted, summoning the fugue. If visualizing a magpie had helped her shift into one, then she hoped thinking about her human form would enable her to shift back. Her hardly-knobby-at-all knees came to mind, and it didn't take long for the jarring sensation of her bones shifting and growing under her skin to take over. The towel under her feet, when she had human feet again, tickled her soles. Like a new parent, she counted fingers and toes, making sure she had the appropriate number after this rebirth, this regeneration. She dispelled the fugue with a thought and scooped up the towel.

Weasel finished getting to his feet.

She'd followed each step to shift in reverse order, but in a fraction of the time.

Mavis sucked in a breath.

Weasel's head snapped up. He stepped back, his mouth falling open, and tripped on the log, but righted himself before he fell over. He held up an index finger as if telling her to wait. "That was really fast."

"I know." Her voice wavered as she said it. Was it supposed to be that fast? Maybe she'd done it wrong.

"I mean, good job." Weasel stared.

A grumbling noise broke the tension. Mavis' hands flew to her stomach.

Weasel smiled. "Hungry?"

Mavis sat to eat the extra food Weasel had given her in the cafeteria. "Now what?"

Weasel squinted at her, his head turned to the side, considering. "You up for trying something different?"

The whole morning had been unique, but what she said was, "Okay."

Weasel slipped his phone from his pocket and tapped away at the screen until he found what he wanted. "Here we go." He handed her his phone. The image of a red-tailed hawk filled the screen. "What do you think?"

Mavis studied the display. She scrolled down to see another photo of the same bird from a different angle. "I'll give it a shot." She passed his phone back.

In a moment, she entered the fugue. Eyes closed, she called up the image of the red-tailed hawk. Her body, wracked by the odd but not painful sensations, shifted into the form of the raptor. Her eyesight sharpened. Her body was larger as a red-tailed hawk than it had been as a magpie, and though she had just eaten, the idea of finding a juicy mouse crossed her mind unbidden. She pushed the thought aside. On the ground she spread her wings and estimated a span of about four feet from wingtip to wingtip. She dispersed the mist with a thought. The talons at the end of her toes, made for catching prey, plucked at the towel.

They hadn't discussed her shifting back to a human right away. She walked with a high-stepping gait away from the towel and lifted her wings away from her body. A few deep beats of her wings, and she was up and soaring.

Mavis circled the treetop not far from the clearing, picking out a branch to settle on. Her eyes strayed toward the mountains, the panorama hazy and inviting. A flicker of movement from below had her head turning toward the clearing. No sign of Weasel. The sight of a slender, furry body as it undulated over a downed tree revised her thinking. No sign of Weasel as a human, but he was there in his ferret form from earlier. His little body poured over the trunk of the felled tree and raced along the ground until he stopped to inspect something.

Another movement caught Mavis' eye. There, through the grass, slid a scaled body, making its way toward Weasel. She opened her beak to cry a warning. It came out as a high pitched *sheeeeee*.

Weasel kept moving. So did the snake.

Without thinking, Mavis hopped off the branch into a steep dive, letting out another cry. She swooped down over the furry body and picked it up in the middle, circling back to the clearing, her one desire to get Weasel away from danger. Weasel, the ferret, writhed and twisted in her talon-tipped grasp, but she didn't let go until they were back where they had started. Mavis flew in low and released Weasel. He dropped, rolled, and scurried away as fast as he could.

The air around him blurred.

Mavis landed, entered the fugue, and made the shift back to human form. Finished, she parted the mist and picked up the towel, wrapping it around herself.

Something was wrong. Weasel, returned to human form, sat and twisted around to look at his back. When he saw her, he cringed. "What was all that about?"

"There was a huge snake." She stepped around him to see scratches on his back. A few of the deeper ones bled. "I didn't mean to hurt you, I just wanted to get you away from there before it—"

Weasel harrumphed and stood, stepping into his jeans. His feet bare, he stalked off into the woods in the direction of where she'd scooped him up. She followed.

He spoke to her over his shoulder. "I smelled something off and wanted to check it out. I've taken on snakes before, you know. I can handle myself in any form." He stopped next to the downed tree, hands on his hips, staring at the ground.

Mavis kept her distance. "Other side."

He walked around the twisted roots of the felled tree. The deadwood stood taller than he did. He stopped as a rattling noise filled the air. Mavis watched him swallow. Slowly, he stepped back until he reached her side. "Yeah, all right. That's a big one." He dragged his gaze away from the tree to look at her. "Thanks."

"Sorry about the scratches."

He shrugged, the movement pulling at his torn flesh. He winced as they headed back to the clearing.

"So, if you're injured in your other nature, you're still injured when you shift back?" she asked.

He nodded, sober as she had ever seen him, his brows arched upward. "And if you die in your other form—"

"You're dead," she said. The long red welts crossed his back from one side to the other. "I'm sorry," she said. "Did you think I was trying to hurt you?"

Weasel pulled his shirt over his head, avoiding her gaze. "I've heard stories."

"What kind of stories?" Mavis hopped on one foot, tugging up her underwear.

"Older shifters. Their second nature can get the better of them and they can have a hard time knowing friend from food." He shook his head. "It's hard to explain, but you knew it was me just now, right? When you grabbed me?"

"Right. I didn't think there was another ferret around."

"Good. Since some hawks have been known to eat my

kind, you can understand why I might have been a little worried."

Mavis' brow pinched together. "But don't some weasels eat birds?"

"Ah, well, small birds and their eggs, yeah, but I'd like to think I wouldn't eat a friend." He raised his gaze and stared at her with something like wonder on his face. Or perhaps concern.

Mavis glanced around, suddenly more uncomfortable than she had been all morning. "Why are you looking at me like that?"

"You said you never shifted before yesterday?"

"Not that I know of."

"I've never known someone so new to shifting to be able to do it so quickly. And more than one species is impressive. Only more experienced shifters can do that."

Mavis wasn't sure what to make of that. Shifting felt good, if a bit strange, like a deep stretch after a long workout. She didn't know switching from a magpie to a red-tailed hawk was supposed to be such a big deal. No one had ever told her. If the collection of feathers in the cup on top of Mel's desk was any indication of the number of different types of bird she could turn into, she wondered how long Mel had been shifting before she disappeared.

"So that was some kind of test?" she asked.

"I didn't mean it to be, as such, but you said before you used to be someone else." He shrugged, eyebrow raised. "It was worth a shot. Did you know you could do it?"

"No, I didn't, so quit looking at me like that," Mavis said.

Weasel blinked, glancing away.

Her stomach rumbled. Mavis looked down. "Seriously?"

CHAPTER 20

C lean silver countertops and industrial appliances gleamed in the hospital kitchen. Working together, Mavis and Weasel mixed up more chocolate-chip cookie dough than she had ever seen in one place, including the grocery store. And that was after she helped herself to more than a little of the dough before it hit the oven.

Like Weasel said, shifting sapped her energy, but food helped. They'd grabbed lunch and then started to make cookies, which helped even more. They took turns shuffling trays in and out of the oven and rotating cookies on and off of cooling racks. From the racks, the cookies went onto a large serving tray or into containers. Kitchen staff came and went the entire time, so it wasn't odd when a man she'd never seen before stopped to sniff the air. His eyes drifted closed in appreciation as he approached.

A tingling sensation started in Mavis' lower back and raced up her spine to the back of her neck, making her shoulder blades move closer together. The man raised his eyelids, revealing reflective pools of blue as he smiled with a lopsided tilt of his lips, his manner easygoing, but there was something just below the surface. It vibrated faster than the rest of him, a barely constrained eagerness she could in no way see, but she could sense. Almost as if he had too much energy for one person.

Weasel pointed his chin at the man. "Where have you been hiding?" he asked.

The man smiled. "I had a late night."

Weasel chuckled in a way that had the other man ducking his head.

The man scratched his jaw. A white speck of shaving foam clung to his neck, up by his ear. "Not that kind of late-night," he said. "The boss had me out." The man pressed his palms together. "May I please have some cookies?" His gaze bounced from Weasel to her.

Weasel waved away his plea. "It's fine with me, but you should ask Mavis. Have you two met?"

Mavis shook her head and stuck out her hand.

The other man took it with a firm grip. "We sort of already have."

The beginnings of a frown puckered Mavis' brow. She would've remembered meeting this person.

Weasel introduced them. "Mavis, this is Harley. Harley, Mavis."

Harley? As in werewolf Harley? The one who had been watching her apartment? Her smile drained away as she tried to reconcile the orange-eyed black-and-gray wolf from the night before with the man in front of her. The two did not mesh.

Harley let go of her hand. "Nice to meet you. Sorry if I scared you last night."

"What happened last night?" Weasel asked.

Harley glanced to the side with a one-shouldered shrug.

"The doc asked me to watch Mavis' apartment, and she caught me keeping an eye on the place."

"That *was* you," Mavis said.

Weasel's gaze bounced between the two of them. He raised his hand. "Two questions. Why did the doc want you to watch her apartment?"

"When I shifted for the first time yesterday, it was because someone pushed me off a balcony."

Weasel's eyebrows shot upward. "Wow. Okay."

"What was the second question?" she asked.

Weasel turned to Harley. "How did she see you?"

Harley ducked his head. "I have no idea. The doc's given me no end of grief about it."

Mavis didn't apologize for spotting him. Seeing him as a wolf the night before had given her a shock, but his being there may have helped her feel safer and get a decent night's sleep. He didn't need to know that, though. Neither did the doc.

Harley reached for a cookie. "But you didn't see me this morning."

Mavis blocked him. "Excuse me? What about this morning?"

Harley's gaze darted from her hand to her face and back again. When her hand didn't move, he frowned. "You didn't see me this morning. I followed you here from your apartment. Can I have a cookie? Please?"

Mavis' hand lowered enough for Harley to grab a cookie, her mouth set in a firm line.

When she'd left her apartment, she hadn't thought to check for a tail. Her mouth quirked at the unintended pun. Harley was too busy eating his cookie to notice, and Weasel was watching Harley with a thoughtful expression.

"What if someone had seen you?" Mavis asked.

Harley smiled and grabbed another cookie but didn't answer the question. Her eyes narrowed.

Weasel cleared his throat. "If someone caught a glimpse of Harley's wolf running through town, they would have thought he was a dog."

Harley glared at the implication until he had another cookie in his hand.

Weasel continued. "A large dog, but just a big, hairy mutt nonetheless. Not a wolf. Not unless they stopped to get a real good look at him. Harley probably wasn't drawing as much energy from the pack as he needed to conceal himself from you. You spotted him because you're not human. Not entirely."

Harley muttered under his breath and grabbed another cookie.

"What?" Weasel asked.

Harley waved a cookie in the air as he backed away. "It won't happen again. Thanks for the cookies." He left the way he had come.

Mavis wondered if that meant he was through with watching her. Or did he mean she wouldn't catch him again if he was? She vowed to pay more attention to her surroundings, especially when she was on her own.

Weasel piled up a stack of cookies on a small plate. "I'm going to run these up to Forrest. I'll be back in a minute."

Mavis pulled the last tray of cookies out of the oven making room on the counter, shuffling cookies around like she was doing some kind of hat trick. The dirty mixing bowls went into the industrial-sized sink. The lunch rush had passed creating a lull.

When the kitchen door banged open, she jumped. The same tingling sensation she'd felt when Harley came in earlier prickled along her spine but with greater intensity. She glanced over her shoulder and met the gaze of a leather-clad biker. Instead of wearing solid black from head to toe as he had the first time she'd seen him, his leather motorcycle jacket covered a white t-shirt, while his leather chaps wrapped around faded blue denim.

Broderick stalked forward. The door closed behind him. "Mel," he said, stopping next to her in front of the sink. "I heard all about your little adventure the other night and your trouble yesterday. You seem to have bounced back. No harm done."

Mavis had to tilt her head back to meet his eyes. At first, she thought they were dark brown, but up close she saw they were a deep blue, darker than the jeans he wore. His eyes crinkled at the corners as if he were enjoying himself, meeting her like this. When she realized she'd locked eyes with him for too long, she glanced away.

"My name is Mavis." She turned on the faucet to run hot water into the sink and held out her hand. "I don't believe we've been formally introduced."

His mouth curved upward in a lopsided grin. "Right." He slid his large, rough hand against hers and squeezed, but not too tight. "Mavis. Nice to make your acquaintance. I'm Broderick. As if you didn't know." He did not release her hand.

"How did you get in here? Is the hospital neutral territory?"

"Even if it wasn't, I would always be welcome in the house my father built."

Gloin built the hospital? That was interesting. How many of the patients knew about werewolves? How many of them were werewolves? The thought slipped away as his hand continued to hold hers.

As they stood there, the lines around Broderick's eyes smoothed, and the skin between his brows puckered with the beginnings of a frown. Still, he held her hand long past the time when it would have been appropriate to have let go.

Mavis let him hold her hand, telling herself he could hold on for as long as he needed to convince himself that she was not, in fact, Mel.

Steam billowed from the hot water pouring into the sink. The smile drained away from Broderick's face in fits and spurts. And then, all at once, he dropped her hand as if scalded and stepped back. Mavis turned off the water. When she turned back, he was staring at her—or, rather, through her.

His voice sounded loud without the noise of running water. "Aitch said Mel was dead. I didn't want to believe him. Chase said you don't remember. I didn't want to believe that, either."

"Did you know her?" Mavis asked.

His gaze sharpened as he focused on her. "A long time ago."

"What was she like?"

A muscle ticked below his right eye. "You're not her, are you?"

"I—" Mavis stopped and squared her shoulders. She raised her chin. "I don't think I am, but I really don't know. I don't know what Melisandrea was like. At all. I don't remember anything about her or who I was before I woke up here. No one will tell me."

"The only person who could tell you what she was like is dead." He turned away as if he couldn't stand the sight of her.

Mavis had wanted to know what kind of person the mysterious Mel had been. She thought maybe Broderick could tell her. She could have asked the doc, but the thought of talking to him about the woman he'd slept with—when that woman could pass for her—made her queasy. Why didn't anyone know more about Mel?

"You're talking about Gloin," she said.

"Of course."

Mavis bit back her frustration. Katrina had told her the same thing, insinuating Mel thought herself above making friends with any wolf less than the Aldwulf. "I don't understand why Gloin would be the only one to know what Mel was like. She must have known other people. She and your brother were... seeing each other."

Broderick looked her way again, his gaze roaming over her from head to toe and back again. His expression was unchanging, which made her think he wasn't being lewd or suggestive, just curious. "No one knew why Mel kept everyone at arm's length except my father. Didn't matter if she was sleeping with my brother—I doubt it meant much of anything to either of them. No one knew her like Da. They were very old friends." His head jerked to the side. "If you're not her, then you can't help me. If my father doesn't return by tomorrow night—" He turned away and slammed his fist down on the metal counter with a ringing thud.

Mavis jumped. "What?"

Broderick kept his back to her. "I'll do what I have to do."

Mavis recalled his threat from the night before last. "Kill anyone who stands in your way so you can rule over all werewolf-kind?"

He whipped around to face her, moving with inhuman speed. The sudden movement made her tense, but she didn't flinch. She'd already been two kinds of bird that morning. He was going to have to work harder than that to unnerve her.

"Never," Broderick said. "The packs need a leader to unite them. We'll tear ourselves apart unless we have one. If my brother won't do it, then I will."

"Even if it means killing him?"

Broderick took a slow, deliberate step forward. "If I have to, I will. It doesn't matter if half the blood running through his veins is the same as mine. I suggest you stay out of the way so you don't get hurt." His gaze roamed her features, settling on her neck, where she could feel her pulse beating away. His focus lingered there for an uncomfortable moment before it slid away and he removed himself. The door banged shut behind him

Minutes later, Mavis scrubbed at a particularly stubborn spot, elbow-deep in hot soapy water, her jaw clenched. From time to time, she muttered to herself.

Weasel returned and helped finish putting cookies away. "I'm sorry, did you say something?" he asked.

"No," she said without looking at him.

"Then who are you talking to?"

Mavis glanced over. Weasel made a show of looking over first one shoulder and then the other. Seeing nothing, he picked up a rag and wiped down the counter.

"It's nothing." Her teeth ground together.

Weasel kept wiping. "Doesn't seem like nothing."

"I don't know what to do." She threw up her hands, suds flying. "Unless someone can find Gloin, there's going to be a big fight tomorrow night to determine who gets to be Aldwulf. But no one knows what happened to him. Mel disappeared at around the same time, and she just happens to be me. Except I don't remember a damn thing about being her." Mavis stacked the clean dishes to the side with a *bang* and grabbed another dirty bowl to start scrubbing.

Weasel stayed silent for a minute. Then he cleared his throat. "I'm not sure I caught all that, but I find that when I have a large problem that needs tackling, sometimes it's best to start over at the beginning."

Mavis snorted. She'd started at the beginning plenty of times, and all she remembered was darkness, blinding pain, and waking up in the hospital. There was nothing else to remember. Not for her.

Her hands froze. She tilted her head back and closed her eyes. "Not for me," she told the ceiling.

"What?" Weasel asked.

She set the dish she was holding back into the sink. "I think I know what I need to do."

CHAPTER 21

The ground rolled by below her as Mavis climbed up and away from the woods behind the hospital on magpie wings. The trees swayed and dipped below her. She breathed in the sap-scented air of the pines, relishing the chance to sink into the landscape, flying farther than she had that morning. The mountains in the distance begged to be explored, but she pushed the thought aside.

Catching a thermal, she rode it higher, wings stretched wide, achieving maximum lift. A few of the trees were starting to get the message about the change in season. She pushed forward. No going back.

She couldn't take much with her, but she had wanted to bring the silver leaf necklace. The chain was wound half around her leg, half gripped in her foot. It was her first time trying to take something with her, and she didn't want to worry about dropping the necklace, so she had Weasel help her secure it after she shifted. He would hold on to the rest of her things for her. Her red-tailed hawk might have been a better choice for carrying the jewelry, but her magpie form came to her more quickly and easily.

She could have tried another bird altogether, but she had places to be. Experimenting further would have to wait.

Mavis beat her wings and flew toward town. The closer she got, the more the straight angles of man-made structures interrupted nature's chaos. Where the trees thinned, patches of gravel showed through. These stretched into roads that led to oily black ribbons of asphalt. From a distance, Eustace Park was easy to spot, the treetops replaced by peaked roofs and concrete.

From above, Mavis oriented herself. She flew straight down the center of Main Street then she banked hard to the left and flew in the opposite direction, spotting the garage below her. She flew lower. The lights were off and the sign in front read "Closed." She turned and pushed herself higher.

Her apartment complex came into view. The courtyard sat like a square-cut emerald oasis in the arms of the building. The blue pool and fountain bubbled in the center.

Mavis flew onward, following the main road out of town to the west. It bent and twisted, but she flew straight, keeping it in sight, trying to remember how far Aitch had driven the night before last. When she thought she'd gone far enough, she circled the area.

Through the trees, she caught sight of a meandering gravel track. She flew lower and followed it.

At the end of the track was a house. Closer, she recognized the log exterior of Aitch's home. She pushed herself higher, convinced she was in the right place.

Far behind the house, a clearing caught her attention. She took a minute to fly over the bare spot. It was roughly circular, with a couple of cut logs laid out in it. It was probably where Aitch had cleared the land for the timber to make his cabin.

She dipped a wing and turned back toward the house.

Mavis landed in the middle branches of a pine tree. A

light shone from inside the house, a good sign. She winged down to the ground and summoned the fugue, shifting. The mist dispelled. Mavis stood in the trees across from Aitch's front door, the silver necklace wrapped around her ankle. She unwound the chain and clasped it around her neck.

As no one was around to see her naked, she ran up to knock on the front door and scurried back to the protection of the trees. She hopped from one foot to the other, her arms crossed over her chest, waiting for Aitch to open the door. With no feathers and not a stitch to wear, her skin began breaking out in gooseflesh.

The door opened. Aitch stood inside, his hand on the door, ready to close it again. The frown was plain on his face.

"Aitch!" She waved her arm and ducked behind a tree.

"Mavis?" Aitch left the door open as he stepped outside and came toward her. "What are—did you fly here?" He took in her state of undress, his eyebrow ratcheting upward as he shook his head. "You could have just called."

What she wanted to ask him was better done in person. "Well, I—" She glanced away and when she looked back he was gone. He'd walked back into the house, leaving the door open behind him.

Was she supposed to follow? The thought froze her in place. Maybe she could sneak into the kitchen and grab a hand towel. It wouldn't cover much. This was a terrible idea. She should just shift and fly back to the hospital. She couldn't go straight back to her apartment, not without having the pockets to carry the keys she needed to get in.

Mavis was still standing there when Aitch came back holding a t-shirt identical to the one she'd slept in the night before last. Mavis suddenly wished for a much bigger tree to hide behind. As he strode closer, she tucked herself behind the too-slim bark as best as she could. Aitch stopped a good seven feet away and thrust the t-shirt out at arm's length. He turned his face the other direction.

Mavis crept forward and grabbed the t-shirt. His head started to turn and she squeaked, "Don't look!" As quickly as she could, she slipped the t-shirt over her head, but her arm went through the neck instead of the sleeve and she fumbled. How did shirts work again? Finally, she got it sorted, the t-shirt longer than some dresses. "Okay, now you can look. Thank you."

A muscle twitched in his jaw. She couldn't tell if he was laughing at her or not, but when he turned toward her, he did not appear amused. "What's going on?"

She folded her arms, shifting her weight from one foot to the other. "Aren't you going to invite me in?"

Aitch huffed, turned, and walked away. It was all the invitation she was likely to get. She hurried after him and closed the door behind her.

Inside, Aitch faced her across the kitchen. "What happened? Why fly out here?"

"I ran into Broderick. I get the feeling he doesn't want to kill anyone, including the doc, but he will if he has to. If we could find out what happened to Gloin before tomorrow night, maybe we could stop a whole bunch of bloodshed."

Aitch crossed his arms. "'We'?"

"Well, yeah, I need your help. You said you were the one who found me and brought me to Shady Creek. Can you remember where? Do you think you can take me there?"

What Weasel had said about starting over had made her think. Her beginning started in the hospital, but she knew her history went further back than that. Aitch was the only lead she had. He might very well be the only person who could help her.

He blinked, and she got the sense she'd surprised him.

Perhaps not much, but a little. "Why, Mavis? What do you think is going to happen?"

One hand went to the front of the borrowed shirt. Her palm settled over the outline of the silver oak leaf beneath the fabric. "I don't know."

"You don't have to do anything. This werewolf mess isn't your problem."

"But what if it is? I—Mel disappeared at the same time as Gloin. I don't think that's a coincidence. What if taking me back to where you found me jogs my memory?"

"Do you really think that will happen?"

Mavis clutched the pendant through the shirt, fabric and all. "I don't know. It could."

"Do you want to remember?"

How could he even ask? "Yes."

He crossed his arms. "Even if you don't like what it is that you remember?"

She couldn't pick and choose memories. She would have to take the good with the bad. Perhaps there was a very good reason Mel had never let anyone get too close to her. Mavis would be foolish not to wonder how bad some of Mel's memories might be, but in her mind, the decision was made. "Yes. Even then. Because maybe we'll find out what happened to Gloin and no one will have to die."

Aitch straightened. "Afraid something might happen to the doc?" His eyes narrowed, and his jaw clenched.

Why was he asking? Could Aitch be a little bit jealous? The thought made her want to laugh, but it didn't seem like the time, so she choked it back. "I want to help because if someone dies, I'm not sure where it'll stop or with whom. You said so yourself. Changes in leadership can get messy."

Aitch's gaze slid away from her. "I'll make a call, see what I can arrange. But you have to know there's no going back."

She opened her hand and smoothed the wrinkled fabric of the shirt. "Great. Do you have any food?"

Aitch pointed to the fridge and told her to help herself, then stalked off down the hallway toward the bedrooms. A few minutes later, she heard him on the phone.

Mavis foraged in the pantry and pulled a loaf of bread from the keeper on the counter. Her stomach made noises, threatening to eat itself. From the fridge, she pulled out whatever looked good, which meant everything. Eventually, jars and bottles of condiments landed on the table. A drawer filled with meats and cheeses got emptied, along with a few containers she had to pop the lids open to see what was inside. She took it all to the table.

Aitch had a lot of food for a single man who lived alone, but he was a big guy. At four inches past the six-foot mark, not only was he taller than her, but he had to outweigh her by at least fifty pounds of muscle.

Mavis ate one turkey and cheese sandwich and then made another, that one roast beef. There wasn't anything special about the food, but it filled a void. Anything might have tasted as good, but after shifting multiple times and flying farther than she ever had, she imagined it tasted like the finest of five-star cuisine. Eyes closed, she hummed a little tune to herself, rocking side-to-side.

"If I knew food made you so happy, I would feed you more often," Aitch said.

Mavis' eyes popped open. She covered her mouth because it was too full to speak.

Aitch walked past her into the kitchen, opened a cabinet, and pulled out a plate. He set it in front of her and sat at the other end of the table.

She swallowed. "You practically buy me lunch every day. This is good, though. Thank you."

"Glad you're enjoying it. I can take you tomorrow morning. If you stay here tonight, we can get an early start."

Mavis chewed that information over as she took another bite of her sandwich. It was getting dark and she was tired. If she stayed with Aitch, she wouldn't have to fly back to the hospital tonight, collect her things, and get back to her apartment just to have him pick her up in the morning. What came out of her mouth was, "Is it very far?"

"No."

"Can we stop by the hospital in the morning, then? I want to pick up the stuff I left there."

"Shouldn't be a problem. It's on the way."

She glanced down at the t-shirt she wore. "I might need to borrow some more clothes."

Aitch sighed. "Fine."

"You don't mind taking me?"

He grunted, which she took as a no. He'd known Gloin. It wouldn't surprise her if Aitch wanted to know what happened to the Aldwulf as much as she did.

"Can you pass the mustard?" she asked.

Aitch slid the container down the table. She squeezed some on her sandwich and pushed the container back toward Aitch, but she pushed too hard and the bottle sailed off the edge of the table. "Sorry," she said. Aitch waved away her apology and bent over to pick up the condiment.

He had to stretch to reach the fallen bottle and didn't sit up right away.

A long moment passed of Mavis sitting comfortably before she remembered what she was wearing—or rather, what she wasn't. She gasped and snapped her knees together. Something banged against the table and Aitch sat up, rubbing the back of his head, refusing to look at her. She blushed to the roots of her hair. Aitch's blush stopped at the top of his ears.

Mavis set her sandwich down and pushed the plate away, her stomach tight all of the sudden. "Maybe I'll just, uh, go to bed." She stood.

Aitch wouldn't look at her.

She had to pass by him to get to the hallway. It couldn't be more than fifteen steps, but it might as well have been a football field away. She tugged at the bottom of the borrowed shirt and started that way, but slowed to a stop next to Aitch's shoulder. "Why did you tell Broderick Mel was dead?"

Aitch kept his gaze lowered. "Because the Mel he knew is gone. You look like her, but you're not her."

"How do you know?"

He shook his head. "You can't be her."

Mavis hesitated. "But how—"

Aitch shot to his feet forcing Mavis to take a step back. He caught the tops of her arms to keep her from falling on her backside. "I just do. Now let it go."

Mavis stared up into his face, confused. Anger made him tense, but underneath was something else. He was afraid. Stable, she settled her hands lightly on his forearms, but he didn't let go. He stared down at her, his gaze searching her upturned face, stopping on her lips. In the next instant, his mouth was on hers.

She'd never kissed anyone before. Mel probably had, but Mavis hadn't. The shock wore off as Aitch stepped in close, his lips moving over hers. And *oh*, it was good—his lips soft and warm. One of his hands drifted down from her shoulder to settle on her waist. She couldn't stop herself from leaning into him.

His head tilted and his tongue stroked her bottom lip. A small gasp escaped her, and he took advantage of the hastily indrawn breath and her parted lips. At some point, his other hand cupped the back of her neck, holding her in place as he moved his tongue against hers with bold strokes, there and back again, getting lost in the sensations. One particular jolt hit her low in her belly.

Then Aitch stopped. Just like that.

He left Mavis standing there—confused and wanting more, her chest heaving—while Aitch seemed unaffected. Or so she thought until she saw him swallow. His head dipped toward hers again, his gaze on her lips, but he stopped himself and leaned back. She didn't know why. She would've been fine to continue. He let go of her waist and retreated a step, sliding his hand from behind her neck. The loss left her cold in an instant.

"You should go to bed," he said.

"Alone?" The question popped out before she could stop it.

"I'll wake you when it's time to go."

"You could just nudge me." Her eyes widened in surprise at her audacity, but he didn't see it.

"Good night, Mavis."

All right, so they wouldn't be continuing their little make-out session. A part of her wondered why they had to stop, while another, more rational part of her was glad they did. As she walked away, the rational part should have grown louder, but it was drowned out by the beating of her heart.

CHAPTER 22

Early the next morning Aitch pounded on the door to the guest room, startling Mavis awake. Outside, it was still dark. With a sense of déjà vu, Mavis stumbled to the bathroom. How did her closing her eyes for a few minutes keep turning into several hours?

The toothbrush she'd used was still there. Either Aitch had thought she'd be back or he hadn't had the time to get rid of it yet. She suspected the latter, even as she hoped for the former. She'd laid in bed replaying his kiss in her head over and over long past the time she should have fallen asleep. When she'd finally drifted off, she still didn't know what to make of it.

In the living room, a set of dark gray sweat pants and a zippered hooded sweatshirt were folded over the back of the sofa. She kept the t-shirt on, slipping into the sweater and zipping it up to the chin. The pants she cuffed until they weren't quite so long. As she lifted her hair free, Aitch pushed his way inside through the front door. He held a pair of rubber galoshes in one hand.

"These'll do for this morning." He set them on the tiled

floor by the door. "Oatmeal's on the stove. Help yourself." He strode past her down the hallway and out of sight.

Mavis watched him go. Despite the early hour, Aitch wasn't his usual cantankerous self. He hadn't grunted once. In silence, she sat on one of the stools at the kitchen island, her ears straining to hear what Aitch was up to. The pre-dawn quiet lay like a blanket over everything. As she finished with breakfast, he strode back into the room.

"If you're done, we should go," he said.

Mavis narrowed her eyes. "What's going on?"

"What do you mean?"

She glanced around the kitchen. "Why are you being so nice all of a sudden?"

"I don't know what you're talking about."

She threw her head back with a loud guffaw.

"We should probably get going," he said.

Close. That sounded more like Aitch, but still not quite right. When he didn't say anything more, she rolled her eyes. "Fine. Let's go." She stuffed her feet into the borrowed galoshes. They were huge and awful and made strange squelching noises as she walked. Outside, the air was still and cold. Nothing stirred except for Mavis and Aitch, their breath curling into a fine mist. She only tripped over the sloppy boots a couple of times.

Mavis hopped into the passenger seat of Aitch's truck. "What were you doing while I was eating?" she asked.

Aitch started the truck, switching the heater on. "Nothing."

"You were avoiding me."

"I was not avoiding you. I already ate. There was no reason to stand over you and watch you. I've got better things to do."

Closer. "Oh, okay, good. You weren't avoiding me because you kissed me or anything." Her statement hung in the air.

Aitch grunted.

There he was.

He flicked on the headlights, putting the truck in gear. "No. That was a mistake."

Mavis sucked in a breath, glad he was watching the road and not her. "Avoiding me? Or kissing me?"

"I wasn't—that kiss should never have happened. I'm sorry."

He was apologizing? "Is that why you were trying to be nice? Because you're sorry you kissed me?"

He wouldn't look at her. "Maybe. A little."

"Was it that bad?"

"No—" The leather of the steering wheel creaked where he gripped it. "But nothing can come of it."

Mavis turned away to stare out her window, an ache in her sternum. She shouldn't want Aitch to kiss her again, but she did. Aitch didn't feel the same. He was her boss. They couldn't be together. He didn't want to go around kissing his employee, which was a shame. It would make the workday go so much faster.

She leaned her forehead against the cool glass and did her best to ignore him. He ignored her right back.

The skies began to lighten when they reached the hospital. Refusing to look in Aitch's direction, she let herself out of the truck and headed inside. When she returned, the truck sat idling. Mavis wore her clothes from the day before, carrying the ones Aitch had loaned her as well as her backpack. She got back in the truck, setting the borrowed clothes on the seat between them and her backpack on her lap.

Aitch drove out of the parking lot. They were near the main road when Aitch spoke. "Mavis, why is your bag moving?"

She kept her head turned away to peer out the passenger side window. "Hmmm?"

"Your bag. Why is it moving?"

"Oh, are we speaking now?"

Aitch hit the brakes.

Mavis braced one hand against the dash and held on to her backpack.

"Talk. Now," Aitch said.

"Calm down," she unzipped her bag.

The small, buff-colored face of a ferret popped out.

"Is that—what the hell is Weasel doing in your bag?"

"Well, if he was human, he wouldn't fit, now would he? He's a lot lighter this way." Mavis stroked the fur on the ferret's forehead. Weasel squeaked and hunkered down in her bag.

"Why is Weasel a ferret right now?"

"I asked him to come along, okay? I want him to take a look around. His senses are heightened this way, and I could use all the help I can get. There's not a ton of room in here. He suggested shifting into a ferret beforehand. That way, he won't have to shift when we get to wherever it is we're going."

Aitch started to speak, stopped, and shook his head.

If it kept Aitch quiet, Mavis was happier than ever to have asked Weasel along. "Where are we going anyway?"

Aitch took his foot off the brake. The truck rolled forward. He turned onto the main road. "This way."

The hum of the road under the tires combined with the weight of the backpack in her lap made Mavis sleepy. Then she remembered why she hadn't slept well and cracked the window to help keep her awake. Eyes wide, she took in the passing scenery. She'd never been this way and watched to see if anything looked familiar. Nothing did.

Mavis chewed her bottom lip. There was a very good chance she wouldn't remember anything, but she was lying to herself if she didn't hope something jogged her memory.

At a curve in the road, a group of buildings sat clumped

together. Apart from this knot of civilization, the road was unremarkable. A mile or two farther along, Aitch turned onto a dusty two-track road. The ride got a lot bumpier, and falling asleep was no longer a concern. The track went straight until it reached the trees, and then it wound through them, climbing in elevation. The track turned back on itself as the trees grew dense on either side. A little farther up, the truck crested a small rise and came to a stop. A small clearing stretched out in front of them. Down the rise sat a log cabin, a curl of smoke rising from its chimney. Through the trees, Mavis caught a glimpse of a long, grass-filled meadow.

"Is this it?" Mavis asked.

Aitch turned off the truck, opened the door, and stepped out. "Not quite." He shut the door.

Mavis got out, backpack over one shoulder, and followed Aitch down to the cabin. Around front was a deep porch with a swing and a couple of chairs. An old yellow lab, face more white than yellow, lay under the swing. Aitch stepped onto the porch, and the dog came alive with a woof, its tail thumping against the wooden boards. It pushed itself to its feet and rushed down the stairs past Aitch to Mavis, tail wagging. She didn't hesitate to bend down and pat the dog on the head, receiving the swipe of a tongue across the back of her hand in return. She scratched the dog under the chin and bent down close to its face. "Hello, sweetie. What's your name?" .

Aitch knocked on the screen door.

Inside, they heard someone walk to the door. "Some guard dog you are, Rusty," an older woman said as she pushed the screen door open and stepped onto the porch. Her long silver and white hair trailed over one shoulder in a single plaited rope. The sleeves of her dark blue chamois shirt were rolled up to the elbow, the tails tucked into a long, patterned skirt. On her feet were a pair of dark brown moccasins. "He likes you." She nodded to Mavis. Her dark-brown eyes shone bright, despite the lines etched into the skin around them.

Mavis wasn't sure how much stock to put into Rusty's character assessment as she had never met an unfriendly lab. She smiled and petted the dog some more.

Aitch, standing on the porch, towered over Rusty's owner. "Essa, this is my friend, Mavis. Mavis, this is Essa."

Did Aitch's voice trip over the word *friend*? She couldn't be sure.

Mavis straightened. Essa couldn't be more than five feet tall. Mavis stepped up onto the porch and held out her hand. Essa came forward to squeeze her fingers in a tight grip, leading Mavis to discover she was tiny, but by no means frail.

"Pleased to meetcha. How can I help you?"

Trust Aitch to cut to the heart of the matter. "Do you remember that exotic bird you asked about in town last spring?"

Essa's brows drew together. "Well, that wasn't me. I never did clap eyes on the thing. My grandson was visiting at the time. He saw it, down the valley a ways. He asked around town if anyone knew what it was, and because he's my grandson, they must have thought it was me doing the asking."

Aitch nodded. "Would you mind if we took a look around? Mavis here has a keen interest in ornithology." He didn't look at her as he said it, the joke meant for her ears alone. Mavis kept her expression neutral. Keen interest, indeed.

"I don't see why not. When you're finished, come on back up to the porch. C'mon, Rusty."

The old dog whined but followed his mistress through the screen door.

"Where to?" asked Mavis.

Aitch stepped off the porch, headed toward the meadow. "This way."

CHAPTER 23

The trail away from Essa's cabin led alongside the meadow next to the tree line. Mavis hiked behind Aitch, telling herself not to enjoy the view, or at least to try not to enjoy it too much. Aitch had made it clear nothing was going to happen between them. Her head knew it. She just needed time to get the rest of her body on board with the decision.

Mavis stifled a sigh and focused on their surroundings. Past the end of the meadow, the trail faded away to nothing, and they picked their way through the trees, moving uphill.

They were a good distance away from the cabin before she asked, "How do you know Essa?"

Aitch answered without turning. "She's an artist. I have a couple of her prints."

Mavis wondered what pieces she'd seen around his home might be Essa's work. "And she doesn't know? That you found me out here?"

Aitch glanced back at her over his shoulder. "No. Essa's cabin sits at the head of this valley, which runs into a larger canyon. I started in the canyon and worked my way here. I didn't realize until later how much of this land Essa owns."

Mavis had a decent sense of direction, but the trees were beginning to look alike. The terrain grew steeper. "What made you think to look out here?" she asked.

Aitch paused in the middle of the incline they were on. "Gossip. I heard someone say that Essa had seen an exotic bird—or her grandson had—and I came out here to check." A few minutes later, he crested the sharp face at the top of the hill and turned around, extending his hand to her.

Mavis caught up and stood there, ignoring his hand as she caught her breath. "An exotic bird? That's it? That's all you had to go on?"

"I did know about Mel's other nature," he said, as if that explained everything.

Mavis' hands went to her hips. "Wasn't there anyone else looking?" Why had this particular search fallen to Aitch and not someone else?

Aitch sighed and lowered his arm. He squatted down on his haunches. "The doc had wolves looking for both you and Gloin across the state. Hell, across the country. I don't know." He rubbed the palms of his hands over his thighs. "I guess I just thought you wouldn't travel too far from home."

Mel's room at Shady Creek implied she must have had ties to the area, but had she considered Eustace Park as much of a home as Mavis did? Mavis had no way of knowing. "But how did you find me in all of this?" She took in their surroundings, lips parted.

"I got lucky," he said, offering her his hand once more.

Mavis took it, and Aitch hauled her up next to him. The ground was much flatter on the hilltop. She peered through the trees to the drop-off on the far side of the small jut of land where they stood. The ground sloped toward its edges less than thirty yards away.

"This is it," Aitch said.

Mavis twitched, surprised to find she hadn't yet released his hand. She turned loose and walked through the trees to take in the view. The canyon opened and spread out below, the treetops turning into a lush green carpet. Despite being warm from the hike, a coolness licked down her spine. She had the strangest desire to step off the edge into the nothingness below. Could she shift in time, or would her second nature take over on its own again? What would it be like to fly over the canyon as a magpie? As a hawk?

A movement in her backpack had her easing away from the edge.

She turned her back on the panorama. Her backpack slid from her shoulders with a tug, and she unzipped it. Weasel slinked his way out. "This is it. Take a look around and let us know if you find anything. Thanks, Weasel."

He scampered away with a rustle of leaves.

Aitch joined her at the edge, frowning at the steep drop.

"What's the matter?" Mavis asked.

"Nothing. It looks different, is all."

"I'll bet. You would have found me before most of these trees had leaves. Lots of evergreens around, though." She twisted around. "Where did you find me?"

Aitch stepped back from the edge and surveyed the trees with a frown. Then he pointed. "There."

As they started up the slope, Mavis kept an eye open for Weasel.

Aitch stopped at an evergreen, glanced around as if trying to get his bearings, then nodded. He spread his hands, palms down, and patted the air in front of him. "Here. This is where I found you. You looked like you were asleep. I checked to make sure you were breathing, that you had a pulse. Then I picked you up and carried you down. Went straight to the hospital from here."

Mavis stared at the ground, trying to imagine herself sprawled at the foot of the tree. Weasel's long ferret body flowed over the ground toward them. He stopped and sniffed along the way.

"Weasel, did you catch that? Make sure you check over here, please."

Mavis turned to face the way they had come, stepping in close to the base of the tree. The vertical lines of the trees interrupted the view, except for—she squinted and did a double-take.

Aitch noticed. "What is it?"

Mavis double checked and waved him closer. "Stand right here." She pointed to the spot at the base of the tree. He took her place and looked toward the edge. Mavis watched his face. Was it just her? Could he see what she saw? He stared for about fifteen seconds. Then his chin lifted and the skin around his eyes relaxed. She knew he saw what she had.

"Huh. I never would have noticed that," he said.

Standing on that spot, facing the canyon, there was an open path straight through the trees to the edge of the cliff. A runway. On either side of the clearing at the end, the trees fanned out. A part of her found the near-symmetry of the trees orderly and soothing. Another part had no trouble seeing the trees as black bars against the morning light when what she longed for were clear horizons.

She could understand why she would have found this spot so desirable, given her love of the balcony at the hospital. How much of her choice of location had to do with her second nature? Mavis had always enjoyed the outdoors. Now she had a better idea why. Perhaps it went along with her interest in werewolves. She had known the Aldwulf, or Mel had. If Mel knew what happened to Gloin, how had it led her here?

Mavis took in the runway and stared out over the rest of

the terrain. "How could you have found me?" She couldn't keep the wonder out of her tone. The area was huge. Even if the sighting of a strange bird had given Aitch a clue, there were still hundreds, if not thousands, of acres to search. So how did he do it? He said he got lucky, but there must have been more to it than that.

Aitch stepped away from the tree and peered down at the ground: the spot where he'd said he discovered her. "It took me longer than you think. I had to come back three times. I hate to think of how long you were out here on your own. I should have—" He stopped, wiping a hand down his face.

Mavis hugged her middle. "What?"

"I should have gotten to you quicker."

"I'm happy you got to me at all."

Mavis stayed where she stood. She didn't press her lips to his cheek to thank him. In Mel's old room, she kissed him purely on instinct. Last night he'd kissed her and made plain this morning that it had been a mistake. Did she want to kiss him again? Yes. Though, a kiss on the cheek was one thing— throwing herself at him was another. She remained out of arms' reach, and hugged herself tighter. Pressure built up behind her eyes, but she blinked several times and it passed.

"You saved my life, you big hero."

Aitch lifted his gaze to hers, the edge of his mouth curling like he found her words humorous. "I don't think so. You're stronger than you think. Like I said, I just got lucky."

The leaves rustled at their feet, and Weasel rushed into view. Mavis knelt in the dirt. "You okay, Weasel?"

"You know he can't answer you," Aitch said.

"Duh."

Weasel squeaked, which she took to mean he was all right.

Mavis opened her backpack beside her. "Okay. If you didn't find anything, get in the bag, otherwise lead the way and we'll follow you."

Weasel's nose twitched. He climbed into her backpack.

"I guess our luck's run out," Mavis said. She took one last look around as she slipped her bag back onto her shoulders.

They hiked back down to the cabin without speaking. As soon as they were within sight of the front door, Essa opened it and set a pitcher of iced tea on a side table next to some plates and flatware. The old yellow dog, Rusty, ran down the steps to greet them and escort them to the porch. Essa stepped inside and returned with a cutting board bearing a loaf of bread and a small baking dish. She set both next to the tea and smiled. "You all might think it's a little early for cookies, but I got this banana bread we can cut into. And a little bit of egg casserole. Anybody a vegetarian?"

Mavis and Aitch shook their heads.

"I am, so the casserole only has cheese and veggies in it. Have a seat. Did you all find what you were looking for?" She poured iced tea into tall glasses.

Aitch snagged the chair, so Mavis took a seat on the swing, setting her bag on the ground near the edge of the porch. Rusty didn't pay any attention to her bag as he sat at her feet with a doggy grin. She bent forward to rub his furry ears, unsure of how to answer Essa's question. The bird they had told Essa they were looking for was sitting on her porch swing, just in human form.

"Not really," Aitch answered.

"Did your grandson ever describe the bird he saw?" Mavis asked.

Essa handed out glasses of iced tea and cut the banana bread into slices. "Not so much. He didn't recognize it. It was early spring then, you know. I think the bright colors are what caught his eye." She joined Mavis on the swing. "I don't get to town much. Have you lived in Eustace Park long?"

It was hard for Mavis not to smile at Essa's easy-going

manner. Mavis relaxed against the swing. "No. I've only been there for about six months."

"Oh, where you from, then?"

Aitch took a bite of banana bread and coughed.

Mavis smiled. "That's a good question. I don't really know. I don't remember anything from before I woke up at Shady Creek."

Essa recoiled, but not in disgust. Her eyes held nothing but sympathy. She might not get into town much, but her reaction told Mavis that she knew about Shady Creek and what kind of hospital it was. "Oh, my! Is that so?"

Mavis nodded. "I recovered and was discharged about four months ago."

Perhaps sensing his mistress' distress, Rusty whined at Mavis' feet. She patted him on the head.

"And you have no idea who you were before?" Essa asked.

Mavis shook her head.

"How intriguing. Have you been working hard at reinventing yourself? Deciding who you want to be?"

Mavis used the excuse of petting Rusty to not answer right away. The word 'reinvent' didn't sit well. It made it sound like Mavis knew more about Mel than she actually did. Instead, Mavis was inventing herself, learning new things about who she was all the time. In that way, she was deciding who she wanted to be. Her wanting to find out what happened to Mel had less to do with trying to remember who she was before and more about trying to help potentially stop werewolf bloodshed. When she glanced over at Aitch, she saw he watched her with an intensity that made her swallow before she turned to Essa and answered, "It's a work in progress."

Essa chuckled. "I hear that."

"Do you live out here by yourself?"

Essa scoffed. "I'm not alone. I've got old Rusty there. He

gave me a good scare a while back. Thought I was gonna lose him, but he rallied, thank goodness. And my grandson comes and visits fairly regular. His mother, too, when she can get the time off."

Essa told Mavis about her art and how she kept busy after her husband died and her daughter moved away. Her husband had built the cabin with her help when they lived outside of Denver. It was supposed to be their summer place, but then her husband got sick. They sold their other home and moved to the cabin to make the most of the time he had left. When he passed away, she couldn't leave. That was when she started taking pictures and painting.

"But that was a long time ago. I don't mean to keep you all." Essa sat forward. "I forget, being retired, you young people probably have better things to do."

"You said you made the banana bread?" Mavis asked. She'd tried a bit of both the bread and casserole as they talked.

Essa smiled. "Did you like it? You can take the rest with you."

"Thank you." Mavis stood. "Would you mind sharing the recipe?"

"You like to bake?"

Aitch stood. "Her cookies are pretty good."

Essa's smile broadened, her eyes taking on a gleam as she glanced between them. "I guess I'll have to send the recipe along with you if you liked it that much. Or are you going to write a book and pass it off as your own?"

"If I wrote a cookbook it would have to be called, 'Mavis' Stolen Recipes from Around the World,' or something like that."

Essa laughed. "I'll wrap this up for you all. Back in a jiff." She stepped inside. Rusty stayed at Mavis' feet, his tail sweeping the boards.

Mavis picked up her backpack. It felt lighter than it had before. The zipper was open. She checked inside. "Uh-oh."

Aitch eyed her bag. "What?"

Essa came back with the leftover banana bread wrapped in foil. "If you can't tell, I don't get many visitors. You all come back anytime." She handed Mavis the shiny parcel.

"Thank you," Mavis said.

Aitch came forward and took Essa's hand in his. "Thanks for having us on such short notice. If that old truck of yours gives you any trouble, you call me and I'll take care of it for you."

"Well, now, I might just do that." She patted the hair in her braid into place. "Rusty, stay."

The dog whined, but he lay down as they stepped off the porch and headed toward Aitch's truck. Essa waved and went inside.

Aitch caught her elbow. "What's the matter?"

She lifted her shoulder with the backpack on it.

"I'm one Weasel short."

"We can't leave without him."

"I know that." In a breathy whisper, Mavis called, "Weasel —where are you?"

A rustling and a squeaking reached her ears. It sounded like it was coming from behind the cabin.

Rusty jumped off the porch. Would the old dog hurt Weasel? He didn't know Weasel wasn't a ferret full-time. Mavis put herself between the dog and the sound. Aitch followed her.

"Hey, Rusty," she whispered as the dog came nearer. "Easy, boy. I'm just looking for a friend."

Aitch patted Rusty on the head to distract him while Mavis turned to the row of bushes behind the cabin. The squeaking came again, and Weasel rushed toward her from under one of the larger bushes.

She dropped to a knee and opened her bag. "Weasel, come on. It's time to go."

He stood on his hind legs for a second before toppling over backward and retreating the way he had come.

Mavis shared a look with Aitch and followed. It was a tight fit. At least she didn't have to worry about Rusty following her as she crawled under the bush on her belly. She pushed branches out of the way to follow Weasel. It was dark under the bush, which made the bone lying there on the ground practically glow.

CHAPTER 24

The bone was about six inches long, curved, and yellow-white. If Mavis had to guess, she thought it could have been a rib bone. What she didn't know was whether the bone had belonged to a human or an animal. She gulped, reached out, and picked it up. It hardly weighed a thing. She wiggled out from underneath the bush, turned, and showed it to Aitch.

When he saw it, his jaw clenched.

Mavis stared at the curved fragment. One end was ragged as if it had been broken. There could have been any number of reasons for a bone to be out there under a bush behind Essa's cabin. Maybe she'd given Rusty a rib bone and it ended up under the bush, except Essa had said she was a vegetarian. Mavis' mind jumped to the worst-case scenario. "Do you think it's Gloin's?"

Aitch winced and shook his head. "Why would you think that?"

Mavis' brows hiked upward. "Why wouldn't I?" She looked toward the cabin as if she could see around it to the woods beyond. "You found me here. Mel and Gloin disappeared at about the same time. Either way"—she lifted the bone higher—"it's a bad sign."

"No. It's just a bone." He patted Rusty on the head one final time. "Bring it with you."

Weasel scooted into Mavis' backpack. Rusty saw him and whined, but didn't try to eat him, for which Mavis was grateful. She patted Rusty on the head. "Good boy. It's okay. We'll be on our way."

The dog watched them get in the truck.

Mavis found a clean rag in the cab. She wrapped the bone, slipping it inside her backpack next to Weasel. As they drove away, Rusty trundled back to the porch and lay down.

"Should we get the doc to take a look at what we found?" Mavis asked. "Maybe he could tell us something about it."

"He's not that kind of doctor," Aitch said. "But there might be someone who can tell us more about it. Let's head to the garage. Weasel can change, and I can make a call."

Weasel didn't squeak or otherwise put up a ruckus, so Mavis figured that plan was okay with him. Back at the garage, Aitch went to the front to make a call while Mavis took Weasel to the office so he could change. She brought the extra set of clothes she'd borrowed from Aitch that morning, set them on the chair, and left him to it. Aitch hung up the phone out front when she came out.

Mavis glanced at the time. It was after nine. "Should I flip the sign over?" Fridays were busy, but she didn't know what Aitch had planned. Maybe he wanted to take the bone to his friend himself.

"Go ahead," he said.

Mavis opened the shop for business. Weasel joined them from the back. He hadn't bothered with the t-shirt, instead leaving the hooded sweatshirt unzipped over his bare chest, rippling torso on display. The pants he had rolled at the waist and cuffed at the bottom so he wouldn't trip over them in his unshod feet.

"What's the plan?" Weasel asked.

Aitch's hand rested on the phone in its cradle. "I'm gonna open up shop. You need to get to Beauryan," he told Weasel.

"What's in Beauryan?" Mavis asked. It was the next biggest town to the west of Eustace Park. She'd never been there. There was no way of knowing if Mel had or not.

"Another hospital. I have a friend there who agreed to look at the bone and tell us what she can about it. Weasel, did you find anything else out there? In the clearing or back at the cabin?"

Weasel tilted his head to the side. "Nothing at the clearing. Didn't catch sight or scent of anything interesting until we got back to the porch. That's when I stuck my nose out and found the bone."

Aitch nodded. "My friend's expecting you. Can you drive?" he asked Weasel.

"Sure."

"Come on, I'll get you the keys to the loaner. You can take Mavis with you."

Aitch kept a four-door sedan in the back lot for customers to use if they needed a vehicle while he worked on theirs. Why did he want Mavis to go with Weasel rather than stay? She would have asked to go along anyway, but the way he suggested it made her feel dismissed.

Aitch and Weasel were speaking in low tones in the office where the keys were kept, but they stopped as soon as she joined them.

Weasel's eyes widened as he glanced from her to Aitch and back. "Are those terrible rain boots still in the truck? Be right back." He scooted out of the room without meeting her gaze.

Mavis watched him flee, then turned back to Aitch. "What's going on?"

He kept his expression blank. "Nothing."

"Then why do I feel like you're trying to get rid of me?"

Aitch stepped forward, and the room seemed to shrink. "I'm not trying to get rid of you. I think you should talk to my friend. Her name's Carol. She works in the basement of the hospital."

What was so special about this friend he wanted her to meet? "Is she a werewolf?" She couldn't imagine Aitch letting just anyone examine the bone, especially if it had anything to do with Gloin's disappearance.

"No, but she is two-natured."

Mavis glanced around the office, reluctant to leave. "You're sure you don't need me to stay?"

"I did run this shop on my own before you showed up. You know that, right?"

"Maybe I can't afford to take the time off," Mavis said.

"Seeing as how you've never taken a sick day, I think you're covered."

"What did you say to make Weasel rabbit out of here like that?"

Aitch uncrossed his arms, taking another step forward. "I told him to watch out for you and what would happen to him if he didn't."

Mavis held her ground, eyes narrowed. What was Aitch hiding? He didn't expect her to believe he threatened Weasel over her safety, did he? There had to be something else.

"But we do need to talk," Aitch said.

She was right. "About what?"

Instead of answering, he lifted his hand to the nape of her neck, fingertips grazing the skin around the collar of her shirt. Her breath halted. She was proud of the way she didn't lean toward him, even as her heart rate doubled. Was that what he wanted to talk about? The strange chemistry between them that seemed to be getting worse instead of better? He pulled the chain with the silver leaf he had given her until the pendant was free of her shirt.

"It can wait," he said, his voice no louder than a deep purr, with his gaze on the pendant one moment, shifting to her mouth the next. One more step and they'd be as close as they were the night before, pressed against each other. He was the one who pushed her away earlier. Was he having second thoughts?

From the doorway, Weasel cleared his throat.

Aitch let the chain spill through his fingers until the pendant fell against the outside of her shirt. He lifted his head and backed up a step. Mavis sucked in a breath, maybe just a little bit mad at Weasel for the interruption.

"Ready to go?" Weasel asked.

"I'll see you later," Aitch said.

The pitch of his voice rumbled through her.

CHAPTER 25

They got in the car, with Weasel behind the wheel. However, the road under their tires wasn't the only rumbling they heard.

"We'd better stop," Mavis said.

Weasel shifted in his seat. "I'll be all right," he said, even as his stomach announced how empty it was again. He had to be hungry after shifting a couple of times already that morning.

It was half-past nine and about a forty-five-minute ride to Beauryan. She pointed to the side of the road up ahead. "We'll make it quick; I promise. Pull over there."

Weasel stopped the car, and they got out. Mavis led him to the door of the Main Street Bakery. "Have you ever been here?" she asked.

He shook his head, his gaze roving the storefront.

Inside, the breakfast rush was in full swing. They grabbed the last two open seats at the end of the counter. Wes worked the room, a coffee pot in each hand, refilling cups. Other servers rushed to get food on tables. As Wes slipped behind the counter and caught sight of Mavis, his eyes widened. He set the carafes back on their warmers and took the order book from his apron pocket. "Hey. What can I get you?"

"Can we get two—"

Weasel cleared his throat.

"Make that four egg sandwiches to go. Two bacon, two sausage. American cheese, please."

Wes scribbled on the pad and turned to put the order in. Then he swung back, pen stuck behind one ear. "How was your day off?" he asked.

"Good," Mavis said.

"Missed you last night." His gaze flicked to Weasel and back, one brow raised in question.

If he had missed her, that meant he'd probably come by wanting to know if she was free for dinner. When she didn't answer, he must have figured she had other plans. She knew he would never lecture her on how she spent her free time, but of course, he would be curious about who she spent her time with. And here she was, grabbing breakfast to go with someone he didn't know. Her cheeks heated.

"This is—" She stopped, smiling to cover her hesitation. Did she introduce Weasel as Weasel, or...?

"I'm Eugene," Weasel said, raising a hand in greeting.

Wes assessed Weasel from the top of his head to where his torso disappeared below the counter. Weasel had zipped the hooded sweatshirt up, but not all the way. An expanse of flesh remained exposed between the parted metal teeth. Mavis should have insisted he put on a shirt before entering the diner. Her cheeks grew warmer.

Wes relaxed and nodded. "Eugene, huh? Well, is there anything I can get you to drink while you wait for your order, Eugene? Mavis?"

Weasel asked for coffee. Mavis declined. Wes poured a fresh cup and pushed it across the counter before he went to check on other customers.

Weasel took four packets of sugar and unloaded them into the coffee.

"So," Mavis said. "Eugene."

"You can still call me Weasel. Or Gene. Only my mother calls me Eugene." He took a sip from his cup.

The diner was loud with conversation and the sound of cutlery striking plates. While Weasel drank his coffee, Mavis snagged the front section of the local paper abandoned behind the counter. Above the fold, a story about Concerned Citizens United and the meeting planned for that night took up half the page. The accompanying photo showed Lydia Shaw folding pamphlets like the ones she had left at the garage.

Mavis frowned as she read the copy. From her research, Mavis knew the anti-werewolf organization had sprung up after werewolves came out. CCU started with chapters in most major cities and spread from there. However, all they seemed to do was sow fear and discord, turning neighbors against one another. Following meetings like the one they were holding tonight, reports of stalking and intimidation always spiked, including requests for restraining orders.

The article stated that tonight's meeting for Concerned Citizens would be open to anyone who wished to discuss the impact of werewolves on the community. But if that were true, why hold the meeting on the night of a full moon, when werewolves would presumably be too busy with the change to join the conversation?

Weasel nudged her with an elbow. Mavis showed him the article. He took the paper from her and read. The skin around his eyes tightened as his gaze moved down the page. He finished and returned the paper, sipping his coffee.

"What do you think?" Mavis asked.

"It's not good, but there's nothing to be done about it right now."

At least there might be something that could be done eventually. Gloin had decided to expose the werewolves, but what about the two-natured? People like her and Weasel? Keeping her voice low, she spoke in Weasel's ear. "Do we have someone in charge like the werewolves? Like an alpha or Aldwulf?"

Weasel chuckled. "Yeah, right. There aren't enough of us, not like the werewolves. The day you get all of us together in one room would be a trick. The best we could hope for would be a representative, but we would all have to agree on one, which would probably never happen."

"How many shifters are there?"

"Depends on the species. You're the first bird I've ever heard of. I'm the only weasel, but there are other small and furry things out there." He paused. "In fact, I've heard some of the shifters have what they consider to be roy—"

"Here you go," Wes set a white bag in front of them.

Weasel tossed back the rest of his coffee.

"Can you put it on Aitch's tab, please?" Mavis asked.

"Sure," Wes said. "You headed back to the garage?"

"Uh—later. We've got an errand to run. Thanks for the food."

Mavis all but fled. If Wes got a second, he would ask where she had been last night. Mavis just didn't know where to start or what to tell him. The only reason they got away easy was because the diner was busy.

Outside, Weasel started the car and pulled away from the curb. Mavis handed him a sandwich from the bag.

He finished the first one before he spoke. "Is there something going on? Between you and Aitch, I mean." He kept his eyes on the road.

Mavis nibbled on her sandwich. "Why do you ask?"

"I'm just curious. He seems very protective of you, is all."

Aitch had kept her at arm's-length since she started

working for him. Then, when they spent just a little more time together than usual, he kissed her and told her it was a mistake. Now what? Did he think they could go back to their previous employer-employee relationship? Mavis wasn't so sure. Not after what she'd learned about Mel and all that had happened since, but she liked her job, and she wanted to keep it. "I don't know. It's complicated."

"Nah, yeah. Aitch strikes me as the complicated type."

"How do you mean?"

"Nothing. He just seems a bit set in his ways."

Weasel didn't add anything more. She handed him another sandwich in the middle of their drive and a third when they hit the outskirts of Beauryan. When she offered him the rest of hers, he took it.

They pulled into the hospital parking lot and went in the front entrance. The main hospital here had a different feel from Shady Creek. Visitors, patients, and medical staff bustled about.

Things were much quieter when they stepped off the elevator down in the basement. Mavis consulted an information board. Dr. C. Krall's office was listed beside a room number.

The office sat empty when they found it, lights off, door locked. Aitch had said that the doctor was expecting them. Across from the closed office stood a set of solid double doors. Mavis cocked an ear forward. Music played. She didn't think it was the radio—reception wouldn't be too great in the basement. Weasel tipped his head forward and nodded. He heard the music also.

The right-hand door was unlocked. Mavis pulled it open. The music got louder and as soon as she glanced inside she knew why. The sound bounced off the painted cinderblock walls and reverberated around the rectangular room. A desk with a lamp and computer sat in the corner, across the room from a wall-sized refrigerating unit with a series of square doors cut into the front. In between lay three stainless-steel tables the size of doors. A body occupied the middle one. Whoever was on it lay covered from head to toe by a white sheet.

A figure in a white coat and light blue scrubs bent over a file at the desk, back to the door. They had short dark hair and, as Mavis watched, their backside grooved along to the doo-wop music spilling from the computer's speakers.

"Excuse me," Mavis said.

They turned, and Mavis saw that the person in the white coat was a woman. Her dark hair was cropped close in the back, but was longer on top and combed to the side. A pair of spectacles dangled from around her neck, and she held a pen poised above the paper in the file she was going over. Her lips pinched together at the interruption, but Mavis noticed that her bottom half continued to move with the music. "Yes?"

"We're looking for Dr. Carol Krall."

The woman's features relaxed, and her body stopped gyrating. Her face was unlined, but her hair was dark enough that the one or two gray hairs threaded through it stood out. Her eyes were intense dark pools of brown that seemed to take in everything about the two of them in an instant. "Have you got a bone to pick with me?" she asked.

Mavis blinked. If it weren't for the slight emphasis she put on the word 'bone,' Mavis would have thought she was asking them if they had a problem. From the corner of her eye, she saw Weasel go still, but he didn't say anything, letting her take the lead.

"Yes," Mavis said.

"Good." The woman tossed the file onto the desk. "I'm Dr. Krall. Call me Carol. I've been expecting you. Heinrich said you were on your way." Carol dialed the music down on the computer's speakers and reached into the pocket of her coat for a pair of latex gloves. As she pulled them on, she crossed to one of the unoccupied tables and turned on a bright light at the end of an adjustable arm.

Mavis noted her use of Aitch's full name and removed the bundle with the bone inside of it from her bag. In the harsh light, the bone looked whiter than before. "What kind of doctor are you?"

Carol's gaze fixed on the bone as she carefully lifted it from Mavis' hand. "The terrific kind. I'm also a forensic pathologist."

Weasel cleared his throat. "So that's a dead body?" He stared at the figure covered by the sheet on the other table.

"If he wasn't dead before the autopsy, he certainly is now," Carol said, smiling. The corners of Mavis' lips curled upward in response, but when Carol glanced at Weasel, her smile faded, a frown taking its place. "If you're going to pass out or throw up, I'd appreciate it if you did it outside."

Weasel swallowed. "I'm not going to pass out."

Mavis wasn't so sure. "Are you okay?"

"I'm fine. Where's the—"

"Down the hall," Carol pointed with her chin.

Weasel went through the door without a backward glance.

Carol waited for the door to close behind him. "You'd think he'd have a stronger stomach, being two-natured and all."

"Aitch told you?" Mavis asked.

"He mentioned it." Carol held the bone under the light and bent close to get a better look.

"What else did he mention?"

"Not much. Only that two of you were bringing me a bone to examine." She didn't glance away from doing that very thing.

Carol rotated the bone under the light, taking it in from all angles. The minutes crawled by. Carol's face came within centimeters of the bone. At one point, she perched the glasses from around her neck on the end of her nose, but only for a moment.

"Can I ask you something?" Mavis said.

"Mmm-hmm," Carol said without looking up.

"What's your other nature?"

Carol raised her gaze without lifting her head. "You can't tell?"

Mavis shook her head. She got nothing like the feeling she had yesterday in the kitchen with Harley. "Should I be able to?"

Carol raised her head. "Sometimes the two-natured can sense the second nature in others. For instance, your friend gives off a small, furry vibe with the potential for something bigger, but not the same as me, so I'm guessing he belongs in the mustelid family." Carol narrowed her eyes. "You, on the other hand, are something completely different."

Mavis shifted her weight from one foot to the other, glancing away. "I only just found out I'm two-natured."

Carol stood up straight. "How could you have just found out? Most of us know by puberty and, no offense, you look a little old to have just gone through that."

Mavis wasn't sure how much to tell her. She didn't want to go into her life history—of which, admittedly, she knew very little anyway—but Aitch had said he wanted her to speak with Carol. She trusted him, but at the same time, she'd only just met Carol. "Funny story. I woke up in the hospital about six months ago with no memory. I didn't know I was two-natured until recently."

As she spoke, Carol's features faded into a frown, her mouth falling open. After a moment, she snapped it shut. "What was your name again?"

Mavis hadn't given it, which made her wonder if Aitch

had. She didn't see any reason to keep it to herself. "Mavis. Corvid," she added after a beat.

Carol's eyes widened. "Did someone give you that name or did you pick it?"

"I picked it." After Mavis had realized she'd lost her memory, she'd known she needed a name. She didn't want to be known as a Jane Doe or Patient X for any longer than she had to, so she'd asked for a list of names. A nurse had handed her a tablet. She'd brought up a site and picked Mavis, not because she particularly liked the sound of it, but because it felt right. Her last name she'd come up with as well, although she was sure she'd seen it written down somewhere. Her mind must have latched onto the letters.

Carol set the bone down on the table and stripped the gloves from her hands. "Are you familiar with taxonomy?"

"Isn't that the way animals get classified? Or something like that?" If she was right, it was just one of those things she knew. How much of what she knew came from Mel, she couldn't be sure, but at least some of it had to come from past self.

Carol went to the desk and pulled down a book from a shelf. "Taxonomy is indeed the science of classification pertaining to all organisms, living and extinct." She opened the book, flipping through several pages and stopping when she found the one she wanted. Staring at the page, she nodded and held the book out to Mavis. "You turn into a bird, right?"

Mavis hesitated.

"I was being modest before. Not a lot of us can tell what other shifters' second natures are. It might just be me. I don't know. But I get a strident, flappy vibe off you," Carol said. She frowned and lifted the book a little higher.

Mavis took it. It was the kind of book that shoved as

much information onto one page as it could, in tiny print. She didn't know what she was supposed to be looking at.

"Check out the class name for birds," Carol said.

Mavis frowned down at the pages.

Carol took pity on her and pointed to the information she wanted her to see—*Class: Aves.*

"Okay," Mavis said.

"Your name. *Aves* sounds like Avis. I don't know why you put the *M* in front, but you have to admit it's awfully close."

Mavis stared at the page. She had a good idea of why she would put an M in front. Carol didn't need to know that, though. Mavis schooled her expression into something she hoped appeared neutral and looked up. "Okay," she said again, drawing the word out a hair longer than needed.

Carol held up her index finger and smiled. "But wait. There's more. You said you just found out you're two-natured. Do you know what kind of bird you shifted into the first time?"

Mavis blinked. She didn't see what difference it made. "A magpie."

"Very good. Extremely smart birds. And it starts with an M. Just saying." Carol took the book from Mavis and flipped through a couple more pages before she handed it back to her. The smile hadn't left her eyes. "Take a look at what family the magpie belongs to." She pointed to the page.

Mavis looked down. *Family: Corvidae.*

Mavis snapped the book closed and held it shut for a moment before she handed it back to Carol. "I don't see what difference it makes. I just didn't want to go around being called Jane Doe. Could just be a coincidence."

Carol set the book on her desk. Her smile turned into a smirk. "Coincidence? I think not. Don't you think it's interesting that the names you picked for yourself relate so closely to the taxonomy for birds?"

"You think I was subconsciously trying to tell myself I was two-natured." Mavis wasn't sure how else to explain it.

"It's interesting, either way. Incidentally, would you consider yourself much of a singer?" Carol asked.

"No. Why?"

"No reason."

"You never said what your second nature is."

"No, I didn't."

The door opened and Weasel stuck his head inside. "Finished up yet?"

Carol smiled. "Just about."

Weasel stepped into the room but stayed close to the door.

Carol returned to the table where she'd left the bone. She used one of her gloves from earlier to pick it up. "It's not a human bone. It belonged to an animal. I really can't tell you much more than that without studying it longer."

"Is that all?" Mavis asked.

"Well, if I had to guess, I would say it came from a medium-sized mammal. Something like a large dog."

CHAPTER 26

W hat was a werewolf if not a large dog?

Mavis thanked Carol for her time, collected the bone, and left with Weasel right behind her. She kept it together until they were outside. Her strides grew longer across the pavement. She reached the car first, bracing her hands against the frame as her breathing grew shallow, her chest heaving.

Did Weasel's discovery mean Gloin was dead? Was Broderick going to kill his brother and become the new Aldwulf? If he did, Katrina was sure he would start a war with humanity. Mavis' head grew so light that she wondered how it remained tethered to her body.

The weight of a hand on her shoulder brought her back to herself.

Weasel stood next to her. "You don't look so good. What's going on?"

Two deep breaths shuddered in and out of her. "Gloin is dead, and there's no way to stop what's going to happen tonight."

Weasel gripped her shoulder. "Slow down. Why do you think Gloin is dead?"

"You were standing right there. Weren't you listening? Carol said the bone could have come from a large dog. What if it came from Gloin? Now a whole bunch of other wolves may die. And people, too."

"Whoa, whoa, whoa." Weasel unlocked the car and let go of her long enough to swing the passenger-side door open. "Take a seat." As soon as she did, he squatted on the pavement in front of her and held both of her hands in his. "Slow down. I found that bone, and we've got no way of knowing where it came from. Besides that, there's something you should know."

Weasel waited until her gaze found his. From his position, crouched in front of her, his head was lower than hers. His green eyes stared into hers in earnest. He squeezed her fingers. "I've lived and worked beside werewolves for a while now, so I know that when a werewolf dies in wolf form, they revert to human. You know what that means, don't you? That bone couldn't belong to Gloin. No matter what."

Mavis closed her eyes. Weasel's hands were warm—or, she suspected, hers were cold. What he said made sense. If a werewolf remained in their wolf form after death, someone would have found a way to autopsy one and put it on the internet by now. That morbid thought, along with Weasel's presence, helped her calm down.

"What's going on?" he asked.

She told him all that she knew—of Broderick's desire to take Gloin's place as Aldwulf. "There might be more to it than that, but Katrina seems to think Broderick will have to go through her first. She's the doc's second. You get the gist, though."

"And this takeover happens tonight?"

"Yeah, unless..."

Weasel sighed. "Unless Gloin isn't dead and he returns from wherever it is he disappeared to and puts a stop to it."

Mavis stared into the distance over Weasel's shoulder and nodded, her vision blurring. "Yep. Pretty much." She blinked, and the wetness gathering at the bottom of her lids spilled over, sliding down her cheeks.

Weasel squeezed her fingers again. "Hey, now, what's the matter? What aren't you telling me?"

Mavis shook her head and wiped her cheeks. Her panic passed; now she was simply sad and overwhelmed. "It's my fault."

Weasel's chin jerked to the side. "How? How could any of it be your fault?"

She sniffed. "If I could remember what happened to Gloin, none of this would be happening."

"Now hold on. Are you kidding?"

Mavis sniffed again, louder this time. "No."

"Well, stop it. I think you're giving yourself way too much credit. It's been a year since Gloin disappeared. The wolves were bound to have problems sooner or later. You're one shifter."

"But if I could remember—"

Weasel stood with a groan, shaking out his legs. "Haven't you done everything you could to try and remember something—anything—from before you went missing?"

Mavis heard him. She thought back to everything she'd put herself through, willingly and not. Sandra had drugged her, and even that hadn't helped. Mavis swiped at her nose and nodded. "I guess."

"And have you remembered anything?" Weasel asked.

Pained, she closed her eyes. No scrap of a memory from Mel's life came to mind. "No. Nothing."

"Then give yourself a break. It's not your fault. You tried."

Mavis opened her eyes and stared into space, beyond the

parking lot into the distance. Weasel spoke the truth. She had tried, but her disappointment was palpable. "I just wish—I wish I could talk to Mel, you know? Ask her what the hell happened to Gloin. To her."

From the corner of her eye, she saw Weasel go still.

"I know that sounds crazy," she said.

Weasel stuffed his hands into his pockets. He pressed his lips together and tilted his head back.

"Doesn't that sound crazy?" she asked.

Weasel didn't answer. Then, "What if you could talk to Mel?" he said to the sky.

Now he was just making fun of her. Her eyebrows formed a single arc. "That's impossible."

Weasel lowered his chin and turned to look at her. "It might not be as impossible as you think. What time is it?"

Mavis told him. Weasel was around the car in a flash, telling her to buckle up. Back on the road, he drove faster than he had earlier. The sedan hugged the curves through the canyon back the way they had come, crossing the center line more than once to pass slower vehicles.

Mavis braced a hand against the dash. "Do you want to tell me what this is about?" she asked.

Weasel gripped the steering wheel, his focus on the road. "I told you, we have to hurry. What time is it?"

"Two minutes since the last time you asked. Where are we going?"

"Shady Creek."

Mavis accepted the news of their destination with equanimity. She never dreaded returning to the hospital where she had woken up. If Weasel knew of a way for her to somehow contact Mel, where better than a mental hospital? Mel had lived there, after all. Maybe they could light some candles, hold a séance. She choked back a giggle. It didn't seem like the time.

They reached the hospital just before noon. Weasel parked around back, away from the main entrance. "Come on. We have to hurry."

Weasel darted through the back entrance and slipped into the kitchen. Mavis followed close behind. Weasel didn't draw attention to himself, but a few people greeted him as he passed. Every time it happened, Weasel would return the wave or nod, but he didn't stop moving. He led the way up a back stairwell, stopping on the second floor and pulling open the heavy door. He stuck his head out into the corridor, looking one way and then the other. Then Weasel pushed the door the rest of the way open and grabbed Mavis' hand, pulling her along behind him.

About thirty feet from the stairwell, he stopped and knocked on a closed door.

Weasel didn't wait for a response before he pushed the door open, but a voice called "Come in," as they slipped inside.

The room was dark, the shades drawn. It was a private room with one twin bed pushed into the corner to their left. To the right were a closet and the bathroom. The only light came from a halogen lamp on the desk between the bed and the door. Forrest sat in a wooden chair in front of an open book. The remains of his lunch were pushed to the side. His brows drew together at Weasel's interruption. He flinched when he saw Mavis, but didn't say anything.

Why were they bothering Forrest? Mavis smiled and tried to make herself appear as non-threatening as possible. She didn't think of herself as intimidating, but Forrest made her feel that way. How could Forrest help them? And what was it about him that made her think that he needed to be protected and sheltered away, even from her?

Weasel released her hand and gently closed the door behind them. "We need your help."

Forrest's gaze flicked from Weasel to Mavis and back again, but he didn't speak.

Weasel tipped his head in Mavis' direction. "Ask her what you asked me."

Forrest turned back to his book and closed it, refusing to look at them. "Yesterday—that was a mistake—I never should have said anything. The new medication is helping me." He pushed himself away from the desk, the chair's legs scraping against the linoleum floor. His hands shook. He curled one hand into a fist and pressed it to his mouth. A dark lock of hair fell across his forehead.

"I'm glad to hear it," Weasel said, "but I need you to tell Mavis what you told me."

Forrest lowered his hand. "What difference would it make?"

Weasel stepped forward. "I think you can help her."

Forrest shook his head, his shoulders curving forward. "I can't even help myself."

Mavis slid forward to touch Weasel on the arm. "Maybe we should go." She spoke low, afraid to startle Forrest. Their presence appeared to torture him and she thought they should leave.

Weasel stepped toward Forrest. "This is your chance to help someone, and you won't even try."

Forrest shot out of his chair, anger in the square line of his shoulders. "You don't know what you're asking me to do."

Mavis had forgotten how tall Forrest was. He towered over Weasel by half a foot.

Weasel didn't back down. "I'm asking you to think about someone besides yourself."

Forrest stared at Weasel, his chest heaving.

A knock on the door kept them from saying more.

CHAPTER 27

Weasel twisted around. He grabbed Mavis' arm and pulled her back, depositing her behind the door so that when it opened, she would be hidden from view. He let go and pressed an index finger to his lips, as though she hadn't gotten the idea she was supposed to be quiet.

Forrest watched the whole thing but remained silent. Without Weasel in his face, his shoulders relaxed, but he didn't sit.

Weasel turned his back on Mavis and opened the door. It completely blocked her from view, but she slipped into a defensive crouch for no other reason than it felt like the right thing to do. She didn't know who was on the other side and didn't know what to do if she was discovered.

"Delivery for Forrest. Hey, Weasel," a man's voice said. "How's it hanging?"

The back of Weasel's head moved in a nod. "Good, Dan. How 'bout you?"

"Pretty good. Just here to give Forrest his meds. Here you

go, Forrest. I'll take this," Dan said, and the sound of a tray sliding across a surface reached her.

"Thank you," Forrest said.

The footsteps retreated.

Weasel let the door swing shut, and the three of them were alone again.

Mavis relaxed. Across the room, the lunch tray was gone and Forrest held a small plastic cup. He tipped the clear container side to side, his gaze glued to the pills inside.

"I'm just asking you to wait," Weasel said. "Not to stop taking them altogether."

A pained expression crossed Forrest's face, followed by one of deep yearning, and Mavis understood Weasel's rush to return to the hospital. Whatever he thought Forrest could do to help them would be affected by his medication, and lunchtime was pill time at Shady Creek.

If Forrest decided to toss back his meds, he wouldn't be able to help them, not the way Weasel thought he could. Mavis knew she wouldn't stop him if that was what he wanted to do. She drew the line at keeping a person from something they needed to function, be it pain medication or whatever it was in the little cup that Forrest couldn't keep his eyes off of.

"Please," Weasel said.

Forrest closed his eyes a moment before opening them and placing the pills in their plastic container on his desk like they were made of the most fragile substance on earth. He braced both hands flat on top to either side, his gaze on the little cup. "What do you want me to do?"

Weasel stepped forward and laid a hand on Forrest's shoulder. "Thank you."

Forrest didn't respond.

Weasel let his hand fall back to his side. "Ask Mavis what you asked me yesterday when I came by with the cookies."

Forrest nodded at the pills and stood up straight, facing Mavis. "Did you have an identical twin sister?"

"Not that I know of. No one's mentioned a twin." She frowned because she couldn't pretend it wasn't possible. It wouldn't surprise her if she had siblings. After all, she didn't remember having parents, either. But an identical twin?

Forrest's gaze flicked over her left shoulder and back to her.

"Why do you ask?" Mavis said.

Forrest swallowed. "Someone who looks just like you died." He blinked. "I thought they might have been your twin sister."

Mavis' breath caught in her chest a second before she drew in two great lungfuls of air. He could only be referring to one person, but Forrest had never met Mel. If he thought they looked enough alike to be identical twins, he must know what Mel looked like. But how?

The way his gaze kept flicking over her shoulder gave her the idea. "You can see this person? The person who looks like me?"

Forrest blinked several times, but his gaze didn't leave hers. He nodded.

"Can you... talk to her?"

Forrest huffed out a breath. "No. It's bad enough that I can see her. That I can see any of them." He rubbed his eyes.

Weasel grimaced in sympathy.

"Them?" she asked.

Forrest pushed his hands through his hair, lacing his fingers together behind his neck. "Yes, them. I've been seeing ghosts for years. I don't know how not to."

Mavis sucked in a breath. "You can see the dead."

Forrest nodded and bit his lip.

He could see Mel, but he couldn't talk to her. Now Mavis knew why he always appeared so uncomfortable around her.

That first time, outside the doc's office. Forrest had come out and seen Mavis, but he'd also spotted the ghost of Mel and assumed she was Mavis' dead twin. He'd even offered her his condolences.

Mavis caught his eye. "I think the person you're seeing is me—was me. It's hard to explain." Mavis didn't know where to start, but she wanted to tell Forrest something. He'd shared his secret with her. "I disappeared about a year ago. A friend of mine found me six months later and brought me back here. I lost my memory. I don't remember anything about who I was before, and I think the person you're seeing used to be me."

Forrest shook his head. "How can you be dead but still be here?"

Mavis nodded toward the chair. "I think you should sit down for this next part."

Forrest looked from her to Weasel and back again. Then he sat down.

Concern etched itself across Weasel's face, but he hunched his shoulders and nodded at Mavis to continue.

"You know about werewolves, right?" Mavis asked.

Forrest sat back in his chair, eyeing her from head to toe.

Mavis smiled. "I'm not a werewolf." She paused, glancing at Weasel. "But I am two-natured."

Forrest frowned, his gaze ping-ponging between her and Weasel. "What does that mean?"

Mavis spoke calmly and clearly. "I have a second nature. I can change into a bird."

Forrest rocked back, frowning. His gaze darted away from Mavis and didn't return. Possibly he was thinking he'd met someone crazier than himself.

"It's true," Weasel said.

Forrest glanced at Weasel and then away.

"Yeah, all right, then," Weasel said, unzipping his hooded sweatshirt. He never had put a shirt back on that morning.

"What—" Forrest began.

Weasel didn't give him a chance to finish. He slid the sweatshirt down his arms as he stepped out of his borrowed boots and shifted.

A blur rent the air.

Forrest gasped.

The mist cleared. The human Weasel was gone. In his place was the slinky buff-colored ferret who crawled out of the sweatpants pooled on the floor.

The shock of the change made Forrest's jaw slide open and stay that way. He bent forward so far that he tipped out of the chair, landing on his hands and knees. Weasel, as a ferret, undulated closer. Forrest stared but didn't reach out. Weasel retreated after a minute and went back to his discarded pile of clothing.

The air blurred around the body of the ferret and grew to human size. Within moments, the human Weasel was back and quickly getting dressed.

Forrest turned to stare up at Mavis, his features rippling in awe. "And you can turn into a bird?"

"Yes."

Weasel finished dressing and crossed the room to Mavis. "You still got that banana bread?"

It took Mavis a second to understand what he was talking about, and then she remembered the leftovers Essa had given her. They were still in her bag. She dug out the foil-wrapped package.

Across the room, Forrest grabbed the chair for stability and crawled back into it. Weasel opened the foil and broke off a chunk.

Mavis lowered her voice to a whisper. "How do you think this helps us?"

Weasel took a bite of bread. Mavis hoped he had an idea and wasn't just stalling. Seated back in his chair, Forrest buried his face in his hands. Mavis knew if he turned around and saw his pills, they would lose whatever chance they had of getting his help to communicate with Mel.

"I think you should take him into the fugue with you," Weasel said.

CHAPTER 28

That was Weasel's big idea? Slip into the fugue with Forrest? She supposed it could be done. Weasel had brought her into the fugue with him that first time, but she hadn't brought someone into the fugue with her yet.

"Forrest isn't a shifter," Mavis said.

Weasel nodded as he chewed. "I know, but it might be the only way to reach Mel."

"He's human. Will it hurt him?"

Weasel ran a hand around the nape of his neck. "I don't know. I don't think so?"

Mavis wondered if Weasel might be having second thoughts about bringing her to see Forrest, because now that she knew he could see Mel and that there might be a chance to talk to her, she had to try.

Mavis went to Forrest. She knelt in front of him, trying to keep his attention away from the pills on his desk. "Forrest?" She kept her voice as low and soothing as possible.

His hands slid down to cover his mouth. His gaze met hers.

She had his attention. "You saw how Weasel shifted just now?"

Forrest nodded, but he didn't lower his hands.

"Did you see how the air went all shimmery when he did?"

Another nod.

"I want to try the same thing with you, but I won't shift into a bird. I promise. I only want to see Mel. I want to see if I can speak to her. Okay?"

Forrest paled as she spoke, his skin going waxy. However, his eyes were bright and clear. He sat up straight, lowering his hands. "What do you need me to do?"

She laid a reassuring hand on his denim-clad knee. "Stand up." She straightened and backed away to give him some room to get to his feet.

He did so. He was taller than Aitch, but thinner. She felt tiny in comparison.

"Weasel will stay here," she said. "He'll make sure no one disturbs us." She looked to Weasel for confirmation.

Weasel went to the door and leaned his shoulder against it. He crossed his arms and gave them an encouraging smile that didn't quite make it to his eyes.

Mavis faced Forrest and tipped her head back to meet his blue eyes. She smiled to hide her nerves. Forrest didn't smile back. He glanced over her left shoulder and shuddered, turning his gaze downward.

Mavis stilled. "Is she there?"

Forrest nodded without looking up.

Mavis didn't know what to think of Mel's haunting her. She'd certainly never felt a presence looking over her shoulder. Not in the way Forrest made it seem with his glancing behind her.

"Here," she said, stepping in close, holding out her hands, palms up. "Take my hands." They would have to have some physical contact if this was going to work. Forrest slid his hands into hers, his long fingers wrapping around her own. They were cool to the touch at first but warmed quickly.

Mavis prepared to summon the fugue. Shifting her feet hip-width apart, she bent her knees and braced her core. And then, before she did anything else, she sent up a silent prayer for safe passage, not just for her but for Forrest as well. Whatever happened, she wanted to bring him through this without causing him any more grief. His strange abilities seemed to cause him enough suffering without her adding to his problems.

"Close your eyes," she said.

Forrest's lids slid shut. He trembled.

Mavis closed her eyes and, with a thought, broke the surface between their world and the fugue.

She opened her eyes.

A wave of nausea moved through her. She dragged in a breath, but it was like being under water and sucking hard through a straw for air. The fugue pressed in on them from all sides, darker than she had ever seen it, but she hadn't summoned it indoors before. The air wavered around them, distorting the sharp lines of the room.

They weren't alone.

Mavis blew out her hard-won breath through pursed lips and turned.

Mel stood over her, and though Mavis had thought herself prepared, her entire body jolted at the sight. Mel's gaze raked Mavis up and down, before the corner of her lip lifted in a sneer. Her mouth moved. Mavis couldn't hear her, but she saw the word 'You' form on Mel's lips with enough scorn on her face that it made Mavis glad she couldn't hear the tone she spoke in. Mel clearly had a lot to say, but Mavis couldn't read Mel's lips beyond that first word.

For a second, Mavis got caught up in the fact that watching Mel was like watching herself rant to a mirror. They were so similar. Mavis hoped she didn't look that unattractive when she was upset, although she probably did. Good to know.

Then she remembered when she had awakened after someone pushed her off the balcony. The scent of disinfectant called her back to that time when she had come around to herself—her face in a mirror, lips pinched, eyes hard. It hadn't been her then, and it wasn't her now. It had been Mel. And now that she knew it, Mavis could pick out the small differences between them. Mel's hair was shorter than hers by a few inches, and there were more lines at the corners of her eyes and around her mouth.

Mavis frowned and shook her head. Mel's mouth kept moving, but Mavis still couldn't hear her.

Mel stopped talking, her chest heaving, which struck Mavis as odd because wherever Mel was, whatever state she was in, she hadn't breathed for a long time.

Mavis shook her head and shrugged. "I can't hear you. Can you hear me?"

Mel finally seemed to understand. She glared and stepped around Mavis to stand next to Forrest. She raised a hand and dropped it on Forrest's wrist. He shuddered, his hands gripping Mavis' harder, his knees flexing.

If he fell, she didn't know if she'd be able to catch him. "Forrest?"

His eyes were squeezed shut. "It's cold."

"I know. Just hang in there, okay?"

He swallowed and nodded.

Mel sniffed. It was a small sound, but it hit Mavis' ear like a thunderclap.

Mel was clearly not pleased with the situation, almost as if she were disappointed Forrest wasn't physically stronger. Still, Mavis noticed Mel didn't touch Forrest more than she had to, which Mavis took as a good sign. At least her former self didn't seem to want to inflict any more harm on Forrest him than she already was.

"So. Are you my twin?" Mavis asked.

Mel glared at her. "Absolutely not," she replied in Mavis' voice, except hers held an extra sharpness.

"But you are dead."

"Obviously."

Mavis paused to see if Mel would try to deliver the speech she hadn't heard earlier, but Mel didn't say anything more.

"What happened to you? Where's Gloin?" Mavis asked.

Mel's brows arched. "What happened?" She barked out a laugh. "I used every ounce of power at my disposal, my considerable knowledge, my physical strength, everything I had in me to avoid an untimely death. And it worked. But not for me. Not for this"—She stopped, her mouth twisting in contempt—"soul." She spoke the word as if coming to terms with what it meant to have one. "Now you get it all." She stared into the fugue, her eyes swimming with banked emotion.

Mavis wasn't sure what to think. By her own admission, Mel was truly dead. What did she mean, Mavis got it all?

Mavis watched as Mel lifted her other hand and stared at the back of it. The edges of Mel's fingers blurred and her hand turned transparent. Mel was fading before her eyes.

"Where's Gloin?" Mavis asked again. They didn't have much time.

Mel focused on Mavis, one corner of her mouth lifting. "I don't know. And do you know what?"

Mavis' eyes narrowed a fraction. "What?"

Mel smiled. "Even if I did, I wouldn't tell you."

Mavis' teeth ground together. She'd dragged the disturbed Forrest into the fugue with her, and against all odds, here she was having a conversation with her former self, but Mel wouldn't help her. "Why?"

"Because you're you and I'm me."

"What—because I'm alive and you're not?" Mavis asked.

The smile faded from Mel's face. "Because all that I have left are my memories. They go with me, wherever I'm going."

Tremors wracked Forrest's body. Mavis squeezed his hands and held on tight.

"That's it? You won't help me because you're jealous I have a pulse and you don't?"

Mel blinked and stared straight through Mavis. "You are everything that I was. You have what you need." She waved her gossamer hand at the shimmering fugue around them. Then her gaze narrowed, her attention returning to Mavis. "I wanted to tell you one thing." Her voice grew faint as she continued to fade. "Whoever you are..." Her brows arched as she shook her head; her anger had drained away, replaced by another emotion Mavis didn't recognize. "You don't deserve it."

Mel let go of Forrest. She departed, fading away into nothingness.

CHAPTER 29

Mavis dispelled the fugue.

Forrest lost the fight to remain upright, and Mavis caught him under the arms before he fell. She was able to prop him up without falling over herself. Instead, they stood in a tense embrace, Forrest's head bent close to hers.

"She's gone," he said.

Mavis shuddered. "I know."

Mel was gone. And with her, Mavis' only opportunity to find out what happened to Gloin. It turned out the only reason Mel's spirit had lingered so long was to tell Mavis off. Not very helpful.

"I'm sorry. I felt it. I felt her go," Forrest said.

Mavis patted his back, and their hug lost some of its awkwardness for her. "Are you okay?"

Forrest lifted his head. "I think I want my pills."

"Yeah." After that, she kind of wanted some too.

She made sure Forrest was steady and stepped out of his arms. He turned and grabbed the small plastic cup of pills, swallowing the contents dry.

Weasel winced as he stood up away from the door. "Did it work?"

"That was—" Forrest shuddered "That was—I can't even call it crazy. For the longest time, that's what I thought I was. But you"—he faced Weasel—"you can turn into a—" He stopped and swallowed. He shifted toward Mavis. "And you can turn into a bird. But you saw her? It wasn't just me?"

"I saw her."

Forrest folded in on himself. He landed in his chair, his face buried in his hands, sobbing.

His cries tore at her, and Mavis took a step closer, her fingertips grazing his shoulder. A second later, Forrest grabbed her around the waist. He pressed his face into her midsection, his tears soaking the hem of her shirt. He muttered something she didn't quite catch.

Weasel stepped forward as if to help.

Mavis patted the air to let him know that she thought they were okay. "What was that?" Mavis asked.

Forrest turned his face to the side and drew a ragged breath. When he spoke, it was in a whisper. "Thank you. Thank you. I'm not crazy."

Mavis relaxed into the hold Forrest had on her. One hand stroked his shoulder. The other combed through his dark locks, soothing him as best she could with her touch. By taking him into the fugue and confronting Mel's ghost, Mavis had confirmed that what Forrest could see was real. His crying grew less intense as he calmed.

Across the room, Weasel tilted his head toward the door. Mavis nodded and slowed her touch to a stop bringing her hand to rest on Forrest's shoulder.

Forrest sniffed and sat back in the chair. He wiped his eyes, his cheeks red. Unwilling to look at either of them, he cleared his throat. "Sorry."

Mavis waited for his eyes to meet hers. "We're going. Get

some rest, but if you need anything, don't hesitate to get a hold of me, okay? I owe you one."

Forrest shook his head. "I heard her. She didn't help you."

Mavis' lips trembled as she reached out to brush her fingertips against Forrest's cheek. "That doesn't matter. You helped me, and I won't forget. Thank you, Forrest. That couldn't've been easy." Mavis bent forward and pressed her lips to his forehead. She didn't know why, but saying it with a kiss felt right.

Forrest closed his eyes, one of his hands coming up to hold hers against his face. His skin was warm under her palm.

"Rest," Mavis said. "We'll see you around."

He let go.

They left, shutting the door gently behind them.

Weasel didn't look at her. "Hungry?"

"Always."

Down in the kitchen, Weasel made them thick turkey sandwiches with lettuce, tomato, and anything else they wanted. They didn't bother leaving the kitchen. Instead, they hopped up on the counter and ate. The mid-day rush was over, and there weren't many staff around.

Halfway through their sandwiches, Weasel caught her attention. "What did Forrest mean about her not helping you?"

"I asked Mel where Gloin was. She didn't know."

He shook his head. "I can't believe it worked." He frowned. "But not."

Mavis told him everything that had happened after she brought up the fugue including not being able to hear Mel until she came into physical contact with Forrest. "She said that even if she did know what happened to Gloin, she wouldn't tell me."

Weasel sat back. "Wow, what a"—he broke off, seemingly thinking better of what he was about to say—"piece of work."

"Yeah."

"Well, then, why did her ghost, or spirit, or whatever, hang around so long?"

"I don't know. Maybe she stuck around to give me a hard time."

"What did she say, exactly?"

Mavis thought about it. "She told me that everything she was, I am, and that I already have what I need. Then she said that she wanted me to know, whoever I am, that I don't deserve any of this."

"Deserve what?"

Mavis took a bite of her sandwich and chewed, thinking it over. "I don't know. To live? Besides that, I don't think she thought I deserved to be able to do the things she could do. Like shifting, maybe. And into more than one species, like you pointed out."

"Was she mad about it?" Weasel asked.

"At first—before I could hear her—she looked pretty upset. But at the end there, before she faded away, she just kind of accepted it, like she was moving on." There had been something else there, too, when Mel told Mavis she didn't deserve this, but Mavis still didn't understand what Mel had been trying to say.

Weasel's brows went up. "Because she was. Moving on." He dipped his head. "Now what?"

"Can you drive me back to the shop?"

Never mind the day was half over—Mavis could put a few more hours in at the shop. The work would take her mind off of things. Her whole exchange with Mel kept playing on a loop in her head.

They finished their sandwiches, lingering over chips and cookies, at odds with the rush they had been in earlier. Weasel changed into his regular clothes. The borrowed sweats went back into Mavis' bag. Without saying more, they headed to the sedan and drove back to the garage in silence.

At least now she knew why she hadn't remembered anything and why she never would. Whatever happened to Mel died with her. All the memories and everything that Mel was, was gone.

Except not; her body was still there and now belonged to Mavis, who wasn't Mel. Her mind, too, lingered, in a way. Mavis figured she only knew what she did because Mel had known those things also. But whatever it was that made Mel who she was—her personality, her soul— that was gone forever.

All this time, Mavis had been struggling to recall memories that weren't hers to recall. Now she knew why she would never remember anything.

The sedan bumped over the drive into the parking lot of the shop. Both bay doors were shut. Mavis checked the front window. The sign was flipped to 'CLOSED,' and all the lights were off. "That's weird."

Weasel stopped the car.

"Wait here, would you?" Mavis asked.

Mavis let herself into the garage. No Aitch. She went to the front and found a short note on the counter.

M—Closed up early. Needed to take care of a few things. Carol told me about the bone. Take the rest of the day off. Tell Weasel he can keep the car until tomorrow—A

They'd never had to close early before. What kind of things did Aitch need to take care of? It must have been important. He wouldn't have closed the shop otherwise.

He hadn't bothered to open the day he drove her to the hospital. Did that make her important? She chewed her bottom lip and tried not to think about Aitch as anything other than her employer and a friend. Either way, she wouldn't have a job much longer if they didn't get back to work soon. She recycled the note.

Outside, Weasel rolled down his window when she walked out.

"Aitch closed up early and told me to take the rest of the day off. He said you can keep the car until tomorrow."

"What are you gonna do?"

Her plan to lose herself in menial tasks didn't seem to be panning out. She shrugged.

"Can I give you a ride home?" Weasel asked.

"Yeah, that'd be great, thanks."

Sitting in the passenger seat again, Mavis gave Weasel directions to her apartment. She stared out the window without seeing the passing scenery. What had Mel said? Mavis was everything Mel had been. All Mel's power and knowledge were Mavis' now, and Mel couldn't do anything about it except watch. The realization struck Mavis so hard she flinched. Mavis would have never known without Forrest's uncommon ability, but she'd seen Mel's anger and bitterness for herself. How infuriating it must have been for Mel to watch Mavis make a hash out of her life, or the life Mel would have had if whatever she had done to cheat death had worked.

But whatever Mel had done, it hadn't worked. She'd forfeited her soul and delivered all that she was into Mavis' incapable hands. No wonder Mel had told her off when she got the chance.

She wasn't Mel; a very freeing thought. Mavis could stop worrying about being someone she wasn't and just be herself, but who was that?

Whoever she chose to be. The exhilarating notion made her stomach flutter.

Who did she want to be?

Was she someone who accepted the way things were and

gave up when the going got tough, or was she someone who stuck it out? So what if Mel hadn't given her the answers she was looking for? Perhaps Mavis could be the kind of person who kept looking and explored every option, even if it did seem crazy.

Not remembering what happened to Mel wasn't Mavis' fault. Was there anything she could do, then, to change what would transpire that night? Without knowing what happened to Gloin—or Mel, for that matter—she didn't know how to stop the fight between the doc and Broderick. Blood would be spilled to determine the new Aldwulf, but where would it stop?

Until Weasel took her to see Forrest, she'd thought she'd tried everything within her power to uncover the past.

"Mavis!" Weasel said. The way he said it, she knew it wasn't the first time. They now sat outside her apartment, the car in park with the engine running.

She turned to Weasel. "I have an idea." When Weasel didn't push her out of the car, Mavis continued. "Can you drive back to where we were this morning? Essa's place?"

Weasel squinted. "I can drive you there if you know the way. I was kind of a ferret at the time."

"I remember. Head out of town past Shady Creek."

While Weasel pointed the car toward the road, Mavis gave her apartment door a long look. It would have been nice to go inside and relax with a book and too many cookies, but she couldn't. She had one last thing to try.

CHAPTER 30

Weasel drove them back through town, heading east. Interesting sights were limited on a mid-afternoon Friday. The days were getting shorter, but summer pressed on, not yet ready to quit.

"Why do you want to go back to Essa's place?" Weasel asked.

Mavis stared out the windshield. "We missed something."

"What did we miss?"

"I'm not sure."

Weasel huffed out a laugh.

"I don't know, okay?" Mavis said. "We missed an opportunity."

"I found the bone."

"There must be something else—something we overlooked. I want to check it out again."

Honestly, Mavis thought, Weasel didn't have anyone to blame but himself. He was the one who had given her the idea. How could she not wonder what else she might find in the fugue if she looked?

They passed the turnoff to the hospital and kept going.

Mavis kept an eye out for the landmarks she had seen that morning. Around a bend in the road, she told Weasel to slow down. They turned down the next dusty entrance. The road was a lot bumpier in the sedan than it had been in Aitch's truck, but Mavis knew they were on the right track.

Essa's cabin came into view. Weasel stopped the car, and they got out. Rusty the yellow lab wasn't waiting this time, but when Mavis knocked on the door, she heard a woof from inside.

"Good boy," she heard Essa say through the door before it opened. Essa started, her mouth snapping closed into a smile when she saw Mavis. "Well, hello, stranger. Didn't expect to see you again so soon." She pushed the screen door wide.

"Hi there. Sorry to stop by unannounced," Mavis said.

Essa glanced over Mavis' shoulder, caught sight of Weasel, and frowned.

"This is Eugene. He's a friend of mine. And Aitch's," she added. "I think I might have left something in the woods this morning. Do you mind if we take a quick look? We don't mean to bother you."

Essa's features relaxed into an easy smile. "It's no bother, I expect. Go on ahead."

Rusty slipped past her onto the porch.

Mavis scratched him behind the ears. "Hey, boy."

Tail wagging, Rusty went to sniff Weasel, who pet him.

Essa shook her head. "Rusty may keep you company."

"Thank you, Essa. We'll stop back by on our way out."

"Take your time. I'm not going anywhere." She pulled the screen door closed, lifted a hand in farewell, then shut the inside door.

The entire walk through the woods they were quiet. Weasel fell in behind her with Rusty behind him. Eventually though, the dog must have had enough, because he barked and headed back the way they had come. Mavis picked her way through the woods, her neck straining for a glimpse of the spot Aitch had led her to that morning. She headed up a steep incline. The trees ahead looked promising.

Behind her, Weasel sniffed. "I think we're getting close."

"How can you tell?"

He tapped the side of his nose.

Her mouth slackened. "Your nose is that good even when you're human?"

He shrugged. "Yours isn't?"

Mavis tilted her head to the side, considering. Birds weren't really known for their sense of smell. As far as she knew, birds had keen eyesight, but only for finding food. She was on the hunt for information, though—not food.

Mavis crested the top of the rise, tramping out onto a familiar flat area. She stood at the base of two trees, trying to find the correct one. Moments later, she found it. The ground didn't appear disturbed though she knew they had been there that morning. Her tracking skills could use some work.

She craned her neck. "I think this is it."

Weasel sniffed, his nose wrinkling. "I think you're right."

Mavis started to undress. Weasel accepted her clothes and jewelry without comment. She had no towel this time, but she was becoming less concerned with her nudity. For speed and safety's sake, she had to get over herself. She was pretty sure Weasel had seen it all before, anyway, but it helped that he kept his gaze lifted.

Shifting in front of Weasel wasn't a big deal, but no way could she have stripped naked in front of Aitch. He didn't know what it was like. Aitch might have grown up around werewolves, but their change was a lot different from what she and Weasel could do. More often than not, werewolves ripped through their clothes, out of control. It wasn't just that. If she was honest with herself, she was starting to have feelings for the curmudgeonly, infuriating Aitch. He'd kissed her and then pushed her away. It was enough to give a girl whiplash.

She forced thoughts of Aitch away, turning her mind to her search.

"Be right back," she said.

Mavis brought up the fugue with a thought. Before she shifted, she took a good look around, willing her stomach to settle. The world appeared watery and smeared as it usually did whenever she summoned the fugue. Nothing out of the ordinary. She concentrated and began to shift into a magpie, the form that came most naturally.

Her eyesight sharpened, but there was nothing more to see than what there had been with her human eyes. Moments later, she ruffled her feathers and left the fugue.

Weasel towered over her. "Good luck."

She opened her black bill, emitting a raucous call, then beat her wings and lifted off the ground. She flew up and up, circling the evergreen, landing on a branch about halfway to the top. A squirrel chattered at her. She focused on the side of the evergreen facing the valley and hopped from branch to branch, ascending, searching. About three-quarters of the way to the top, tucked up against the trunk, she found a nest. Bits of twigs, grasses, and even string had been woven together to form a deep bowl. However, parts of it had been disturbed and left unrepaired, suggesting the nest was abandoned. She poked around the nest for anything out of the ordinary. Nothing. She hopped closer. Empty.

At least, that was the way it appeared at the moment.

Mavis called up the fugue and looked again.

Inside the fugue, the nest was not as completely empty as it looked. A few delicate, downy feathers were trapped in the bottom. She hopped onto the edge of the nest, dipped her head low, and pulled a feather free with her beak. She placed the feather on the edge of the nest, bending close to examine it. The fugue muted the tones, but the feather was bright red. A breeze stirred the air. The feather curled and crumpled into ash. She let out a squawk, but the feather was gone. One or two remained safe at the bottom of the bowl, but that was all. She parted the mist and looked again, but outside of the fugue, there was nothing to be seen in the nest with her magpie eyes.

Mavis took off from the branch and glided down to the ground. She called up the fugue again. The thought of crispy chocolate chip cookies helped her shift back to her human form, but it also made her hungry. She dismissed the fugue.

Weasel held out her shirt before she was completely done shifting. "Find anything?"

She wasn't sure how to answer that. Whatever proof she thought she had found had turned to ash and floated away. Still, something had been there, invisible to the naked eye but certainly present in the fugue. The place she and other shifters called up to change was a place of transition. Whatever had happened to Mel to make her Mavis had happened in the fugue. The feathers indicated that some type of bird had been involved, but she didn't know if the bird happened before or after Mel ceased to exist and Mavis came into being. She started to speak and stopped, pulling her shirt over her head and peering through the branches above her in the nest's direction. A dark smudge above the treetops in the distance caught her attention. "Is that smoke?"

Weasel turned to look over his shoulder. He frowned. "I think so, yeah." He held out the rest of her clothes to her.

"Is that—"

"Hurry up and get dressed."

Neither of them said it, but the smoke came from the direction of Essa's cabin.

Mavis yelled as she threw on her clothes. "Go. Go!"

Weasel took a step and stopped, clearly torn between

taking off and waiting for her. Mavis hopped on one foot, pulling her pants on.

"Go! I'll be right behind you."

Weasel took off.

As much as she would have liked to have been right behind him, she struggled to get her jeans up and zipped. She wrestled with her socks and shoes and stuffed her necklace into her pocket. By the time she slid her backpack onto both shoulders, Weasel was out of sight, but at least she was on the move toward Essa's cabin.

As she ran, the plume of smoke grew.

The cabin was on fire. The front door stood wide open as flames licked at the roof through shattered panes of window glass. She ran to the porch. The boards under her feet rippled and warped with the heat. She stopped to catch her balance as the screen door flew open and Weasel tumbled out, coughing and covered in soot.

"It's too late—" Weasel coughed.

"Where's Essa?"

Weasel shook his head. "She didn't make it."

"What?" That was impossible. How could she not have gotten out?

Mavis dashed around him. She threw open the screen door, ducking inside, burying her mouth and nose in the crook of her arm. She bent low, trying to get under the smoke as best she could. Across the room, the wall with the fireplace sat engulfed in flames. Orange tongues lapped at the area rug on the floor, the easy chair, the loveseat—everything. Behind the couch, Mavis spotted a moccasin, unmoving. She edged forward, the heat growing unbearable.

Essa lay on her back, arms flung wide. Blood covered the front of her dark blue shirt to the waist, turning it black. Her throat had been torn out.

CHAPTER 31

Mavis' stomach turned over as she cried out. The noise didn't reach her ears over the rumble of the fire. As terrible as the sight was, Mavis couldn't turn away. Essa's unseeing eyes reflected the fire's dancing flames, making her seem alive, though her expression remained frozen in a rictus of fear, mouth open. Essa was beyond any help Mavis could render.

Mavis caught a glimpse of bone amid the tangle of mutilated flesh that had once been Essa's neck. Whatever had torn her throat out had taken it clear back to her spine.

A hand landed on her shoulder. Mavis screamed. Weasel let go and grabbed her free hand, pulling her along through the front door, off the porch, and far enough away from the burning building that the heat no longer threatened to overwhelm them.

They bent over coughing. A timber inside the cabin squealed and broke loose, causing black smoke to belch from the front door and broken windows.

"She's dead," Mavis coughed. "What happened to her?"

Weasel coughed, passing a hand over his watering eyes.

His head turned away from the fire, and he went still. "I think I know."

"What—" Mavis followed his gaze.

A large gray werewolf stood twenty feet away, head low, hackles raised. Its black lips curled back as it let out a deep growl revealing pointed pink-tinged canines. Behind the wolf, another figure stepped out of the trees, one hand behind his back. Mavis squinted. It took a second for her to recognize Harley from the hospital kitchen.

Weasel stood up straight. "What's going on?"

"I'm sorry you had to be here for this, Weasel. Take care of him," Harley said.

The werewolf stalked forward.

With a hand to her upper arm, Weasel pushed Mavis away, sidestepping several times, putting distance between them.

"Weasel?" Mavis' voice cracked, unable to cover her mounting fear.

"Don't worry about me," he said, never taking his gaze off the approaching werewolf. "Worry about him." He pointed at Harley.

Mavis glanced away from the werewolf to find that Harley only had eyes for her. He brought his right hand out from behind his back. He held a gun, the barrel black as night, his finger on the trigger. She backed away, heart pounding.

The werewolf leaped at Weasel. She saw its feet leave the ground, but she didn't see it land, because she was already running. A shot rang out, distinct over the roar of the fire. Ahead of her, the bark of a tree splintered with the impact of the bullet. She refused to lose time by glancing behind her. Instead, she focused on dodging trees, her legs churning, arms pumping. The roar of the fire faded.

She didn't know how far she ran before she stopped, gasping, to press her back to a thick tree.

Harley had shot at her, but he was a werewolf—why

would he need a gun? Regardless, he had no need to rush. He could follow her scent trail for as long as it took him to chase her down. Mavis gulped, trying to quiet her breathing, and peeked around the tree. No sign of him.

Instead of running, Mavis tip-toed forward through a path in the trees.

The thought that she could strip, shift, and fly out of there occurred to her, only to be rejected straightaway. She would not leave Weasel behind, yet there was no way she could keep running. She circled a tree, retracing her steps back the way she had come. When she reached the tree she'd stopped at before, she turned sideways and tucked herself behind it, hoping.

A minute passed. Two. Her body trembled, straining to hear anything. Then, the scrape of a shoe in the distance. She held her breath and edged forward.

Harley held the gun at his side, his eyes scanning from tree to tree, his steps measured and unhurried, as if he had all the time in the world.

As he passed her by, Mavis skirted around the tree, keeping it between them. Bending forward at the waist she kept Harley in sight. He tipped his head back, scenting the air as he followed her trail. He stopped. His head jerked to the side before he readjusted his grip on the gun and continued past her.

Mavis eased back out of sight, waited for a count of ten, and stepped away from the tree back toward the cabin.

A twig snapped.

Mavis froze.

"Doubling back? That was your big idea?" Harley said from behind her.

Mavis did not turn around. "Yeah, I'm a little disappointed, too."

"I thought you would have done the smart thing and flown the coop by now. I don't want to do this," he said.

"So don't."

He laughed, but it was completely without humor. "Turn around."

"You don't want to shoot me in the back?" As the words left her mouth, her stomach cramped. The thought of getting shot made her ill, but the idea of getting shot in the back made her break out in a fresh cool sweat.

"Turn. Around," he repeated, his voice dead calm.

Mavis wondered what he would do if she didn't. She could run again, but she'd tried that, and it hadn't worked. She didn't want to see the gun raised, the barrel of it pointed in her direction, but she had no alternatives. Mavis turned. "Why?"

Harley fidgeted, the gun at his side. "My instructions are to put a bullet in your head. And to tell you Broderick sends his regards—" His words broke off. His face turned red, his neck corded and tense, as if he wanted to say more and physically couldn't get the words out. His arm shook as he began to raise the gun. Mavis tensed, ready to jump to the side. She refused to make this easy for him.

As the barrel reached the height of her midsection, the yellow body of Rusty flew into Harley, taking him to the ground. The gun flew from Harley's hand. Rusty snarled and snapped, but the yellow lab was no match for a werewolf, even in human form. Harley threw the dog off of him. Rusty landed with a thud and a whimper.

Mavis ran for the gun, snatching it up.

Harley got to his hands and knees.

Mavis pointed the gun at him. "What are your orders now?" she asked.

Harley smiled a real smile, one that reached his eyes. Then his back arched high in the air, and his smile fled. A terrible sound reached her ears, followed by a grunt of pain. As high as his back had arched, now it bowed, and Mavis got a look at Harley's face, which was less human than it had been, his hair darker and more than a little longer. The sound of flesh tearing came again as the skin along Harley's forearm split, oozing a gel-like substance that steamed in the open air and revealed something hairy and black beneath it.

Mavis backed away, eyes wide, struggling to blink. She tore her gaze away from the changing Harley and tucked the gun into the waistband of her jeans against the small of her back. She ran to check on Rusty. "Rusty—here, boy."

The dog lay panting on the ground under a tree. He didn't look so good, but when she spoke, he wagged his tail and lifted his head. "We've got to go." Mavis didn't know how long it would take for Harley to complete the change to were-wolf, and she didn't want to stick around to find out. They had to get out of there.

Rusty climbed to all four feet. He wobbled with his first step, but then he took another and another, and soon they were rushing back through the trees.

Flames engulfed the cabin. No sign of Weasel or the other werewolf. Mavis gave the structure a wide berth, staying on the edges of the intense heat. Behind the cabin, Weasel slumped against the base of a tree, his head lowered. As they got closer, his head snapped upright, his hand picking up the ax next to him. He was covered in a mix of deep and shallow scrapes, the worst around his shoulders and torso. His clothes were torn and dirty, the ax head bloody.

"Weasel! Are you okay?"

He dropped the ax, his head thumping back against the tree. He shut his eyes. "I'm alive. That's better than okay. You should see the other guy."

Mavis cast a nervous glance behind her as she crouched beside him. He'd picked up the ax with his left hand because his right was useless, the skin shredded from shoulder to elbow, his forearm punctured from multiple bite marks. "About the other guy. What happened to him?"

"I put him in the fire. Where's Harley?" he asked.

"In the middle of changing."

Weasel lifted his head and grabbed the ax again, this time trying to use it as a crutch, pushing himself to stand. "We gotta go."

Mavis stooped to get an arm under his good side. He didn't let go of the ax. "How did you get him in the fire?"

"I dragged him into it. I'm stronger than I look." As they got closer to the car, he slowed. "But I don't think I can drive."

"I'll have to," Mavis said. She'd never driven before. She stopped herself from asking how hard it could be. "Keys?"

"Pocket."

Propping Weasel against the side of the car, she dug in the right-hand pocket of his jeans for the keys.

"Buy me a drink first," Weasel said.

Mavis ignored him. She got the key ring, opened the car door, and pushed him into the front passenger seat. Then she opened the back door and called for Rusty, who hopped inside, turned in a circle, and laid down.

Mavis slid behind the wheel and locked the doors, turning the car on.

"Have you ever driven before?" Weasel asked.

Mavis checked the mirrors. "Nope."

Weasel groaned. "The gas is on the right. Brake's on the left. Try to keep it on the road and not oversteer."

Mavis nodded and pulled the gear shift into D. The car lurched.

"Foot on the brake," Weasel said.

Mavis did as he said.

"Seatbelts."

She might not have bothered, but Weasel was already injured. The last thing she wanted was for her driving to finish him off. She helped Weasel buckle his belt first, then did hers before pressing down on the gas. Around the first bend, they passed a black SUV parked off to the side out of the way. Harley and the other werewolf must have followed them in it.

"Can't believe Harley tried to kill you. Or sicked a werewolf on me, for that matter," Weasel said.

Now that the adrenaline was wearing off, Mavis shivered. She took her eyes off the road long enough to flip the heater on full blast. "Did you recognize the werewolf?"

"No. It wasn't anyone I knew."

Harley's expression popped into Mavis' head. "I don't think Harley wanted to kill me. At least that's what he said."

Weasel put his head against the headrest. "Only an alpha would be able to make him do something he didn't want to do."

Mavis slowed for a bend in the track up ahead. Harley had answered to the doc when he'd been charged with keeping an eye on her at her apartment, but that wasn't what he'd said just a while ago.

"Any alpha?" she asked.

"Any wolf dominant enough to be alpha. How did you get away?"

"Rusty."

Weasel glanced into the back seat. "Good dog."

Mavis focused on driving. There weren't any other cars, but they were approaching the road. "If Harley didn't want to hurt me, what do you think he'll do after he changes?"

Weasel lifted his head. "He failed, so he'll have report back to whoever gave him his orders."

Mavis turned toward town. A siren sounded in the distance. Mavis glanced back in the direction of Essa's cabin.

A dark cloud hung over the valley. The fire truck passed them, going the opposite direction.

"Lights," Weasel said.

"Huh?"

"It's going to get darker soon. Twist the end of the lever there."

The windshield wipers came on.

"The other one."

Mavis found the lights and turned the wipers off. The inside dash lit up.

"Where are we going?" Weasel asked.

"Where would the wolves meet?"

"Every pack has its own territory."

Mavis concentrated on her driving, slowing down for turns and accelerating out of them. She caught up to a pickup truck and stayed behind it.

"Where would two alphas come together to fight it out for Aldwulf then?" Presuming their land gave them some kind of home field advantage, if each pack had their separate territory, how would they ever decide where to fight each other?

Weasel shifted with a groan. "I don't know."

Mavis gripped the steering wheel. "That's okay. I think I do."

CHAPTER 32

Mavis had failed to find out what happened to Gloin. However, someone was so afraid she might remember that they'd tried to kill her. More than once. Perhaps more than twice. Sending Harley to put a bullet in her brain was the last straw. Because of her Essa was dead, her home burned to ash, and Weasel was hurt.

How had this happened? She remembered the SUV they'd passed as they left Essa's place. She'd been followed. How else would someone have tracked her movements throughout the day? What would those moves look like to someone afraid of her regaining her memory? Once they'd left Aitch's cabin that morning, she'd made him stop at the hospital to pick up Weasel. That had to be where they picked up the tail that followed her to Essa's and every single place after, including the stop outside of her apartment. What if she had given up then and gone inside? Would Essa still be alive? Whoever wanted to keep her quiet must have seen her return to Essa's cabin as proof her memory had returned. They must have decided Essa's property was a nice enough place to commit murder. The older woman just got in the way. The same with Weasel.

When Broderick wanted to meet with the doc, they came to the garage in town. Mavis didn't know how large the pack was, but she figured two of them coming together to fight for Aldwulf was a big deal. That many people would draw too much attention. But if the garage was neutral territory, maybe Aitch's place outside of town was, too.

Had it only been last night that she flew out there? The clearing she'd seen before she landed had been a decent size. Big enough to hold a pack of werewolves or two? She was betting it could.

Mavis drove with extreme caution, especially when they got to town where the speed limit was lower and she had to make turns. Her nerves urged her to go faster, but she couldn't do it. The fact that she sat in the driver's seat directing a pile of metal and glass kept her in check. Her gaze darted between her speed and the road.

Large groups of people gathered downtown. Traffic increased. A bunch of cars vied for a limited number of parking spots. At first, Mavis didn't know what was going on until the flash of a long skirt caught her attention. Lydia Shaw stood on the walk, greeting people as they trickled in for the Concerned Citizens Unite meeting. There were more than a few concerned citizens in the area, by the looks of it, but another face stood out. Louis, among a group of kids his age and older. They made their way inside the building where the meeting would be held.

A harsh sigh of disappointment left her. Despite her own very recent bad experience with werewolves, Mavis didn't believe the CCU had the best interest of the community, werewolves and shifters included, at heart. If she didn't have places to be, she would have stopped the car, leaped out, and pulled Louis out of there by his ear. Her jaw clenched.

Weasel took in the traffic. "What is it?"

Mavis sniffed. "It's that anti-werewolf meeting. There are more people than I thought there would be."

A rumble escaped Weasel. "I'm a bit anti-werewolf myself at the moment."

Mavis turned her attention back to the road and her speed. "You're not going to turn into a werewolf on me, are you?" She glanced at him from the corner of her eye.

He let out a breathy grunt. "No. You have to be human first, and we don't qualify. Besides, to turn a human into a werewolf, the attack would have to be much more savage. This is just a flesh wound."

Mavis pressed her lips together and swallowed. The coppery smell of blood scented the air. "Looks like it hurts."

His chin dipped down to his chest. "It does, but we're stronger than we look, Mavis. Haven't you noticed?" And just like that, he closed his eyes and lost the battle to stay conscious.

Mavis didn't try to wake him, her instincts telling her to let him rest. She had noticed she was strong, physically. Aside from an acute allergic reaction to strawberries, she was the picture of health—now, anyway. She'd overlooked those capabilities before, too focused on her inability to use her legs. If shifters were so physically strong, why hadn't she been able to walk when she first woke up in the hospital?

On the other side of town, Mavis picked up speed as she tried to remember the way to Aitch's place. She slowed down as she approached the turnoff. As she followed the road back into the trees, her anxieties piled up. Maybe she had taken the wrong turn and this wasn't the way. Then she reached the halfway point. A line of empty cars sat parked on the side of the road. They continued to Aitch's front door. Mavis parked in the grass.

A whine from the back seat told her Rusty was awake.

"Stay here, boy," she said. She rolled down the window before she turned off the car. Weasel didn't stir. Honestly, she didn't think he would be much help in his current state, so she left him in the car. He'd done enough. She left her bag with him. Nothing in it would help her here either.

The cabin was deserted. Mavis thought of her flyover the day before and walked around to the back, straight up the hill away from the cabin. She hadn't made it too far when a soft woof sounded from behind her. Rusty padded forward to catch up with her.

"You should have waited in the car." She patted his head. She had bigger problems than shooing the dog away. Besides, she didn't mind his company. Rusty fell into step beside her.

Five minutes through the trees passed. Then ten. Then fifteen. Finally, they approached a clearing. A large number of men and women surrounded it, all of their focus turned inward on what was happening in the middle. Mavis paused from one footfall to the next. The hair on her arms stood up. She should have been prepared for it, but the sensation she got told her every one of them was a werewolf. She pressed on toward the center, passing those who hung farther back. No one tried to stop her. She didn't have time to wonder why.

Closer to the clearing, she saw what everyone else was watching. Two werewolves faced each other, one silvery grey, the other dark brown, both injured and dripping blood. Outside the bare circle of dirt on one side stood the doc. Directly across from him, also outside the clearing, stood Broderick. The werewolves in the middle snapped and snarled at each other, coming together and breaking apart in a flurry of fur.

While everyone's attention was on what was happening in the clearing, Mavis took in the crowd. There were more men than women. Though they appeared to be one large group, this close to the center she could see the division. They were split into two roughly equal-sized factions, those clustered on the doc's side of the clearing and the others around Broderick. Glancing at the faces, Mavis recognized a few from town, but most of them she didn't know. She could make out their expressions, though. A few could barely contain their excitement, panting while they toyed with the buttons on their clothing, ready to tear off their shirts and jackets at a moment's notice to change. Others couldn't hide their disgust. They stayed farther away from the clearing, arms crossed, their noses turned up, though they didn't look away from what was happening. Mavis' gaze skipped around the people gathered. No Katrina. No Aitch.

The fight in the middle of the clearing raged on. Mavis couldn't tell which wolf was winning. The werewolves moved inhumanly fast, their furred bodies rippling one over the other, rolling and throwing up dirt. Then there came a cry of pain and surprise, cut short. The dust settled. The silvery grey werewolf stood over the other, hackles raised, fur bloodied. The dark brown werewolf lay motionless on the ground, dead.

A lonesome call rose from the back of the pack on Broderick's side of the circle, but others joined in from both sides with yips and calls of their own.

Mavis stepped to the front of the crowd, her attention on the dead werewolf. It lay completely still, but only for a moment. Her gaze didn't leave the dead wolf as it jerked and shuddered, beginning its final change back into a human. Wet popping noises filled the air. The dead werewolf's flesh split across its back, the same strange clear gel-like ooze spilling from it as it had from Harley earlier. Mavis swallowed, glancing away as more and more human flesh was revealed.

The silver werewolf trotted back around the circle favoring one hind leg to sit in front of the doc's side. The werewolves' lament became one loud chorus. The howls and yips faded when the body on the ground finished changing back to human. Mavis recognized the figure sprawled on the ground, covered in wounds that would never heal. The last time she'd seen him, he'd been riding a motorcycle away into the night.

Joe, Broderick's second, lay dead on the ground. Nobody moved.

Mavis glanced around the circle. They all seemed to be waiting for something.

The noise hadn't completely died away when two men stepped forward to gather Joe's body and remove it from the circle. As they did, a movement in the trees caught her attention. A different four-legged animal slipped through the waiting crowd. The orange and black stripes of a giant Siberian tiger stood out as it stalked through the standing werewolves and into the middle of the clearing. The pale golden eyes took in the dead body, expression inscrutable. Then it laid its ears back and opened its massive jaw, growling long and deep. The ears flicked forward as the large predator walked the perimeter of the circle. Mavis watched its progress along with the rest of the two packs.

When the tiger got to her, it stopped, tail lashing the air. This time it growled, showing off its two-inch canines.

Mavis sensed the werewolves easing away from her. She froze in place, hoping not to draw any more attention to herself.

Then the air around the tiger blurred with a shimmer.

The mists parted, and where the tiger had been moments before, Aitch stood, naked. Mavis' mouth opened, but no sound came out. Her breathing halted, all she could do was blink.

Aitch was two-natured.

It would have been nice to know, but no. Not one single word. She'd had no clue. Now it made sense. The wolves wanted to meet on neutral territory. What could be more neutral than land owned by another, larger predator—a freaking shifter that could turn into a tiger?

She didn't have time to say anything before Aitch stepped in close, wrapping a hand around her upper arm.

He glared at her with tired eyes.

"You shouldn't be here," he said. The grip he had on her bicep removed any doubt as to how upset he was with her. His touch reminded her to draw breath, at last, and she gasped.

Aitch pulled her closer, lifting her onto her toes. "You need to go."

Rusty whined behind her.

"Essa's dead," she said.

Aitch froze. "What did you say?"

"Essa's dead. She's dead." Mavis flexed her arm and pushed at him with her other hand. "You're hurting me."

He blinked as her words registered, and he let go of her arm. "How?"

Mavis rubbed her arm. She could place where every one of Aitch's fingers had dug into her flesh. "Someone tore her throat out and burned her cabin down with her inside of it."

"Why?"

"Because of me. They were afraid I remembered something," Mavis said. "Or at least I think that's why." It was the only explanation that made sense, the irony being—of course —that she would never remember anything from Mel's life. The thought burned enough to make her jaw clench.

And Aitch was a shifter; Mavis choked back the desire to scream or laugh. She wasn't sure which.

Broderick stepped forward. "Did you find the Aldwulf? Did you find my father?"

Mavis didn't turn. "No. I didn't." She spoke through gritted teeth.

The crowd surrounding them murmured.

"Then we continue," called the doc from his side of the clearing.

Aitch stared at her as he spoke. "Your second has been bested by Chase's, Broderick."

Broderick began unbuttoning his shirt. "Then I challenge my brother, alpha to alpha."

"My second accepts the challenge," the doc said.

"Wait—what?" Mavis turned to peer at the doc. His second had killed Joe, which meant the wolf in front of him was Katrina. "You're going to let Katrina do the fighting for you?" Katrina had told her as much when she came to her apartment, but Mavis didn't actually think the doc would let her go up against another alpha in his stead. Not when she'd already taken on another wolf and been injured. Not when he was supposed to be so in love with her.

A few whispers came from Broderick's side of the circle, where he shrugged out of his shirt.

Mavis stepped around Aitch and into the clearing. "Whoa. Keep your shirt on," she told Broderick. "No one else has to die today."

She hoped so, but surrounded by werewolves on the night of a full moon, she had the sneaking suspicion she was wrong.

CHAPTER 33

Mavis didn't know what she'd done to make several werewolves gasp, but the collective sound of rapidly indrawn breath was her first clue that she might be in trouble. The second came when Aitch's arm wrapped around her waist from behind, lifting her feet clear off the ground as he moved into the middle of the circle. Not how she had imagined being held in his arms, to say the least.

"Put me down." Mavis kicked at Aitch's shins, connecting.

Aitch grunted but didn't let her go. "Ignore her. She doesn't know what she's saying."

Mavis continued to struggle, battering Aitch's shins, taking offense at being manhandled. Shifter-handled?

A sigh sounded from behind them and Broderick said, "Let her go."

Aitch growled in her ear. "You don't know what you've done." His hold on her tightened for the briefest of moments before he lowered her to the ground and withdrew his arm.

"Mel will fight on Broderick's behalf," the doc said.

"What?" Mavis turned to stare at him.

Mel was gone. There was no Mel. There was only Mavis, and she was her.

Aitch's hands landed on her shoulders, but he kept his touch light, which she took to mean he wasn't trying to hold her in place. She let them stay—for the moment. "Her taking his place would be highly unusual, Chase," Aitch said, his breath stirring her hair.

The doc's gaze avoided hers, skipping around the werewolves assembled. "If Mel presumes to break the circle and walk amongst us, then she will assume the role of Broderick's second and accept the challenge."

Aitch growled. "By suggesting she becomes Broderick's second, you acknowledge her dominance in the arena."

The doc scoffed. "The Aldwulf extended an invitation to Mel long ago. She accepted it tonight. Mel entered the circle of her own free will; she can either prove her dominance or face the consequences."

Mavis suppressed a groan. Gloin must have invited Mel to pack events or whatever the hell this was. That was why no one had stopped her from getting close enough to land herself in a heap of trouble. But what was the doc playing at? Did he want her to fight Katrina? He knew she could just turn into a bird and fly away, right? Or could she? She sucked in a breath and blew it out slowly, thinking hard. Would she have time to shift before Katrina got to her? No way. Besides, if she shifted and flew away from this fight, she might as well just keep on flying. She couldn't run if she ever wanted to flap her feathers in Eustace Park ever again. She had to fight.

The crowd around them on both sides murmured, which told her that the doc's suggestion was highly unusual. Shifters probably didn't participate in too many dominance fights. Especially not, well, shifters that could change into birds.

Aitch's fingertips on her shoulder twitched. "Only if Broderick agrees."

Mavis' gaze turned toward Broderick. Vertical lines creased the center of his brow, but he didn't take his eyes off the doc. She wondered if he was trying to figure out what his brother was up to. At the hospital, Broderick had told her to stay out of the way. He'd spoken of uniting the wolves, not ruling them as Katrina said he wanted to do. While Broderick pondered Mavis' fate, she glanced at Katrina. Blood from the kill darkened her silvery muzzle, and she didn't look as hurt as she did before. Did Katrina want to fight her? Her wolf gaze revealed nothing. Mavis knew Katrina would love to take a bite out of her regardless of what form she took, but she'd had the chance to do it at Mavis' apartment and hadn't. Now Katrina sat at the feet of her alpha, prepared to do his bidding.

What did it all mean?

The doc stood behind Katrina, stone-faced, his gaze on his brother. He refused to even glance in Mavis' direction.

No; he'd called her Mel because that was who he believed she was and would always be. He didn't see her as Mavis.

Mavis spun and faced Aitch. "What happens if Broderick doesn't agree?"

The doc answered instead. "Your invitation will be summarily revoked and you'll be cast out. With force."

"Is that true?" she asked Aitch.

He stared down into her upturned face and nodded.

Mavis faced Broderick. "I'll do it," she said.

"You don't know what you're agreeing to," Aitch said.

"Yes, I do."

Broderick tore his gaze away from his brother, taking in Mavis from head to toe. He frowned harder.

He wasn't going to do it. Broderick wasn't going to let her fight, and she was going to get tossed out.

She was about to lose her chance to change how this night

turned out. She had to convince him. "I am all that Melisandrea was. Please," she said.

Broderick's gaze flickered between Aitch and Mavis

"Let me fight," Mavis begged.

Broderick's stared at her a long moment, then he dipped his head once.

"You have to say it," Aitch said.

Broderick raised his chin. "I agree."

Aitch exhaled sharply. "Now you've done it." He took her by the shoulders. "I can't help you. Do you understand? You're on your own.."

Mavis stared at the hollow of Aitch's throat. How could he have not told her he was two-natured? How could she have not figured it out? "I know," she said.

He squeezed her shoulders, then let go, turned, and walked to the edge of the circle. Heart in her throat, she couldn't even enjoy the view of his backside as he walked away. Someone handed him a pair of jeans. She held back a sigh and shook her head.

"Why, doc?" Mavis asked without turning to look at him.

When he didn't say anything, she faced him. His gaze met hers.

"Why do you want to be Aldwulf?" she asked.

He lifted one brow. "I do not. Gloin is Aldwulf."

That was the problem.

Gloin was Aldwulf, but he wasn't freaking here to deal with any of this.

Mavis turned away, glancing at those assembled outside of the clearing without seeing them. That was it. He wasn't there. Gloin was missing, and that was the way the doc wanted it.

Mavis spun slowly in a complete circle until she faced the doc again. "Where is he?"

The doc smiled. "I have no idea."

Mavis could have groaned. Her palm itched to smack her forehead, but she resisted, curling her hands into loose fists. The doc had probably been waiting for someone stupid enough to ask him that question, and there she was. If he knew where his father was and lied about it, every werewolf there would have smelled it. Yet, he didn't know, and he relished the opportunity to say it out loud—to have everyone know he spoke the truth.

"Mel knew. Didn't she?" Mavis asked.

"Do you?" he asked, still smiling.

Mavis' teeth ground together as her hands tightened. "Melisandrea is dead."

A confused murmur went through the crowd, and Mavis had to wonder what the doc had been telling everyone about her.

The doc's smile fled. "You are Mel."

"No. I'm not."

The murmur dialed up to a dull roar. Every werewolf there would be able to smell the lie if she spoke one.

The expression on the doc's face told her and everyone else there that he didn't want to believe it. She had to be Mel. She must be Mel. They looked so much alike—how could she not be? Everyone could see the doc was locked into a state of denial, refusing to believe what his nose told him. To him, she was Mel. And if she remembered what happened to Gloin, she might be able to bring him back. The hiss of whispers joined the roar of the crowd.

Mavis rocked back on her heels. Without a new Aldwulf, Broderick was convinced the werewolves would tear themselves apart. If chaos was what the doc was after, seeing his father disappear had achieved that goal. Or it would. The werewolf community had held itself together for a year, but that ended tonight. Chase couldn't risk having his father return, causing peace to break out. The doc couldn't risk Mel remembering what happened to Gloin.

Unfortunately for Mavis, the doc believed she was Mel.

He must have believed Mavis at some point. Probably in the early days, right after she woke up. Maybe after she ate the peanut-laced chocolates Mel would have died from consuming. He was a doctor. He must have been willing to give her the benefit of the doubt in the beginning. The way he'd helped her move out of the hospital and find the job with Aitch so he could keep tabs on her. Just in case. She saw that now.

Then his circumstances had changed. He knew Broderick would challenge him for Aldwulf. The doc had to see if her memory would return. He had to probe what she knew. First, he drugged her. Then he pushed her. He didn't even have to do it himself.

Mavis speared all ten fingers through her hair, hands shaking. She knew he had been having her watched. All he had to do was order some agile wolf to push her from the balcony. Her second nature truly had saved her life. But what else would she remember after she found out she was a shifter? The doc had asked Weasel to help her explore her abilities. Then he had her followed. He must have viewed her return to Essa's cabin as proof that he was correct and she was beginning to remember. Essa was just collateral damage. Weasel would have been, too, if he weren't a shifter. A werewolf attack would have been too obvious and could have led back to him—that was why Harley had to shoot her. Someone might put two and two together. A bullet, however unlikely, was easier to explain away.

Mavis' gaze found Aitch watching from outside the circle. The doc must have realized they were becoming friends. He couldn't have Aitch asking questions.

But why order Harley to tell her he was shooting her on

Broderick's account? If he'd shot her, she'd be dead. Or would she? Maybe the doc had thought he'd gotten rid of the problem once before, only to have it pop up six months later with no memory, unable to walk.

It was her. She was the problem.

Only she wasn't. Mel had been the problem, but Mavis would answer for it all. For the span of a single heartbeat, the situation struck her as unfair, and a part of her wanted to yell and scream that she didn't deserve this. She remembered Mel telling her that very thing. Mel's anger had fled and she had spoken with a grudging acceptance of the circumstances that had befallen her, but there was something else in her final words to Mavis: remorse. Mel knew that Mavis didn't deserve what was about to happen, but she was going to get it because she'd gotten everything else. Mavis wondered if that were true and if she'd gotten enough. It was time to find out. Who did she want to be?

"I am all that Melisandrea was, but I am not her. I don't know what happened to Gloin or where he is." Mavis watched the doc closely. "What will the packs become without a leader? How many people will die?" Chase's eye twitched when she said the word *people*. She tried again. "How many humans will perish?"

The doc glared at her, his lips drawing back from his teeth. "The weak will be purged. Beginning tonight." The doc raised one arm and pointed. "Even now, so-called concerned citizens gather in town."

Mavis' eyes widened. The CCU meeting at the town hall? Louis was there. So were a lot of other innocent people.

The doc raised another finger. "Two wolves are in place. The strong will be turned. The weak will die, and humans will learn to fear us as they should. No more hiding."

Mavis glanced at Aitch. His face was contorted with anger.

"Brother, what have you done?" Broderick's voice wasn't filled with anger so much as anguish.

The doc lowered his arms "What Father would not. Show the world how strong we truly are."

Broderick stepped toward the clearing. "I will not let you do this."

The doc laughed. "You've agreed to abide by the terms of neutrality. You have no choice. Unless you wish to forfeit your right to lead?"

A muscle jumped in Broderick's jaw.

Forfeiting sounded bad. Mavis wasn't entirely clear on the rules, but she was pretty sure Broderick had to let her fight, or the doc would win. Doing otherwise would weaken him.

Mavis was on her own. No one would interfere. One look at Aitch revealed his grimace of frustration. Even if he wanted to help her, he wouldn't be able to take on all the werewolves, not even in tiger form. The moon hadn't risen yet, but when it did, every werewolf there would begin the change. If the doc had his way, anyone who opposed him would die.

The doc stepped forward, bent his head without taking his eyes off Mavis, and pressed his hand against Katrina's side. "Kill her."

Katrina lunged.

CHAPTER 34

"Whoa." Mavis threw up both hands, palms out, and stepped back. She didn't think for a second that would stop Katrina, but she did slow. The hesitation gave Mavis hope. Maybe Katrina didn't want to kill her. She simply had no choice but to obey her alpha.

This was so stupid. Mavis didn't want to hurt Katrina. What would happen if she couldn't put a stop to this? If Katrina killed her? Mavis swallowed, her mouth dry, trying to think.

With her out of the way, Chase would pit Katrina against Broderick directly. He didn't care what his orders might be doing to her. He was just using her.

Katrina stalked Mavis as she retreated.

As sure as the moon would soon rise, Mavis knew if she failed to stop her, Katrina would kill her. All the doc had to do was wait.

"Katrina—you don't have to do this."

There were a few chuckles and several snorts from the crowd.

This was about more than who lived and who died—this was about dominance. Who had it, who wanted it, and how they used it.

They circled each other until Mavis stopped. She stood up straight and put a hand to the small of her back, pulling Harley's gun from the waistband of her jeans. She held it with two fingers from the grip, showing it to Katrina, who growled, baring her teeth.

"Look—I don't want to hurt you." More snickers from the surrounding crowd. Mavis ignored them. Without taking her eyes off Katrina, she tossed the gun to Aitch, who caught it and held it at his side.

She couldn't be certain there were silver bullets in the gun. If there weren't, it'd be useless against Katrina. The only ones who could be killed by gunfire were her, Aitch, and Rusty. She didn't want to shoot anyone and that included Katrina.

Several people in the crowd leaned one way or another to see around the person in front of them. Making a show of her peaceful intentions might work more favorably for her later.

Her empty palms on display, Mavis spoke. "The doc is using you, Katrina."

Silence from the crowd. Katrina growled, inching closer, her head low. Mavis stood her ground.

"Remember when you came to my apartment?"

The doc shifted, drawing her gaze for a millisecond. He frowned. He must not have known about their little chat.

"You didn't try to kill me then," Mavis reminded her. "It was just you and me. We were fine. I know you've never liked me much, but the only times you've ever had a serious problem with me have been when the doc has been there." She stabbed the air in his direction. "He did this to you. He's doing it now. He feeds your insecurity. He encourages it. And I know why. Do you?"

Katrina leaped.

Mavis was ready for it. She spun away and fell on Katrina's back as soon as she landed, sweeping the wolf's feet out from underneath her and taking her to the ground. Mavis pressed her left arm across Katrina's neck to keep from being bitten. The crowd made shuffling noises, but if no one would interfere on her behalf, they wouldn't interfere on Katrina's, either. Mavis sprawled across Katrina's back, using all of her body weight to hold her down, but the wolf continued to snarl and snap her jaws, growing more enraged by the second.

"I'm sorry!" Mavis shouted over the ruckus. She dug into her front pocket, her fingertips scrabbling for purchase, and yanked out the silver leaf pendant. When she pressed it into Katrina's shoulder, the wolf released a high-pitched cry. The metal grew warm under Mavis' hand but didn't hurt her. However, Katrina howled and thrashed in pain, whining in the back of her throat. Mavis let up the slightest bit.

It was a mistake.

Katrina broke free. The silver necklace flew from Mavis' hand across the clearing. The fur where the pendant had touched Katrina was matted with blood, the flesh below it blistered and pulsing. Katrina whined and shook her head as if to clear it before she growled again. Mavis found herself on all fours, face to face with a very angry werewolf.

Mavis put out her hand. "Listen to me, Katrina. He doesn't love you. Not really. He uses his love like a weapon. He's using it to control you."

Katrina charged, forcing Mavis onto her back. Mavis avoided tooth and claw, sinking her hands into the ruff of Katrina's neck and holding on tight. Katrina's jaws snapped inches away from her face and throat.

The scent of blood and meat lingered on Katrina's breath. Her claws tore through Mavis' clothing, scratching her wherever they met. Mavis held on for all she was worth, but the weight of Katrina on her chest made it difficult to catch her breath. Still, she didn't let go. She met the yellow-brown eyes of Katrina's wolf and tried to reach her one more time.

"The doc pretended to love you so he could control you. You're more dominant than he is, Katrina. You are stronger than him. Don't let him use you to destroy the world."

Katrina's fur slid through her fingers, her hot breath moving closer. In one quick motion, Mavis kneed Katrina in the chest and threw up an arm in front of her face. Katrina's teeth sank deep into Mavis' forearm. Mavis screamed, even as her grip tightened on Katrina's fur, refusing to give the wolf the slack she needed to rear back and, on the next lunge, tear into Mavis' throat. If Katrina wanted a piece of her, Mavis would give her more than she could handle. She would feed the wolf her arm if it slowed her frenzy long enough for Mavis' words to sink in. If they didn't, the fight would be over for her soon enough.

"Am I lying?" Mavis asked. The question came out no louder than a whisper from between her gritted teeth. Katrina froze.

The moment stretched.

Then the pressure on her arm eased.Katrina's werewolf teeth burned just as badly sliding out as when they went in. Mavis gasped, her muscles convulsing from the need to hold on so tight for so long, but when Katrina didn't take another bite out of her, Mavis slowly released her, keeping her hands raised. Katrina growled and snapped as she struggled, but not directly at Mavis. As the weight of the wolf left her, Mavis scrambled backward on her one good arm, her other a bloody mess between wrist and elbow.

Katrina stopped growling and circled the clearing toward the doc.

Sitting on the ground, a movement caught Mavis' attention. A gray-and-black wolf filtered through the crowd—

Harley. He wove his way through the standing figures on Broderick's side of the clearing around to the doc's where he sat well away from what was happening. Still, there could be no doubt as to whose side he was on and who gave him his orders.

"What are you doing?" The doc roared. "Kill her!"

Ten feet away, Katrina paused, but then kept moving straight toward the doc. Mavis was right. Katrina was stronger than him. She didn't have to do what he said. Not anymore.

"Stop!" the doc yelled and raised his hand, palm out.

Katrina stopped. Who knew why? Maybe she was giving him one last chance.

The doc drew his arm back as if to backhand her across the muzzle.

Karina emitted a low, terrible growl. An instant later she was airborne, hitting the doc square in the chest with all four feet. Mavis couldn't see all that happened from where she sat, but during the brief tussle, the sound of teeth rending flesh and choked screams reached her ears.

When it was over, a group of people surrounded the body.

"Is he..."

"He's dead."

"But he could still heal—"

"No. He can't. There's no coming back from that."

"I can see bone."

The crowd stood silent after the exchange, stunned. Katrina loped around the periphery, her fur rippling and shaking, agitated. Then the howling started. Yips and other cries joined in. Mavis might have imagined it, but she didn't think the calls were as loud as before, nor did they go on as long as they had for Joe, Broderick's second.

Mavis cradled her right arm in her left and wondered why the doc hadn't put up a fight. Perhaps he hadn't thought

Katrina would do it. Had any other wolf turned on their alpha in such spectacular fashion? Mavis didn't know what this meant for Broderick. Was he Aldwulf by default, or would someone else challenge him? She glanced around the clearing. No one stepped forward.

Rusty padded over to Mavis on silent paws. She patted his head while he sniffed her wounds. Besides her torn-up arm, Rusty licked a few of the deeper scratches from Katrina's claws. Her entire body hurt, but she had survived, which meant that Weasel was right. She was stronger than she looked.

The old yellow lab whined and rested his head and a paw on her lap.

Then the air around the dog shimmered.

CHAPTER 35

I t was a good thing she was sitting down.

Rusty, the old yellow retriever, was shifting.

Mavis sought Aitch in the crowd. His was the only face turned toward her. Everyone else was staring at the doc, dead on the ground.

Aitch's mouth dropped open.

When the mists of change cleared, a man's head lay in her lap. With his face turned away, all Mavis could see were longish sandy-colored locks.

Across the clearing, she saw Aitch shudder at the same time that an electric charge seemed to spread through the crowd. Several people gasped and turned to one another in confusion. When someone noticed the man with his head on Mavis' thigh, they cried out as their knees hit the dirt at the edge of the circle. More cries of surprise rippled through the night air. Some stood in shock, their mouths hanging open. Others threw themselves to the ground, and not just in surprise. Meaty popping noises meant that more than a few people in the crowd had started to change.

The man raised his head from her leg, and she saw his

AMBER BOUDREAU

profile for the first time. Something about his features was familiar.

Broderick stepped into the clearing, eyes wide, his gaze locked on the transformed Rusty.

Mavis remained still, unsure of what to do.

Closer, Broderick dropped to his knees. "Da?"

Mavis recoiled with a shiver even as she stared. That was why he looked familiar. She'd seen his picture in Mel's old room. Rusty was Gloin, the Aldwulf returned, alive and well.

Broderick's gaze darted in the direction of his brother's remains, then back to his father.

Gloin blinked. "Aye," he said. The word came out in a low burr. A breath shuddered in and out of him with that one word, but otherwise, he showed no other reaction to having watched one of his sons perish right in front of him.

There were shouts of "Aldwulf!" and "Gloin!" along with yips and howls of joy.

Having the Aldwulf back must have meant more to them than the demise of one alpha, but Mavis couldn't join in the celebration. For one thing, she hurt all over, and not just her arm. She couldn't forget that people in town were still in danger. There were two werewolves in town set to ravage anyone at the CCU meeting. With a grunt, Mavis pushed to her feet using her one good arm. Aitch was at her side before she was completely vertical.

"We have to get to town," she said. "Louis is at that town hall meeting."

The Aldwulf stood, from a crouch to upright in one smooth motion. "Wait," he said and closed his eyes, tipping his head back. "The wolves there have begun the change, but they won't hurt anyone. Those orders died with Chase."

She leaned into Aitch. "How—how does he know that?"

"The pack bonds," Aitch said. Mavis wasn't sure what he

meant by that, but it wasn't the first time she'd heard the bonds mentioned.

The Aldwulf opened his eyes and stared at her. "You have a lot of questions. As do I." He dragged his gaze away from her to take in the crowd. "But now is not the time."

Mavis followed his gaze. The crowd had begun to change, except for Broderick and Gloin. If she and Aitch stayed, they would find themselves surrounded by werewolves in wolf form.

One figure stood out as solitary and unmoving. Katrina had ceased her pacing and lay stretched out on the ground in front of the doc's dead body, head resting on her paws, waiting. Mavis glanced from her to Gloin. The Aldwulf's gaze had come to rest on Katrina as well. His face was impossible to read.

Mavis swallowed. "What happens to Katrina?"

Gloin focused on Mavis, and she almost wished she hadn't asked. His hazel gaze had weight, and as their eyes met, he tried to drag her down. With Aitch at her side, she didn't need to worry about falling over, so she locked her knees. Gloin blinked, and the sensation passed. Perhaps he hadn't meant to make her kneel, but then again, maybe he had.

"She will come to no harm," Gloin said. His voice carried, and it sounded like a decree to all the wolves. Mavis believed him.

Moonlight flooded the clearing. It was time to go.

Aitch swept Mavis' good arm up and over his shoulders and started walking. She got the sense he would have dragged her from the clearing if her own feet weren't taking her in the same direction. Mavis couldn't resist looking over her shoulder. Broderick had begun to change, but Gloin remained standing tall among the rest of the werewolves.

Aitch and Mavis were halfway back to the cabin when the howling started.

"What's going to happen?" Mavis asked.

"The pack will run and hunt till morning."

"Did you know?" she asked.

Aitch glanced down at her but didn't stop moving. "About Rusty? No." Then, "Tell me what happened to Essa."

Mavis told him all that she knew also letting him know about the injured Weasel in the car. By that time, they could see the back of Aitch's cabin. They walked around front to check on Weasel, Aitch easing Mavis' arm from around his shoulders to set her against the driver's side door. Weasel was out cold, his wounds in the middle of healing. Even in sleep, he kept a hand wrapped around the handle of the ax next to him.

"Did you drive?" Aitch asked.

"Somebody had to."

Aitch grunted. She had kind of missed that.

"He should be okay with some rest and food. Lots of food," Aitch said. "You too, for that matter."

"Why didn't you tell me you were two-natured?" Mavis asked.

Aitch stiffened, refusing to look at her. "I had my reasons."

"Was it a test?" Mavis asked in a small voice. She had to know.

Aitch's brows drew down into a deep vee. "What?"

"You know what I mean."

"I'm not like Chase. I don't play games."

Mavis could understand why he hadn't said anything when she didn't know about shifters, but what about after? "Then why not slip the fact that you're a shifter into conversation somewhere? 'Here's the mustard and, oh, by the way, I can change into a tiger.'"

He turned toward her. "It's more complicated than that."

"Did Mel know?"

"Yes, she did. And that's how I knew you weren't her. I never felt a thing for Mel. Not the way I—" He cut himself off. Whatever his feelings, he didn't sound happy about them. Aitch stepped in front of her and pressed his body to hers from chest to thigh.

With the car behind her, Mavis couldn't go anywhere, not that she wanted to. Her eyes widened as she looked up into Aitch's golden gaze.

He sucked in a breath. "You don't even know well enough to be afraid."

"What are you talking about?"

"This." He kissed her.

Mavis' lids drifted closed with the sensations Aitch stirred to life within her. His hands buried in her hair, he cradled her scalp, tilting her head to the side. His mouth plundered hers, but Mavis gave as good as she got, her uninjured hand resting against the hard planes of his chest.

Finally, Aitch lifted his mouth from hers, both of them breathing hard.

Mavis instantly felt the loss, but he didn't stray far. His hands tilted her head back, exposing her throat as his lips moved downward. He licked the skin at the base of her neck where her pulse pounded away.

"I like you, Mavis, but it doesn't matter."

The words penetrated her lust-fogged brain, causing a frown to form. She opened her eyes, but all she could see was the top of his dark, curly head.

Aitch spoke to her neck, saying, "As much as I like you, a part of me will always want to tear you apart."

His tongue stroked the flesh of her neck again, except this time she felt the edge of his teeth.

Mavis could have lost herself in the sensation, but his words echoed in her ears, reverberating across her thoughts.

She summoned her strength, using it to straighten her unin-jured arm and push him away. "Stop."

Aitch stumbled back, chest heaving.

"Why would you say that?" she asked.

Aitch settled, though he still breathed hard. "It's true. It doesn't matter how I feel about you—our second natures can't coexist. You need to understand that. There's a part of me that will always want to rip you open and tear your insides out."

She huffed out a breath. Why was he saying such terrible things? The backs of her eyes stung. She had to leave before she did something stupid—like cry. He already knew she was vulnerable; no reason to let her tears fall and erase all doubt. Mavis pushed away from the car and started walking.

Aitch growled. "Where are you going?"

She spoke over her shoulder. "What do you care?" In the trees, she snaked her undamaged arm inside of her shirt and peeled it over her head, popping the button on her jeans and toeing off her shoes. Good enough.

She summoned the fugue, her eyes wet and vision blurry. Then she shifted.

CHAPTER 36

The injury to her arm didn't stop Mavis from flying. The more she moved, the less she felt her aches and pains. The clearing in the woods where the doc died was empty. Farther along, she caught a glimpse of several sleek, dark bodies through the trees below, hurtling forward, moving together except for one. A pair of lupine eyes flashed in the moonlight. A solitary wolf stood still above the others. As Mavis passed overhead, it threw its head back in a high mournful sound. One howl turned into many. She banked hard, leaving the wolves to their run.

At night, the lights of town were easy to spot. The day had started early and been crammed with blood, death, and revelations. Her thoughts dragged her down. Her wing beats decreased and she lost altitude, alighting atop a telephone pole on Main Street. Emergency vehicles sat, their lights off, parked in front of where the CCU meeting had taken place. Whatever had happened was over. Nothing to be done. Mavis wasn't sure if she should feel relieved or not, but something told her she'd done all she could, even in her absence.

Mavis flew to her apartment. The lights in the courtyard

were out, so it had to be after ten. She landed outside of Wes' sliding glass door and shifted. She scratched at the apartment wall, not wanting to scare him. When Wes opened the door, he found her crouched outside in the dark.

"What the—oh my God, Mavis! What happened?" He bent to her side, hands up as if to reach out, but he didn't touch her.

Mavis took a look at herself in the light spilling from inside his apartment. The worst of her scratches were scabbed over and the rest had already healed, but she was filthy. "I'm okay. It's not as bad as it looks. Do you have something I can wear?"

Their relationship was solid, but she didn't want to stand naked in front of her best friend if she didn't have to. Not that she thought he would care, but showing up covered in blood was already making things awkward enough as it was.

Wes hurried back inside. He returned and settled the blanket from the back of his couch across her shoulders. The crocheted granny-squares were better than nothing. Mavis stood and shuffled inside the apartment. She slipped the blanket from her shoulders and tucked it under her arms, wrapping it around herself like a beach towel.

Wes closed the door. "Do I need to call the police?" His hands fluttered at his sides with what she took for worry. "Should we go to the hospital?"

"No. No, none of that. I'm okay. Do you have anything to eat?"

"You're hungry? You just showed up on my doorstep naked, covered in dirt and—is that blood?"

It was.

"Are you going to tell me what happened?" he asked.

Mavis so very dearly wanted to, but she didn't know where to start, and she didn't know how he would take the news. "I...I—"

"Does this have anything to do with that guy you came in with earlier?"

"Eugene? No, this doesn't have anything to do with him."

Wes raised a finger at her in warning. "Do not tell me you went and got yourself lycanthropy." He really said that.

"What? No, I'm not a werewolf." She motioned outside. "If I were a werewolf, I'd be a wolf right now."

Wes glanced out the window and back. "But you're not."

She waved both hands in front of herself and grabbed the blanket to keep it from slipping. "No. I am not a werewolf."

"Okay." He cleared his throat. "You were saying?"

Funny that he thought she might have been attacked by a werewolf. Come to think of it, he wasn't wrong, but she wasn't going to tell him that. She guessed she had shown an unhealthy interest in werewolves since she'd known him, but Wes didn't need to know why. "I... I want to tell you. I just don't know how you'll take it. Promise me you won't freak out." Her heart pounded as hard as it had in the woods surrounded by werewolves.

"Take what?"

"I have to show you, but I'm going to be really hungry afterward. I'm just warning you."

"Show me what?" Wes asked, exasperated.

Mavis entered the fugue and shifted.

Wes backed up so quickly he bounced off of the wall behind him hard enough for a picture to fall. The glass splintered. He raised a hand, palm out, as if to stop her from coming any closer. "Mavis." His voice shook. "Mavis, are you a bird right now?"

She didn't flap her wings, afraid to terrify her friend further, but blinked magpie eyes and cocked her head to the side. Then she shifted back, stooping low to snatch up the blanket as quickly as she could.

Wes didn't move. He stared at her, eyes wide, chest heaving.

Mavis didn't know what to say, but her stomach decided to do the talking for her. The rumbling noise meant something to Wes. He trembled as he pulled himself away from the wall. He didn't look at her. He went to the refrigerator and opened the door, pulling out covered dishes. What he didn't do was open the front door and throw her out, which she took as a good sign.

Mavis watched as he opened the cupboard over the fridge and lifted down a glass bottle half full of amber-colored liquid. He poured himself a drink and tossed that one back before he poured another. He nodded to himself, and when he turned back to her, she was happy to see his eyes had lost most of their apprehension, but he still wouldn't meet her gaze.

"Okay," he said. "Okay." Then he didn't say anything more.

Mavis watched him sip his drink while she ate cold beef, roasted potatoes, and steamed veggies, all of it delicious.

Wes waved his drink. "What do you need from me?"

The backs of her eyes prickled. Mavis had come to him after dark, filthy and naked but he still asked her what she needed. Mavis was going to have to make this up to him, but she had no idea how. Wes was simply the best.

Mavis swallowed the last bite of food, her hunger sated for the moment. "Do you still have the spare key to my apartment?"

Wes opened a drawer in the kitchen. He rifled through the contents and came up with a frog on a chain ringed to a single key.

"Can I borrow the blanket?" she asked.

"Take it."

When he didn't say anything else, she reached for the key.

He quickly set it on the counter and backed away. "I need some time, okay? But we will talk about this." Then he turned and reached into the overhead cupboard for the bottle again, refilling his glass.

Mavis nodded, though she couldn't tell if he saw or not. "Thank you for the food. And the blanket. And for letting me in."

Wes didn't say anything else. She let herself out his front door, closing it softly behind her, sticking close to the shadows until she was inside her apartment. There, she grabbed the container of cookies out of the kitchen cabinet and brought them into the bathroom with her.

The shower washed away the dirt and the blood, and Mavis started feeling human again. The cookies did the rest. Afterward, she pulled on long-sleeved tee, put on a pair of flannel boxers, and crawled into bed. She didn't set an alarm because she couldn't contemplate going into work the next day. Saturdays were busy at the garage, but as Aitch had pointed out, he'd run the place on his own before she worked there. He'd figure out she wasn't coming in when the coffee wasn't made. Pushing thoughts of Aitch and work aside, Mavis checked the news for anything about what had happened in town. Someone had called the police about a disturbance downtown, but there were precious few details beyond that. Perhaps there would be more to read tomorrow.

No dreams disturbed her slumber. She slept late, but she couldn't say how much longer she would have stayed asleep, because a knock on her door roused her. She sat up. Whoever it was knocked again.

"Coming!" Mavis threw off the blankets and stumbled to the door. Rubbing the sleep from her eyes, she didn't check to see who it was, hoping it would be Wes, ready to talk about what she was. She pulled the door open. The hair on her arms stood up with a little electric zing, as if she'd been hit with a wave of static electricity.

Gloin stood on her doorstep. He wore an unzipped leather bomber jacket over a plaid flannel shirt in shades of hunter green. The color brought out his eyes. His shirt was tucked into a pair of dark blue denims, belted at the waist, that he wore with a pair of hiking boots. He was of average height, with a lean build that made him appear capable of anything from office work to hard manual labor. She knew he was Broderick's father, but they could have been brothers. He didn't look older than his mid-thirties.

Mavis blinked rapidly. Was he really there? She glanced past him into the parking lot, but there was no one else there to bear witness to the fact that the Aldwulf had just knocked on her door.

He cleared his throat. "Sorry to bother you like this. Do you mind if I come in?" His voice was not deep or commanding, but appearances were deceiving. After all, he might not look like he'd been running through the woods as a wolf all night, but he most definitely had to have been. For as nonthreatening as his clothes and posture suggested, no one would have been the wiser.

Mavis swallowed. She left the door standing open and retreated all the way to the sliding glass door, which wasn't far. She pulled the curtain, letting in the morning light.

Gloin stepped inside closing the door behind him. He glanced around her sparse furnishings, his eyes landing on the tangled sheets of her bed. "I didn't mean to wake you."

"It's okay, I'm just gonna—" She edged past him and hurried into the bathroom, closing the door behind her and locking it. "Make yourself at home," she called through the door, wincing at her cheery tone. Didn't he have better things to do the morning after his celebrated return than talk to her?

There was only so much she could do in the bathroom without showering. So, when she ran out of options to stall with, she opened the bathroom door and stepped through.

Gloin stared out the sliding glass door at the courtyard, hands stuffed into his back pockets.

"How can I help you?" she asked, then felt ridiculous for sounding like a customer service rep while dressed in her pajamas in her apartment.

Gloin shook his head and turned to face her, taking his hands out of his pockets. "You have done so much already." His eyes shone bright, though the light filtered into the room behind him. "And you don't even know the half of it." He blinked, clearing his throat. "You should know Essa's family will be notified of her death and all of the arrangements taken care of. Those responsible won't hurt anyone else ever again." He stopped talking, jaw clenched.

"She was a nice lady," Mavis said.

A muscle jumped in his cheek. "She was."

Mavis sat on the edge of her bed. "Did you know her before you became Rusty?"

His mouth curved for a brief moment. "Only by reputation. When Rusty died, I saw an opportunity."

Mavis nodded. Essa had lost Rusty, but she never knew it. That was where that bone had come from. Gloin had assumed the yellow lab's identity and hidden in plain sight the whole time. But why?

"What happened?"

Gloin started to speak, stopped, and motioned to the camp chair she kept collapsed in the corner by the sliding glass door. "May I?"

He snagged the chair, snapping it open and settling it next to the foot of her bed, facing her. He sat leaning forward with his elbows on his knees, one hand kneading the palm of the other. Gloin didn't say anything for a minute. Mavis waited. She didn't want to interrupt the ordering of his thoughts with inane chitchat. She had nowhere to be. They were comfortable. They could sit for a long time.

He didn't keep her waiting.

"A few years ago," he finally said, "someone sent a compromising photo of a werewolf in the middle of the change to a well-known media outlet. An associate stepped in before it could get any traction and convinced everyone it was a fake. The story never happened. Then, about a year and a half ago, a video was given to three separate media networks. You can guess what was on it. Again, certain individuals stepped in and the video never saw the light of day. However, two things became clear. The first was that someone wanted the wolves to come out. They weren't going to stop until we did."

"That was when you gave the firefighter, Andrew Tull, permission to tell the world what he is. What was the second?"

"That the individual responsible had to be close to the werewolves or a werewolf himself. Very few people knew about the attempts to drag us into the light. When no one made contact to take responsibility, I suspected it was someone I very likely trusted. The way things were escalating, I permitted Andrew to tell the world that werewolves exist and to provide whatever proof was needed."

"Then you disappeared."

Gloin sat back in the chair. "Not right away. After talking it over with my consultant, the two of us came up with the plan for me to go away for a while. We thought my absence would eventually flush out the threat so it could be neutralized."

Mavis' eyebrows rose. "Eventually?"

"It wasn't a perfect plan, especially after—" He pressed his lips together.

"After what?"

"After Mel disappeared."

Mavis folded her arms. "Mel disappeared first?"

"She missed our meeting."

"Mel was your consultant?"

The corner of his mouth curled up. "She was. The best, and the most trusted. When she didn't show at our meeting, I knew something was amiss." His gaze slid away from hers as he chewed his lower lip.

Mavis sat up tall. "Is that when you began to suspect your son?"

CHAPTER 37

Gloin's brow smoothed. He huffed out a small laugh and flashed her another smile. "Oddly enough, no. It took me a while. I'm ashamed to say how long. Still, I stuck with the plan and made myself scarce. Over time, I've come to realize Chase's initial reaction to Mel's disappearance was all a show put on for the benefit of one person: me. Chase pretended to be more enthralled with Mel than he was.

"Mel took his attention with good humor, but never any seriousness. They became lovers at his insistence, not hers. If she made one mistake, it was trusting Chase more than she should have, but I don't blame her. We all get lonely from time to time. I believe that in part, she only yielded to his advances because he was my son. And I think Chase tried to get close to her because he thought he would gain some insight into me."

Mavis stiffened. "And why would he think that?"

He tipped his head toward her. "I already said Mel was one of my most trusted friends. We were close, but you can relax, at no time were we ever lovers."

Mavis couldn't stop the way relief rounded her shoulders. The thought of having to meet any more of Mel's old flames filled her with dread, considering her visceral reaction to learning that Mel and the doc had slept together. She sucked in a breath now, wondering if her body had been trying to tell her something she was too dull to pick up on.

Gloin noticed and chuckled. His laughter faded, then he frowned. "I failed my friend because I couldn't see what was right in front of me. I have to ask. Do you know what happened to her?"

Mavis winced. "I have my suspicions, but I don't know exactly. I was hoping you knew."

Gloin's face crumpled for an instant before his features settled into a deep frown. A single breath escaped him.

"I don't know exactly what Mel did, but it took everything she had," Mavis said. "She summoned the fugue to do it."

His brow smoothed. "Of course, she used the void."

"The void?" Mavis asked, confused.

"It's what you call the fugue. It's not bad or good, it just is. It's a place where things end and things begin. Where things are born."

Mavis thought about the nest she'd found and the feathers she'd only been able to find in the fugue. She recalled how the one she'd removed had crumbled to ash. A shiver chased its way down her spine, and she wrapped her arms tightly around herself. "Whatever she did, it couldn't save her soul. It changed her. Into me. I wasn't kidding last night when I said I'm everything Mel was, but I'm not her. She's dead. Dead and gone."

Gloin stared at her, his gaze taking in her features one at a time, seeking perhaps any whiff of a trace of the friend he thought he'd failed. After a moment, he raised one brow. "I understand. You do look an awful lot alike, though."

Mavis' lips curled upward in a humorless smile, but she let his statement go without comment. "Then what happened?"

Gloin drew a deep breath and nodded. "I hid in the canyon, shutting down my ties to the pack as best I could. I couldn't severe them completely. I spent most of my time as a wolf. One night, not too long after I arrived, I heard Essa calling for Rusty. She sounded worried. I found him before she did. I was there when he breathed his last. Then I did something I'd never done before."

"You shifted." Mavis shook her head. "How?"

"Mel. She taught a very old werewolf a new trick. I went back later and buried Rusty near the cabin because I thought he would want to be close to Essa. Afterward, I kept my ears open and my nose down, but when you showed up at Essa's, I thought you'd come for *me*. I almost shifted when I saw you. It was close. You told Essa about your amnesia, and I didn't know what to do. Then you found that bone and left. I was making plans to run away when you came back. I stuck close to you, wanting to find out what happened, but when I heard something from the direction of the cabin, I turned back. By the time I got there, it was too late. You know the rest."

Now she understood why Mel had chosen that particular valley. It led straight to the canyon. Perhaps she'd worked on the nest ahead of time. Mel wouldn't have known exactly where Gloin was. If anyone asked, she could have denied knowing, and it wouldn't have been a lie. Mavis shook her head. They were all too smart for their own good. Things could have turned out much differently. And if they had, Essa might still be alive.

"What's going to happen to Katrina?"

Gloin blinked. "She's going to need time to recover from what Chase did to her. She's under my leadership for now, but I'm not sure she'll ever trust another alpha."

"You're not angry? At her? Or me?"

Gloin stared into Mavis' face. "No. That's what I've been trying to explain—poorly, I guess. Between you and me, I would give Katrina a medal, not that she would take it. Her confidence is shaken. She killed Joe on Chase's orders. She would have killed you, too, and done who knows how many other terrible things. Which reminds me." He stood up and reached into the pocket of his bomber jacket. "This belongs to you." He held out a small, dark blue velvet bag.

Mavis stood and took it. The material was soft under her fingertips. She wiggled a finger into the drawstring opening, making it wider. Tipping it over, the contents spilled into her hand—the silver leaf necklace Aitch had given her. She stared at it, pressing her lips together to disguise their trembling. After last night, she'd thought she'd never see it again.

"I don't make it a habit of giving silver to people, but it's yours and I wanted to return it. You have my permission to use it on any werewolf at any time."

Mavis' hand closed around the pendant. Pressing the silver into Katrina's shoulder had helped the wolf regain her senses and throw off Chase's control. All while his father watched. Mavis had worried she and Katrina would both face retaliation from the Aldwulf for what they'd done. However, it sounded as if he wanted to thank them. He couldn't come out and say the words, but he could show them.

She swallowed and looked into Gloin's eyes. They had done what the Aldwulf could not with the impossible situation Gloin had found himself in. His responsibility to all werewolf-kind had driven him into hiding because he couldn't do the one thing required to keep them all safe—kill his son. She blinked and peered closer. If he had had to kill Chase himself, something would have broken loose inside Gloin. If that had happened, Chase may have gotten what he wanted after all.

Mavis glanced away and opened the clasp of the necklace. She slipped it around her neck and fastened it. "Thank you."

"My pleasure," Gloin said. "I've taken up enough of your time." He stepped toward the door.

"Wait."

Gloin stopped.

"I was wondering if you would do something else for me." She didn't know when she'd have another chance to ask. Mavis told him what she had in mind.

Gloin nodded. "I can make that happen. Shall we say next Friday night?"

After Gloin left she didn't see anyone else on Saturday, including Wes. On Sundays, the shop was closed. Mavis dressed in her shabbiest clothes and let herself into the garage. She kept the 'CLOSED' sign up in the window as she dragged furniture away from the walls. The sea-foam green paint she'd picked out flowed into a tray after she gave it a good mix. She grabbed a roller and got to work.

By midmorning, she was done with rolling the first coat onto the front office, her tongue stuck between her teeth as she trimmed the corners of the walls she'd just painted. A tap on the window made her jump.

Louis waved from the other side of the glass. She set the trim tray aside and opened the door.

"What's up, mama?" Louis asked, slipping inside.

Mavis didn't get a chance to answer before he spewed everything that had gone down at the town hall meeting two nights before. The papers weren't putting out any details, so all she had was Louis' account of the events that transpired. She listened keenly. Apparently, Lydia Shaw had been in the middle of her speech when two guys in the back started howling and carrying on, making a scene. That was weird enough, but then they started to change for real. The place went crazy with people screaming and fighting to get away. Someone call the police—more than a few times—which turned out to be a good thing because the doors had been barred and no one could get out.

Louis had taken out his phone and streamed the whole thing. He showed it to Mavis, talking the whole time. The police had to break down the doors when they got there. By that time, the two guys were just about done changing into wolves. Shaw kept calling them monsters and yelling for the police to shoot them, but the officers wouldn't do it. As soon as the wolves were finished changing, they sat there like they were letting everyone get a good look at them, and then they took off, trotting out the open door into the night. No one tried to stop them. There weren't any laws against changing in public. At least, not yet. Mavis wondered why the video hadn't been shared far and wide already, but maybe she shouldn't be surprised it hadn't, considering the Aldwulf was back.

Mavis handed the trim tray to Louis when he paused for air and put his phone away. "Why were you there in the first place?" she asked.

Louis peered into the tray. "Are you sure about this color?"

"Louis."

He picked up the brush and ran it through the paint. "I was curious, you know? I wanted to hear what they had to say. I wasn't impressed. That lady was freaking out, claiming the wolves were there to kill us all. She looked kind of silly when they finished changing and rolled out of there like friendly mutts."

Mavis crouched near the large paint tray and stayed there. Lydia Shaw hadn't been wrong. Louis and everyone else there might not be alive if things had turned out differently in the clearing Friday night. Her stomach flipped over and she stood back up, holding the roller. "What are you doing here, anyway? It's Sunday."

"Just out and about. Thinking about going to the square," he said, shrugging both shoulders to show her his backpack.

"I don't want to keep you if you have to study."

He dropped his bag onto a chair. "Nah, I don't mind."

The second coat of paint went on a lot faster. They finished, raided the snacks behind the counter, and called it a day.

Mavis returned early the next morning. The paint dry, she put the furniture back where it belonged. The sound of the back door opening echoed through the garage as Mavis hung up the phone. As she made a note on a ticket she was filling out, she heard someone pour coffee into a mug.

Not showing up for work Monday morning wasn't an option. She'd done a lot of thinking over the past couple of days and was willing to follow Aitch's lead—see how things went—but she would be lying if she didn't want things to go well. She liked her job, but she'd come to some hard conclusions.

She was willing to admit she liked Aitch a little more than as a friend. Definitely more than the typical employer-employee relationship allowed. She didn't know what to do about it. Not yet, anyway. She needed time. And possibly space, but she wasn't likely to get any. There was nowhere else she wanted to go.

Mavis finished writing up the ticket and turned. Aitch stood in the doorway, dressed for work in his coveralls with coffee cup in one hand and her backpack in the other. She hadn't seen her bag since Friday night. He peered at the walls with his lips pursed. Even if she blindfolded him, there was no disguising the aroma of fresh paint.

"Good morning," she said.

Aitch grunted and took a sip of coffee. He set her back-pack on the floor near the door. Business as usual then.

She held out the ticket. "Mr. Havemeyer across town needs a tow. He tried jump-starting his car this morning. Didn't work."

His gaze met her over the rim of his cup. "You missed a spot."

Mavis resisted the urge to check. "Did not." She refused to give him the satisfaction of seeing her fret.

He reached for the ticket, careful not to let his fingers graze hers. Then he just stood there.

"What?" Mavis asked.

A muscle jumped in Aitch's jaw, a sure sign he was grinding his teeth.

She knew that look. She didn't want to hear him apologize. Sure, it would be nice if her boss didn't want to eviscerate her for being able to shift into a bird, but she wasn't sorry for knowing Aitch could shift into a cat, either. She held up a hand. "Just don't."

With her back to him now, Mavis switched on the computer so she could start on the invoice.

Behind her, Aitch growled. "You might want to watch who you turn your back on."

She could have sworn she felt hot breath on the back of her neck, but when she turned, he was gone.

CHAPTER 38

The rest of the workweek continued without incident, though Mavis remained hyper-aware of Aitch's presence and he continued to be his curmudgeonly self, which meant they ignored each other as best they could.

She saw Wes. They still hadn't talked about what happened, but they were on good terms. He hadn't run screaming when she'd gone to pick up lunch on Monday. He'd greeted her in the normal way and acted as if nothing was wrong. In other words, he was in complete denial, but that worked for her at the moment. Between sorting through her feelings for Aitch and her preparations for Friday, she had enough to worry about, and she was happy Wes was speaking to her at all. Not only that, but he went shopping with her after work a few days later. She needed something appropriate for a funeral. She thought he might bring up the subject of her being able to change into a bird then, but he did not. Instead, he asked her who died. She told her it was someone from Shady Creek.

That Friday after work, she went home to her apartment,

showered, and dressed in the little black dress and cardigan Wes had said she should buy—the others had been, "too boring." He'd said she didn't have to dress like she was dead just because it was a funeral. Mavis couldn't stop the tiny giggle that had escaped her, covering it with a cough. If Wes only knew. The pair of three-inch spike heels Wes had urged her to purchase completed the look. As long as she didn't have to get anywhere fast, she could walk in them without tipping over. Most of the time.

She almost left the silver-leaf pendant on the bathroom sink, but, at the last minute, she decided to wear it. When she opened the door, she was glad she had. Outside, Broderick leaned against the door of a sleek foreign sedan, all curved steel and chrome. He wore considerably more clothes than he had the last time she'd seen him, and not one molecule of leather, as far as she could tell. He stood up straight and smiled when he saw her. It made his blunt features more than pleasant, but it also made her suspicious. Gloin had said he was sending a car. She hadn't known he was sending Broderick.

Mavis turned away to lock the door, the hair on her arms standing at attention. When she was done, Broderick was right behind her. His dark blue suit matched his eyes and highlighted the width of his shoulders.

"Dad sent me to pick you up and that's what I'm going to do. Look out," he said.

It was the only warning she got. Before she knew it, Broderick had wrapped his arms around her waist, pinning her arms to her sides, and lifted her clear off the ground in a bearhug.

"What are you doing?" she squeaked in protest. "Put me down!"

Broderick might have regretted the embrace when her silver pendant brushed against the skin on his face and neck, raising angry red welts. He hissed as he set her on her feet. "Sorry. I'm just happy to see you." He smiled through the pain.

"Why?"

His head tipped back with a chuckle. Still smiling, he offered her his arm. "I'll tell you in the car."

Mavis took his arm, but only because she didn't have complete faith in her ability to make it without falling over in the new shoes. Broderick played the perfect gentleman, opening the car door before getting behind the wheel and pushing a button to start the engine. Then they were on their way to Shady Creek.

"Why are you so happy to see me again?" she asked.

He glanced at her legs. "Besides the fact that you're a beautiful woman?" He smiled.

She frowned, growing tired of his good mood. "You do know we're on our way to a funeral, right?"

His smile dimmed but didn't go out. "I know. But I never got a chance to say thank you."

Mavis shook her head, mystified. "For what? Because of me, your brother is dead."

"Half-brother," Broderick said, but his expression sobered. Here was the Broderick she knew. "Chase brought what happened on himself. If he hadn't gotten the foolish notion into his head for werewolves to rule the world, he might still be alive. There's no coming back from that particular madness. He's gone, but my father is back where he should be. Now we can get back to the business of living without the threat of being exposed as the bloodthirsty beasts we are."

"Wait, what?" Mavis frowned.

"All werewolves struggle to make peace with their beast. The ones that can't are put down by the pack, as they should be. That's part of the Aldwulf's job. Now he can get back to it. I missed him. Dad can't come right out and say it, but I will." He took his gaze off the road to meet her eyes. In a solemn voice he said, "Thank you, Mavis. Thank you for saving my father and bringing him back to us." He faced forward to watch the road again.

Mavis was speechless. It didn't feel right to accept his gratitude, especially given her part in his brother's death so she remained silent, and he didn't say anything more for the rest of the trip.

Outside the hospital, Broderick helped her from the car and politely escorted her inside. He guided her with light touches to her lower back, though she knew where she was going.

Ahead of them the doors to the Shady Creek chapel—in actuality a nondenominational sanctuary—stood open. She paused just inside the doors. The altar in front held a large spray of yellow and pink roses, as well as a picture. Mavis was prepared for the sight, but it still gave her a jolt. Someone had cropped Gloin out of the photo from Mel's desk and enlarged it to focus on Mel's smiling face. Presumably, that same someone had replaced the picture glass Mavis had cracked in the frame.

Mavis glanced away from the altar and saw that the some-what small room was crowded with people. There wasn't much space to move. She hadn't expected such a turnout, but she did see a few familiar faces. The fact that the air seemed electrically charged told her more than a few of those faces belonged to werewolves.

Broderick left her side to go and speak to his father, who sat in the first row. Gloin's eyes were closed, his manner completely at ease. Either that or he was doing a good job of pretending to be. He wore a simple black suit, perfectly tailored.

Weasel, fully recovered, stood speaking with someone off

to the side. He excused himself and headed in Mavis' direction. Two feet away, he stopped, mouth opening in wonder and appreciation as his gaze raked her from head to toe. "You look amazing," he said. "And tall. No, don't slouch."

Mavis' lips curled upward despite herself as she straightened her spine. "You look a lot better than the last time I saw you."

"Nah, yeah, I just needed some rest and a hot meal. I got the recipe you sent. Everything's ready to go."

"Great. Thank you. I appreciate you taking care of the food."

"Not a problem. I had lots of help."

Mavis glanced around. "Do you know who all these people are?"

"Some of them work here, but I do believe a good number of them are Gloin's associates."

In other words, she really was surrounded by werewolves. Taking a closer look, a few of the faces might have stood out from the rest. It was hard to tell. Maybe if she saw them against a backdrop of trees, she would recognize more of them. Heads kept turning her way. She could feel eyes on her from every angle, but she did her best to ignore them. This event had been her idea, after all. There was nowhere else she would have thought to hold it beside Shady Creek. Mel had felt comfortable enough to take a room there. The thought of living around so many werewolves obviously hadn't bothered her, but maybe there was another reason. Perhaps the other residents or patients had a reason for being there that was connected to being a werewolf or having a second nature. Mavis didn't know for sure, but it wouldn't surprise her. She wondered if any of the others suffered an affliction similar to Forrest's. Maybe Weasel knew.

Gloin caught Mavis' eye from the front pew and nodded.

It was time to start. As she made her way to the front, people shuffled in and out of the rows in search of seats.

Mavis paused in front of the altar before she faced those assembled. Standing up in front of the sanctuary, she gazed out over a sea of faces. The crowd consisted of mostly younger to middle-aged men and women, but a few heads were covered in gray hair.

Mavis blinked. Katrina sat in the row directly behind Gloin, her gaze steady but unfocused. The way Katrina held herself, arms wrapped around her middle, made it clear she didn't want to be there. Mavis suspected only a sense of obligation kept her in place. Toward the back, on the opposite side of the center aisle, Forrest sat next to Weasel. When their eyes met, his mouth curved before he ducked his head. She wondered how he was getting along without the doc and if his new medication was still working.

The doors to the sanctuary had just started to close when a hand grabbed one and held it open. Aitch stared around the room before he glanced down at himself, as if he was unsure of how he got there—and in a suit, no less. A shorter woman stepped around him into the sanctuary. Mavis' eyes widened. She hadn't expected to see the forensic pathologist from Beauryan in attendance, but there Carol stood, dressed in a black button-down shirt dress, the sleeves rolled up to her elbows. Both of them found empty seats in the back and sat down together.

Mavis cleared her throat. The sounds of settling faded into quiet. She smiled and tried to remember to speak loudly, clearly, and not to rush. She clasped her hands in front of her waist. "Thank you all for coming. We've gathered this evening to pay our respects to someone I didn't know very well, even though we look alike. Some would say we could have been sisters, if not twins, but—definitely related." There were a few soft chuckles. "The truth is, I didn't know Melisandrea at all." Mavis stopped and swallowed. "She and I never met. From the little I know of her, it's clear Mel lived a life far from ordinary. That life is what we're here to celebrate tonight. Thank you for helping me honor her and lay her memory to rest. Without Mel, I know I wouldn't be here." Now for the tricky part. "Would anyone like to share a memory of Mel?"

She'd told herself to be prepared for no one to speak on Mel's behalf and to transition to the food and drink, so she was surprised when Broderick stood and came to the front of the room. Mavis sat down in the front row across the aisle from Gloin, who watched his son.

"I didn't know Mel very well, but I do know she was one tough cookie. She could handle herself, that was for sure." He inclined his head the slightest bit in Mavis' direction. "She will be missed." He returned to his seat, back to being a man of few words.

Mavis gathered her energy to stand, but she didn't have to. Gloin was on his feet and in front of the room. The Aldwulf faced those assembled, and if it had been quiet when she and Broderick spoke, now it was absolutely silent. Mavis wasn't the only one curious about what Gloin had to say. The air filled with a sense of anticipation.

Gloin smiled at the crowd and it bled a little of the tension out of the air. "Melisandrea was a true friend. I trusted her with my life and could not have chosen more worthy or capable hands." He'd told Mavis as much when he'd come to see her, but from the shifting in the crowd, it might have been news to at least a few of them. "I will miss her company and pray that, wherever she is, her soul is at peace."

Mavis hoped that, too. After all, funerals were for the living.

Gloin continued, "The truth is Melisandrea saved my life when we first met. I've never forgotten that small kindness."

His audience stirred with the admission. "I tried to repay her over the years, only to be thwarted at every turn." A few people chuckled at this, but sadness pinched Gloin's features. "Melisandrea saw the world in a way I never could. Let us remember her as an ally to our community. The past is gone. We cannot reclaim it, nor should we try. I will cherish the memories I have of my friend, but we must move forward. Let us do so with hope and grace."

He drew a deep breath and began to sing in a rich, clear tenor that rose to fill the room.

Mavis didn't know what language the song was in, but the music hit her in the solar plexus. It stirred to life a sadness deep within her she'd ignored until now. It swelled, consuming her full attention, causing the tears to spill over her lashes onto her cheeks.

The song continued.

As it did, Broderick's deep voice joined in, adding depth to the melody and raising the song higher. The last note rang off the walls around them and the room fell quiet once more, but not the same deep reverent silence as before Gloin spoke. For a moment, no one stirred. Mavis eventually heard shuffling and sniffling as people blew their noses. She wasn't the only one affected by the song. She dabbed the corners of her eyes with a tissue.

The quiet soothed her as much as the song had.

Broderick rose and stood next to his father, directing everyone to the cafeteria. Mavis waited with him and Gloin while the room cleared. She lost sight of Aitch and Carol first. Katrina left without a backward glance. Weasel waved on his way out with Forrest behind him.

Mavis turned to Gloin. "Thank you for that. It was beautiful."

"It was the least I could do, Mavis."

Broderick snagged the picture of Mel on their way out

and brought it with them. He set it on the corner of a long table filled with the food Weasel and the staff had prepared. People served themselves. At the end of the dessert table, Gloin jerked to a stop. Mavis' crispy chocolate chip cookies sat on a tray surrounded by other sweets. Gloin grabbed one and took a bite, smiling even as crumbs fell onto his clean shirt. "These are my favorite."

"They're very good," a voice said behind her.

Mavis turned. Carol stood close by, holding a clutch purse in front of her with both hands.

Noise flew around the room from several conversations, but Mavis swore the volume dipped and they had everyone's attention.

"Hi, Carol. Thank you for coming," Mavis said. She assumed Aitch must have been the one to tell her about the service, but she wasn't sure why Carol had come. Mavis was pretty certain she hadn't known Mel.

"I'm sorry for your loss," Carol said, her gaze skipping around to each of them.

Gloin made the rest of his cookie disappear. "Thank you, Doctor. And thank you for coming." He held out his hand.

The room quieted further. Mavis had no idea what was going on, but Carol smiled and placed her hand in Gloin's with a dip of her head. With the sleeves of her dress rolled up, Mavis could see the inside of Carol's right forearm for the first time. Black ink ran across her skin. The silhouette of a crown with—Mavis had to squint to see—a long hairless tail running from underneath it. Mavis knew Carol was two-natured, but she'd never said what her second nature was. The tail was too long to belong to a mouse, but it could belong to a rat.

"I wish it could have been under happier circumstances," Carol said, still holding Gloin's hand. Or maybe he was holding hers.

"Perhaps we can do that. Meet under better circumstances," Gloin suggested.

Carol nodded once. "I would like that."

Their hands parted.

"Da, we should take care of that other thing," Broderick said.

Gloin sighed. "Of course. Please excuse us, Carol. Mavis, will you come with me?" He tilted his head in the direction of the door. His tone was cordial enough, but Mavis got the impression that she shouldn't refuse. She noticed he snagged another cookie on the way out.

CHAPTER 39

"What's going on?" Mavis asked, glancing between Gloin and Broderick.

"Just a little business to be taken care of," Broderick said.

She walked between the two men down the hall to an office she'd never been to. Broderick opened the door; it was dark inside. Gloin went in ahead of her while Broderick closed the door behind them and turned the lights on.

In the middle of the room, a man sat tied to a chair with several loops of stout rope wrapped around his naked torso. He wore a pair of jeans, but his feet were bare and dirty. Mavis didn't need to be a werewolf to smell the desperation and hopelessness in the air. In addition to the rope, several heavy chains were wrapped around him.

"What the hell is going on?" asked Mavis, eyes wide.

Broderick slapped the man on his chest. "Wake up."

The man in the chair jerked and raised his head.

Harley saw her and jerked against his constraints.

"Be calm," Gloin said. The words might have been kind, but the steel behind them indicated that it was a command.

Harley relaxed in an instant, his breathing deepening, but Mavis could see that he was still afraid. She looked from Broderick to Gloin. Broderick remained next to Harley, while Gloin leaned back against the wall, his arms crossed.

Gloin nodded to Harley and said, "Tell her."

Harley whimpered. "I pushed you from the balcony that day. I climbed to the roof and changed. And then I waited. The doc was sure you would come out there sooner or later. I laid low, and when I saw you, I slid down the roof and pushed you."

"And?" Gloin prompted from his place against the wall. His eyes were half-closed.

Harley gripped the chair arms while he spoke. "The doc told me and Jack to follow you. Then he told us to make sure you didn't come back. We had to make it look like an accident, but the old lady was a mistake. Jack doesn't—didn't—have very good control over his wolf, and he killed her before I could stop him. I lit the fire to cover our tracks."

"Jack? That was the name of the wolf Weasel killed?"

Harley's eyes widened as he nodded. Maybe he thought that Mavis had killed Jack instead of Weasel.

"You could have killed me," Mavis said. "What stopped you?"

Harley's hands clenched into fists. "I didn't want to, so I changed. There would have been no way for me to do it without making it look like a werewolf killed you then. By the time I was done changing, you were gone." He whimpered again.

Smart.

Mavis turned to Gloin. "Is he telling the truth?"

Gloin lifted his lids. "As far as he knows it." His eyes were a shade more golden than they had been before Harley started talking. Hearing about what the doc had ordered

Harley to do seemed to upset him, but he was keeping his emotions in check.

"So why is he tied to a chair?"

Broderick answered. "He tried to kill you, Mavis. More than once. We thought you should decide what we do with him."

Mavis' shoulders slumped, suddenly weary. She hadn't expected to decide anyone's fate today. The only thing she knew was that she was tired of death. "Killing Harley won't bring Essa back. If Jack did it, then he's already paid the price for her death. Let Harley go. The doc used him just like he did everyone else."

Neither Gloin nor Broderick moved.

"Are you sure?" Gloin asked.

Mavis was about to say yes when she stopped. How many times had Harley tried to kill her? "Did you leave me chocolates in the hospital after I woke up?" she asked Harley.

His head waved from side to side. "No. No, I never left you any chocolates. I've never bought anyone chocolates."

Mavis believed him. Broderick sniffed and said, "That's true."

She turned back to Harley. "And you don't have any idea what happened to Mel?"

Harley hesitated.

Gloin stood up straight away from the wall and took a step forward. Broderick stepped in close to Harley and grabbed him by the hair, pulling his head back and exposing his throat. His pulse beat wildly at the base of his neck, and the scent of perspiration grew.

Broderick lowered his voice to a whisper. "She asked you a question."

Mavis snapped, "Stop. Let him go."

Broderick's eyes met hers.

"Please," she added.

He let go of Harley's hair, but he didn't step back.

Harley stared at Mavis. "I—I didn't see what happened."

"Tell us what you can," Mavis said.

Harley swallowed. "I was headed back to the hospital late after a run when I heard the doc and Mel arguing off in the woods." He closed his eyes. "I thought they were breaking up because I heard Mel say they were done. Then the doc said, 'Don't walk away from me,' and there was a loud bang." Harley blinked his eyes open. "Mel cried out. At least, I think it was Mel. It sounded human at first, but then it changed into some kind of screeching. The doc never said a word about seeing Mel that night, and I never let on that I heard anything. That's all I know, I swear."

Mavis waited for a beat, processing what Harley had said. Could Mel have found out what the doc was up to and tried to put an end to his grab for power? Could Chase have shot his lover in the back? She knew the answer to that.

"Let him go," Mavis said.

Gloin nodded to Broderick, who got rid of the chains and untied Harley. He didn't stand up but instead threw himself onto his knees in front of Gloin, head bowed. "Thank you."

Broderick snorted and rolled his eyes.

"You should thank Mavis," Gloin said.

Harley turned toward Mavis and said, "Thank you." Then he threw himself at her feet so low that his forehead touched the floor.

Broderick shook his head. Gloin sighed.

"You can get up now." Mavis took a step back. Harley's groveling made her uncomfortable. She didn't want to be the kind of person who enjoyed having a grown man throw himself at her feet.

Harley got up, gaze lowered as he rubbed at the skin around his wrists.

"Shall we?" Gloin motioned toward the door.

Broderick stepped around Harley with a warning. "You got lucky. Stay out of trouble."

They left the room and Harley behind, heading back to the cafeteria. The conversation there flowed at a normal volume, despite the somber occasion.

Gloin headed back to the dessert table while Broderick called out to someone he knew and mingled with the crowd, leaving her side with a brush of his hand on her arm.

Katrina sidled up to her from the shadows, sipping punch out of a clear plastic cup. With heels on, Mavis towered over her despite Katrina's spiked footwear. Katrina had paired her lethal heels with a black pencil skirt and fluttery white blouse. "Nicely done," she said, and Mavis caught a whiff of something stronger than punch on her breath.

Mavis wasn't entirely sure what she was referring to and shook her head with a frown.

Katrina tilted her head in the direction of the hallway. With her enhanced hearing, all Katrina would have had to do was step into the hallway to hear what had happened. Katrina's eavesdropping didn't bother Mavis. Everyone would know she'd let Harley live sooner or later.

"You, too," Mavis said.

Raw emotion flashed behind Katrina's eyes, but Mavis noted they remained their normal shade of brown.

"A word of warning—" Katrina began.

Mavis' brows drew together. What now?

Katrina waved her cup toward the food. "Stay away from the cheesecake. It's strawberry. I seem to recall"—she hiccupped—"I seem to recall you're allergic to strawberries. Not Mel, though. Mel was allergic to nuts." Katrina's mouth turned down at the corners as her eyes met Mavis', and she blinked.

Mavis' head tipped back in understanding. Katrina had

left the chocolates for her—well, for Mel. And she wasn't proud of it.

Mavis relaxed and dipped her head once in acknowledgment. "Thank you. For telling me."

Katrina toasted her with her cup and glided away, which Mavis didn't think was fair. Katrina had been drinking, but it didn't impair her ability to get around on heels in the slightest.

Mavis searched the cafeteria but didn't see the person she was looking for. However, she did spot Weasel. She tilted her head toward the side of the room, and he joined her. "Have you seen Aitch?"

"He was here, but he stepped out." Weasel started to say more and stopped, a concerned expression settling on his features.

"What?" she asked. Annoyance crept into her tone.

"Can we talk? Out there?" He led her into the hallway and spoke quietly. "Aitch made me swear not to tell you he was a shifter." Weasel's expression went sheepish. "I might not have been as out of it as you thought when you came back to the car that night. I heard what Aitch said and he's right. A relationship between you two, given your other natures—well, it's not a good idea. For what it's worth, I think he cares for you in his way, but it comes down to biology, doesn't it?"

"Now wait a second." Her voice took on a challenging tone. "I had the chance to disembowel you, and I didn't take it."

"True, but age affects these things, and you're like a new soul knocking around in an old body. Aitch has been around a while in both body and spirit. I'm not saying it could never happen, but you might not want to poke that particular bear."

Mavis heard the words that were coming out of his mouth but didn't feel the need to heed this particular warning. She pasted a smile on her face. "I don't want to poke the bear," she said. No, she wanted to pet the kitty.

Mavis left the hallway.

Full dark had fallen outside, but harsh orange sodium floodlights lit the parking lot out front.

Mavis found Aitch leaning against the side of his truck, staring up at the night sky, but she didn't think he was seeing anything beyond the end of his nose. His dark suit was well-tailored, showcasing the breadth of his chest and his trim physique. He hardly looked like himself, and she wondered if she wouldn't have preferred him in boots and coveralls for this conversation.

"Hey," she said. As opening gambits went, it wouldn't win any awards, but it was something.

Aitch straightened away from the side of his truck, stuffing his hands into his pockets. "I wanted to talk to you."

Mavis picked her way forward, careful not to turn an ankle. With the heels, she was only a few inches shorter than Aitch, and she liked the height advantage. "I wanted to talk to you, too. Thanks for coming. You clean up well."

Aitch cleared his throat, but he didn't return the compliment, his eyes taking her in with one glance before his gaze slid away.

This wasn't going the way she thought it would. Mavis chewed the inside of her lip. Despite what he'd said about their second natures not getting along, they'd worked together all week without a problem. Yes, Aitch was a taciturn curmudgeon as usual, but she was used to it. They could work together, but was that really what was best for them? Best for her?

Gathering all her courage, she drew a deep breath and asked, "Would you like to go out with me?"

Aitch frowned. Okay, frowned harder. "Like on a date?"

"Uh-huh," was all the reply that came to mind because a part of her sensed this wasn't going well.

"No, Mavis, I don't want to go out with you," he said.

Mavis didn't think he had to say it like that—like the idea was completely ludicrous.

"Wow," she thought, and she sucked in a breath when the word hit her ears.

"Look, I'm sorry," Aitch said.

Mavis took a step back, the rejection hitting home, but the worst was yet to come. When Aitch started apologizing, nothing good followed.

"I'm sorry, too." She knew what she had to do.

"We can't do this anymore—"

"I know we can't," Mavis said, surprised at how firm her voice sounded.

"Mavis—"

"Aitch—"

They spoke over each other.

"You're fired," Aitch said.

At the same time, Mavis said, "I quit."

They stared at each other, both surprised by the other's words.

Mavis recovered first. "Don't worry. I won't ask you for a reference." She didn't look back as she went inside. Maybe she could get Weasel to give her a ride home. She had to start looking for a new job.

Gloin waited for her just inside the large oak front doors. He was alone, the reception area deserted after hours. "I'm sorry." With a tilt of his head, he indicated the parking lot.

An exasperated noise left her. "Of course. Of course, you heard that. Because...because." She struggled to remain cogent.

"I can see that you're upset, but there were a couple of things I wanted to discuss with you in private," he said.

Mavis sighed. "Like what?"

"I have some information for you, but I also wanted to talk to you about a job of sorts. It would require some travel, but I could use your assistance."

The newly returned Aldwulf needed her help? And she might be able to get out of town? This she had to hear. "Tell me more."

The End

THANK YOU

Thank you for reading *Second Nature*.
Please consider leaving a review so that other readers can find this title.

ACKNOWLEDGMENTS

I've never written in a vacuum, but I have to assume it's pretty rotten. I enjoy connecting with fellow writers and readers and have many to thank. Much of my gratitude belongs to the members of my long-time writing group, Tuesdays With Story. They read more than one version of the beginning of this story and saw it through to the end. I also have to thank my beta readers and critique partners Diane Boles, Tracey Phillips, Becky Crookham, and Marianne Flynn Statz. A big thanks to Tracey Gemmell, who talked about story structure with me before she decided to decamp to her native England--I still hope to visit someday. In addition, it would be remiss of me not to mention the editorial team at GenZ for their assistance in getting this manuscript together. Thank you to everyone there who had their eyes on it.

A special thank you to my sister, Amanda Lahners, who answers all my questions about birds no matter how silly they are.

Thank you to my husband, Armand, who reads what I give him and offers feedback and emotional support. And to my kids for reminding me every day that they are mine.

Finally, a big thank you to you, the reader. I hope you've enjoyed this story. If so, please mention it to someone and consider writing a review. I don't want to write in a vacuum, so I look forward to hearing from you.

www.ingramcontent.com/pod-product-compliance
Lightning Source LLC
Chambersburg PA
CBHW020539020726
47494CB00006B/1829